'Reading *The Voids* is a sensory ex[...]
too much, it never lingers. There i[...]
O'Connor's lightness of touch, the[...]
are all perfect, all harmonious, po[...]
blackest of moments. Part of me i[...]
the sunlight through the fire exit d[...]
and perfect. I want to say this is a [...]
PAUL BUCHANAN, The Blue Nile

'Luminous … a writer capable of revealing the humanity in everyone …
In an era when contemporary fiction is leaning ever more towards
identity and relatability, it's gratifying to know there's still a place for
a literary ride as wild as this.' **BENJAMIN MYERS, *The Guardian***

'A startling debut … Benders are integral to the Scottish literary
tradition, but O'Connor sets the bar high in a series of absurd, visionary,
uproarious episodes … A triumph of the grotesque … Comedy at
its most existential.' **JOHN BURNSIDE, *TLS***

'Finely written … O'Connor creates a world *ex nihilo*, showcasing the
lives of the forgotten … He writes with compassion and honesty about
his characters, from drug dealers to prostitutes, lecherous drunks to
addicts.' **SARAH GILMARTIN, *The Irish Times***

'Poignant, poetic, and compassionate, *The Voids* is a tender tale
of alienation, and the need to escape and, paradoxically, to belong.'
LISA HARDING, author of *Bright Burning Things*

'A sensory portrait of the city, set in a dizzyingly surreal Glasgow.'
KATIE GOH, *i-D Magazine*

'At times disturbing, and at others hilarious, there are characters
that appear for a page that have haunted me ever since. A wild
ride that journeys through the underbelly of our society.'
PAUL MCVEIGH, author of *The Good Son*

'It is rare to discover a book that is simultaneously beautiful and
devastating, where characters are frightening to behold but also
worthy of compassion. *The Voids* is a brilliant emotional tapestry
woven by a writer of immense talent.' **SIMON VAN BOOY, author
of *Night Came with Many Stars***

'There are echoes of J.G. Ballard in the setting, and of Don DeLillo in the prose. But *The Voids* is distinctively and brilliantly Ryan O'Connor's own, rich with precise observations, full of haunting images, and replete with deft vignettes of character, place, and context. This is a novel that confidently generates its own unnerving atmospheres. Extraordinary work.' **KEVIN POWER, author of *Bad Day in Blackrock***

'In the space of a few pages, I was there, right in the world of *The Voids*, in its chaos and sadness, its life and humour. Melodrama and sentimentality have no place in Ryan O'Connor's writing. Instead he gives us warmth and bleakness, humanity and beauty. The "voids" might be empty but this novel is brimming with feeling and perception.' **WENDY ERSKINE, author of *Sweet Home***

'Ryan O'Connor succeeds in conjuring beautiful imagery out of a desperate situation. A whirlwind tour of Glasgow, in the wake of a protagonist plagued by addiction and failure is lifted by the narrative's breakneck pace, and frequent moments of real humour. Reminiscent of James Kelman's work, *The Voids* should be on everyone's reading list.' **POLLY MARKHAM, Golden Hare Books**

'One to watch!' *The Bookseller*

'A wild, magical, and magnetically mad picaresque … it had me bellowing with laughter on one page and needing to weep on the next. I tore through it, and it through me. A brilliant debut.' **NIALL GRIFFITHS, author of *Sheepshagger***

'An engulfing read.' **HEATHER MCDAID, *The Skinny***

'What is exceptional, and admirable, is that, in a field where it would be so easy to take an imitative route, *The Voids* is an original work in its own right.' **JOHN BURNSIDE**

'An unflinching yet poetic portrait of addiction, this bleak tale is leavened by glimmers of hope and humour.' **DAN SHAW, *Happy Mag***

'Beautiful, and both explicit and allusive, *The Voids* is a brave and moving work.' **PENELOPE COTTIER, *The Canberra Times***

THE VOIDS

RYAN O'CONNOR received the Scottish Book Trust Next Chapter Award in 2018; later the same year he was Highly Commended in the Bridport Prize short story category. He currently lives in Glasgow with his partner and young sons.

THE
VOIDS

RYAN
O'CONNOR

SCRIBE
Melbourne • London

Scribe Publications
2 John St, Clerkenwell, London, WC1N 2ES, United Kingdom
18–20 Edward St, Brunswick, Victoria 3056, Australia
3754 Pleasant Ave, Suite 100, Minneapolis, Minnesota 55409, USA

Published by Scribe 2022
This edition published 2022

Typeset in Fournier by the publishers

Printed and bound in the UK by CPI Group (UK) Ltd,
Croydon CR0 4YY

Scribe is committed to the sustainable use of natural
resources and the use of paper products made responsibly
from those resources.

978 1 913348 44 1 (UK paperback)
978 1 913348 43 4 (UK hardback)
978 1 922310 35 4 (Australian edition)
978 1 950354 94 8 (US edition)
978 1 922586 28 5 (ebook)

Catalogue records for this book are available from the
National Library of Australia and the British Library.

scribepublications.co.uk
scribepublications.com.au
scribepublications.com

For *you*

As I sit here writing this, everything has already happened. The past and the future no longer exist. Either for me or for you. Nothing remains but the words.

If it were possible to disintegrate time, I could show you how easily things fall apart. If it were possible to disintegrate time, I could show you how easily life disintegrates.

1

I was living on the fourteenth floor of a condemned high-rise. I was all alone up there. One of the few remaining tenants in the building. The others, a character known as the Birdman and several pensioners who hadn't set foot on terra firma for years, were scattered throughout the floors below.

At some point all maintenance had ceased. Then the lifts had been decommissioned. Then the intercom system stopped working. It was only a matter of time before they disconnected the utilities. After this, those of us who remained would be cut off altogether. We were the irredeemable. The unremembered.

The Birdman was in his late forties and had a flat on the fourth floor that he shared with a flock of pigeons. Regardless of the weather, his living-room window was always open to allow the birds to come and go. Every morning he'd be there in his guano-covered dressing gown, dragging his oxygen tank back and forth as he fed the pigeons jostling and cooing loudly on his windowsill. I'd call up to him from the car park and ask how things were, and he'd smile and respond with the same answer every time.

'Look around,' he'd yell with his arms outstretched like some profane Christ the Redeemer heralding catastrophe, 'can you no see? It's shite. The world is full of shite and getting shite-er.'

Then he'd laugh himself into a coughing and wheezing fit and start groping for his oxygen mask while being engulfed by a storm of wings.

As for the pensioners, I would never have known they were there if I hadn't looked up as I walked towards the high-rise and caught sight of them standing at their windows. Sometimes there'd only be one or two, at other times there would be several of them scattered across the great geometric sweep of its façade. Forgotten sentinels hovering behind clouds or sunlight reflecting off the glass, like ghost figures in double negatives.

The only people I came into direct contact with were the heroin addicts. Desperate for their fix, they'd shoot up as soon as they managed to get inside the building and were usually too strung out to make it up more than a few flights of stairs. I'd pass them gouching in the foyer or dragging themselves up the stairwell. Emaciated, dying of a thirst that would never be quenched, like pilgrims lost in the desert. One guy made it as far as the seventh floor once. He was slouched in the corner of the landing and nodding off as I came down the stairs towards him. Hearing my footsteps, he looked up and asked, 'Am ah there? Have ah made it?'

'Made it where?' I asked him.

'The top of the world,' he replied.

I didn't want to lie to a dying man. At the same time, I didn't have the heart to break his high and what was left of his spirit by explaining that he'd only managed to crawl a third of the way up a condemned high-rise.

'Nearly. You're headed in the right direction. Don't give up. Keep going,' I told him. The fire in him had almost been extinguished. I half-expected to see it flicker and burn out right there and then. Instead, a beautiful smile lit up his ravaged face and illuminated the entire high-rise. I'd seen him a few times before, but after that day, I never saw him again.

When demolition was first mentioned, most people said they would never leave, that they would fight till the end. When it was confirmed, a petition was launched and residents' meetings were held. One of my neighbours, a gigantic brute with a head like a smashed pumpkin and huge, spade-like hands that looked rusted from all the roll-ups he smoked, was the first and last to sacrifice himself for the cause.

Out on life licence for attempted murder, Mondo wasn't much of a conversationalist. What he did have was a predilection for grand idiosyncratic statements and capital letters. I knew this because the summer afternoon he moved in, he forced a huge Christmas card through my letter box with *I AM YOUR NEIGHBOUR AND I LOVE YOU NOW* scrawled inside the mangled card. I didn't know whether to be touched or terrified. When he knew I was home he'd leave his front door ajar and have music playing at just the right volume. Never too loud, it seemed purposely set to lure me across the landing into his flat, like a tacit invite. It was usually a Meat Loaf song, most often 'You Took the Words Right Out of My Mouth'. I wondered if this was how he used to serenade his fellow prisoners. Mondo's was a classic case of a body that had been freed, but a mind that was still deep inside.

As it turned out, we never did get the chance to know one another. When demolition was proposed, he expressed himself no less emphatically on that front too, scuppering any possibility of forging a friendship. On a huge banner fashioned from several white sheets that he hung from his living room window he declared — *I WILL MOVE OUT OVER MY DEAD BODY!* Unfortunately for Mondo, the public declaration of this impossible threat broke several of his bail conditions, and when the police turned up to arrest him an altercation ensued. A small group that had gathered outside his door to support him cheered in solidarity as they heard him yell, 'Pick a windae, ye fucking bastards! Yer leaving!' to the police officers. But the only person leaving was Mondo, in a brutal restraint hold via his front door.

Mondo's suppression and swift removal only increased the residents' rage and sense of injustice. 'Free Mondo' meetings were held. People wore T-shirts with a blurred image of his face printed on the front like some parody of the Turin Shroud. Photocopies of the same image with *MONDO NEEDS YOU* emblazoned beneath his mugshot, were stuck on lamp posts and bus shelters. Intended as recruitment posters, they looked more like Victorian-era wanted posters and scared the shit out of the local kids and the elderly. Plans were made to set up roadblocks and to barricade the entrances to the high-rise. Exhilarated by these events and giddy with righteousness and rebellion, people vowed to fight to the end. Some even swore they'd lay down their lives if they had to. Then the cheques started arriving for those who had applied for home loss and disturbance payments. When word of their financial windfall got out, it spread through the building like a disease everyone was dying to catch. Overnight, Mondo went from being a travesty of justice to simply being a travesty. Soon after, an unholy exodus ensued.

In less than a month, occupancy in the high-rise went from full to almost empty. It started slowly enough. A couple of people one day, a few more the next. I didn't really pay much attention in the beginning. Then entire families started bailing out with their belongings any way they could. Clothes jammed into swollen suitcases. Linen stuffed into bursting black bin bags. Shoes, toys, pots and pans piled high in stolen shopping trolleys. Pillowcases filled with bric-a-brac and tied around bicycles like packs strapped to mules. Heirlooms carefully laid out on duvets, then rolled up and carried into the lifts like the dead. Huge items of furniture secured with ropes and lowered down the outside of the building. Small children and pets wheeled out on hand carts and trucks. It went on like this, day and night. A steady stream of people and possessions flowing out of the high-rise like grains of sand from a broken hourglass.

While the exodus was in full swing there was a carnival atmosphere. Protests mutated into parties. Teenage scouts, who'd previously patrolled the perimeter watching for hostile bodies, were instead sent out on booze runs. Communal lunches and dinners were cooked on disposable barbecues that burned around the base of the high-rise throughout the day and smouldered through the night. Within days the place began to resemble an encampment of disparate communities displaced by war. The wretched absurdity of it all. Honestly, if you didn't laugh, you'd cry. Not that anyone else was thinking such thoughts. On the contrary, with peace bought and further conflict averted, suddenly everyone was happy and a comrade. Euphoric racists shook the hands of puzzled immigrants, grizzled alcoholics raised a toast with young junkies, Catholics sang songs with Protestants, and the army of security guards laughed at the jokes of departing residents while soft-pedalling their evictions. Everyone behaved as if their hopes and dreams were waiting for them just around the corner. Like they were on their way to Shangri-La. Watching them reminded me of cartoon characters speeding off a cliff desperate to escape some adversary. Their desperation keeps them suspended in mid-air for a time, but the moment they look down, they fall.

Initially, I found the departure of the residents disorientating. When it continued unabated, I began to find it unnerving. The increasing isolation. The haunting silence building itself around me. The intense stillness that resonated throughout the vast interior. It was so quiet I would lie in bed at night listening to my breathing, terrified of all that uninhabited space, feeling myself atomise into the darkness. Sometimes I wasn't sure if the others had left us or if we had left them.

Besides Mondo, there were two families on my floor. A Malawian family and an Iraqi family. During those first days, with the hours moving as slowly as photographed clouds in a photographed sky, it was these neighbours I missed the most. Encountering the aromatic warmth of the food they cooked as I stepped out of the lift onto our landing. Listening to their music drift through the walls of my flat. Hearing their children play in the hallway outside my door in the evenings, their laughter colouring the grey concrete floors and grimy magnolia-painted walls. Sometimes when I closed my eyes and began to fall away in sleep or stupor, I would dream I was in Lilongwe or Nineveh, searching for my neighbours. I loved straying into these terrae incognitae. They were my very own cities of the red night and my heart would sink when I'd wake and find myself back in my flat.

These families were also the most reluctant to leave. The immigrants. The migrants. The refugees. The so-called outsiders. They didn't want the resettlement money. To move on again. They wanted homes. An opportunity to rebuild their lives. They didn't understand why the authorities wanted to tear down the high-rise. To erase all these rooms from the sky. Why they would further disperse the already dispersed and dispossessed.

Late one night, back when demolition was first mentioned, the intercom in my flat buzzed. It was Zamir, my Iraqi neighbour. He'd forgotten his fob for the main door and didn't want to wake his wife and children. He kept apologising for disturbing me and I tried to reassure him that I was awake anyway, but I don't think he believed me, so I decided to wait for him on our landing after buzzing him in. He emerged from the piss-pale light of the lift with his head down and was surprised to see me when he looked up.

'Neighbour, my good neighbour,' he smiled, 'Thank you, thank you. I am so sorry to awaken you.'

'It's fine, really. I was awake anyway,' I told him. There was a fresh cut on his forehead and blood on the yellow sports jacket he was wearing. 'Are you okay? What happened?' I asked him.

'This thing,' he said, pointing to the ceiling, but referring to the cut on his head, 'nothing. Babies, babies who don't understand anything. But the other thing, why are they doing this? This is something *I* do not understand.'

'Doing what?'

'Kaboom,' he said, opening his arms and looking around to indicate he meant the high-rise.

'They call it regeneration.'

'What is regeneration?'

'They tear down old stuff and build new stuff.'

'This is good is it not?' he asked.

'It's supposed to be. But it isn't, not really. The people who live here now can't afford the new stuff, so they get moved on.'

Zamir looked puzzled. Either he hadn't a clue what I was going on about, or else he was trying to understand why they would do such a terrible thing.

'Something does not sound right,' he said.

'I know. I'm sorry. I'm not being very clear,' I smiled.

'No, *I understand you*. What they are doing does not sound right.'

It wasn't. It was basically a land grab. Opportunism disguised as opportunity. Developers in cahoots with the council, they'd been doing it for decades. Reappropriating formerly undesirable areas that were now desired — minus the undesirables.

'It's not right. It's like a trick. An illusion,' I said.

'Illusion?'

'You know, like Houdini?'

'Yes. Magicians.'

'Exactly. They pretend they're doing one thing, in order to hide what they're actually doing. In this case, that they're giving you something better than what you had.'

'Ah, tricksters.'

'Yes, tricksters.'

'Like the people smugglers.' Zamir mock-spat.

'Yeah I suppose, like them. But then everything in life is a dirty trick,' I added.

'No, my neighbour, not everything. Life can be good. *Very good*. Haven't you seen my wife?' He winked and smiled.

'I have, she's very beautiful,' I agreed.

'You've looked at my wife?' he asked angrily.

'Well. No. I just. You know,' I mumbled.

'My neighbour, my neighbour, I am funning with you,' Zamir said, laughing loudly. Then he came forwards and flung his arms around me, hugging me with an embrace full of heart. Just then his front door opened and his wife appeared.

'Zami, in, *now*.'

'Beautiful and the boss,' he said beneath his breath. 'By the way, my favourite trick is the Indian rope trick. It does not seem possible. And yet on they get, and up and up they go.' He said, smiling warmly, before turning and walking towards his wife with his arms wide open.

A week after most of the residents had left, the sense of seclusion intensified. As well as my neighbours I began to miss the things I'd formerly hated about living in the high-rise. The sound of garbage bags and bottles tumbling and crashing down the waste-disposal chute. Front doors slamming shut. The creaking and rattling of the lift cables. People yelling from their windows throughout the night. The senseless violence that would suddenly flair up outside the entrance of the building for no apparent reason, but that I couldn't stop myself watching from above, despite the fact it made me feel sick. I even missed the couple who lived in the flat above mine and who were always fighting with each other. Dead-end battles fuelled by alcohol and hopelessness. The two of them screaming questions neither of them had the answers to. Who'd paid for the booze? Who'd hidden the booze? Who'd drunk all the booze? *For the love of God, how were they going to get more booze?* Crazy altercations that wouldn't stop until one of them passed out or they started fucking, or they both passed out while they were fucking. They'd regularly call the police on one another to report an incident of domestic abuse. You'd hear their door being knocked, then moments later, from lungs filled with love and despair would come that bittersweet duet, when in unison they'd tell the police to 'Fuck off and mind yer own business!' Tommy and Moira, raging like two star-crossed drunks in a Pogues song. Held hostage by dramas they themselves had written and in which they played the lead roles. Crying their hearts out for creating each other's misery.

They lived directly above me. I knew their names and intimacies, yet in all the time they were there I never met them. Which wasn't that remarkable. One of the lifts stopped on the even-numbered floors, and the other on the odd-numbered floors. This meant that unless you went out of your way to do so, you never met half the residents in the high-rise, except briefly in the foyer. A high-rise is like two streets running parallel up into the sky. Two streets that never meet and that you'll never find on any map or Google Earth.

The only people who did mix with everyone, regardless of which floor they lived on, were the alcoholics who rode the lifts with a bottle or a bag of cans. Vertical itinerants, going up and down, drinking and dreaming of the lives they used to lead. There was one old man I was particularly fond of — Pitter-Patter-Pete. So called, because after he'd had a few drinks he'd stand in the corner of the lift singing a song and doing a kind of old soft-shoe shuffle. Pete was different from the others you'd encounter. It wasn't only the dancing. He always wore a suit, only drank White Horse whisky, and never drank it from the bottle. His drink was always in a glass. Pete and his wife Martha had moved from a tenement and were among the first to take up residency in the high-rise. While Martha was alive, I rarely saw him ride the lifts. Following her death, he began to ride them all the time. As far as I knew, he hadn't set foot outside the building since returning from Martha's funeral. Now the lone rider of the lifts, when I'd last spoken to him, he said the day he left would be his last on earth.

After a couple of weeks, I found myself standing outside the *voids* in the middle of the night listening for human activity, for any sign of life at all. Voids are flats that have been vacated, that will never be lived in again. But there never were any signs of life. Only the wind whistling through vacant interiors. The ghostly trill of it passing beneath front doors. The faintest whisper as it spilled across cold concrete and gathered in little pools of loneliness in the corners of landings.

———

After a month, I got used to the fact that there was almost no one in the high-rise. I made a covenant with loneliness and became drawn to the voids *because* they were derelict. I discovered that each one had its own musical composition. Like breath through an instrument, the passage of the wind was altered by what furniture and other remnants were inside each flat. Even wallpaper curling at its edge had an effect. Everything in them combined to produce different notes, tones, and cadences, and I'd move from door to door, listening to them. A multitude of requiems playing simultaneously in a huge, malfunctioning jukebox.

Wandering endlessly throughout the high-rise, I became increasingly fascinated by the voids. They were enigmas, black stars exerting an irresistible force on me. Determined to uncover their secrets, I began to break into them. Once inside I'd look for old messages left by past tenants or hurried dispatches written on the walls by the last occupants during their final days in the high-rise. There were always words left behind. Random inscriptions, notes written somewhere, and no matter how banal or meaningless they seemed, even if it was just a name and a date written in the faintest pencil on the back of a cupboard door, to me these inscriptions had all the substance and magic of love letters or prayers.

After the words, I'd look for objects and begin to compile inventories. This could take a few minutes or sometimes an entire day. People left all manner of things behind. Beds. Wardrobes. Sofas. In one flat the sofa had been too big to fit through the doorway and had been left where it was, trapped mid-air in the door frame. Armchairs. Dining tables and chairs. Coffee tables. Rugs. Vacuum cleaners. Lamps. Paintings. Televisions. DVD players. Video machines. Stereos. Clothes. CDs. Records. Books. Sex aids. A motorbike. A moped. And photographs, so many photographs and shopping lists and letters. In a flat on the nineteenth floor someone had gathered a thick pile of letters, photographs, and utility bills and nailed them to the ceiling like a seven-inch exclamation mark proclaiming the end of their old life.

One evening, I found a wooden rowing boat complete with oars. It was positioned in front of a bedroom wall decorated with photographic wallpaper depicting an expansive loch or fjord somewhere. A thick layer of dust coated the oars and the boat, as if its occupants had magicked themselves into the landscape and sailed off years ago. In another, someone had pre-commemorated the destruction that was about to come knocking. On their front door they'd daubed *END OF DAYS* in red paint and throughout the rooms they'd arranged life size inflatable dolls dressed and posed as if going about their daily routines, like the mannequins you'd see in old film footage of 1950s nuclear test sites.

Domestic integrities and intimacies. Memories flung up in the air and left wherever they landed. Sacred. Inviolate. Until I trespassed. Walking around the vacated flats, examining people's belongings, I felt blessed and cursed in equal measure. Then one afternoon I discovered the paradox of an enigma. To be one, it must remain one. After breaking into a flat through which the wind was singing a beautiful lament and finding nothing in it at all, not even a nail sticking up between the joints of the floorboards, I realised I couldn't crash my way into the mystery of things. That my inventories would never reveal any secrets. Only murder them.

Later that night I stood at my living-room window ripping the pages out of the book containing all the lists I'd compiled. Setting each page alight, I dropped them out of the window and watched them burn and curl, then float away like tiny ashen coracles.

Not that I stopped what I was doing altogether. Instead, I began to move all the mementos and objects I had collected to specific points in the high-rise, where I'd rearrange them and set up my own rooms. Create my own makeshift dwellings. Random spasms of interiors. Vignettes of domestic neurosis. Visions of homes. Lost homes. Broken homes. Longed-for homes. Homes designed as if someone had thrown furniture off the back of a moving van. The high-rise was sited below the flight path of jets leaving Glasgow Airport, and I'd choose a certain window on a particular floor to reveal a specific view towards the airport, to capture each jet in a framed moment of its going.

I'd watch the planes rise north-east, then bank hard right, where I'd lose them for a minute as they looped south, then passed back over the high-rise, before locking into invisible vectors to climb up and out towards their destinations. Sometimes I'd sit for hours gazing at them. If the sun was shining, I'd close my eyes and let it burn me. I'd blink into the light and through barely open eyes, glimpse jets disappearing from one life into the next.

2

Before moving to the high-rise, I'd couch-surfed for several months. Prior to that I'd been living with a young woman and had a job as a journalist. I met Lillian by chance near the end of July. It was one of those cloudless, incandescent afternoons when the sun erases the landscape, burning the heart of time, and with it your presence in the world. Sweltering beneath the khaki greatcoat I'd taken to wearing that summer, I was looking for somewhere cool to shelter from the heat and ended up in the restaurant where she worked as a waitress.

Unsteady and unsighted, I stepped from the blinding light of the street into the darkness of the interior. It took a moment before I was able to get my bearings and cross to a table in the centre of the room, where I believed I'd sat down on a chair. I discovered I hadn't when the world in front of me disappeared in a nauseating rush to the head and I pitched backward and found myself gazing up at the ceiling. In the same place a decade earlier I'd have been laughed at and applauded, or quietly pitied then helped up. Back then this was an old-time boozer. Now it was a fine dining restaurant, and this was Finnieston, where gentrification had whitewashed heritage and banished human fallibility.

All the customers who'd seen me fall — and there were a few — pretended not to have noticed or looked away in disgust. I'd like to say I didn't care, but I did. I felt an almighty wave of shame pass through me and lay there for a

minute before managing to overcome the humiliation and find the will to feel
my way back into my body. I rolled over onto my hands and knees and hung
my head between my shoulders, unsure if I wanted to get up onto the seat or
stay down on all fours and crawl out of there like a dog. I've often used music
to overcome moments when I didn't think I'd make it up off my backside or
over some line. Now, with the help of a half-remembered hymn, I tinkered
with the keys of my emotions again, working them first into sorrow and then a
bruised sense of grace, while singing, *Jesus' Blood Never Failed Me Yet*.

Gripping the edge of the table I pulled myself up off the floor and scanned
the room to see if anyone had anything to say about my fall or continued
presence. They didn't, which was just as well, because the posturing was pure
bravado. My only concern, once I was up and in my seat, was that a member of
staff might have seen me fall and that my visit would be cut short, pushing my
next drink further out of reach.

Viewed from a safe distance, such behaviour is considered tragic, pathetic,
hilarious, or some combination of all three — arranged depending on your
world view. But from my perspective there was an unheralded sense of glory
tinged with pathos in getting wasted in the afternoon. I was under no illusions
as I stumbled around mumbling to myself, that I looked like nothing other than
a loser. Yet I saw these liquid interludes from the life I'd been living less and
less every day since my teens and that I was no closer to understanding, not
as deteriorations or malfunctions, but as departures into unmapped territory.
Forays into the unknown. Attempts to trip the light fantastic into a beat my
heart kept missing.

After ordering a pint from one waiter and a double rum from another,
then drinking both without removing my coat or even opening the menu, the
waiters decided it was best to give me a wide berth. All except Lillian, who
approached my table and asked, matter-of-factly, if I'd like another drink. I
told her I would, and a few minutes later she sat down beside me with a bottle
and poured two glasses of wine, one for me and one for herself. This was a
highly unusual situation. I was accustomed to being escorted from the premises

on such occasions, or to wandering outside and finding myself standing on the pavement with no idea where I was or how I'd got there. But that afternoon I was astonished by one of those rare moments when the universe confounds all your expectations.

Assuming it was the end of her shift, I thanked her for her kindness, but suggested that for the sake of her job she might want to reconsider what she was doing. She said it wasn't the end of her shift, it was the end of her job. That she'd just this minute handed in her notice, effective immediately. What could I say to that? I wasn't conceited enough to think she'd quit on my behalf, but then again.

'Did you see me fall?' I asked.

'Did you fall?'

'I took a tumble when I sat down.'

'I didn't notice.'

'It's just, I wouldn't want you to, you know, do anything because you felt sorry for me.'

She smiled at this suggestion, 'What, like quit my job?'

'Well, yeah.'

'I didn't. Sorry if that's a disappointment.'

'It's a relief.'

'I pretty much quit the night I started. I've just been waiting for the right moment to leave.'

'And this is it?'

'Yeah. If you don't mind me joining you that is?'

'Not at all. But don't they mind you stopping mid-shift and sitting down to drink with a customer? We could go somewhere else?'

'It's fine. The manager's a friend of mine. I think he's more relieved than anything else. I don't do any work anyway. He saw me watching you. He was the one who gave me the wine and suggested I sit down.'

'Very decent of him.'

'Well, this way he gets rid of me and takes care of you.'

'Two birds with one stone.'

'More like two birds with one bottle,' she laughed.

'Decent and pragmatic.'

'He reckons we're a match made in heaven.'

We finished the wine, then left and spent the remainder of the afternoon in the park. We ate ice cream and I sang to her and read her a poem I'd written. Basically, I made a fool of myself in what I hoped was an amusing and touching manner. Afterwards we went to a bar and then back to her flat, where we danced to LCD Soundsystem all night. She had all these plastic instruments, toys really, but toys that worked like real instruments and were childishly glorious. Silver plastic trumpets and clarinets, gold plastic saxophones and trombones, tambourines, egg-shakers, glockenspiels, and plastic mouth organs. We played them all night and made love in the morning, and by the end of the month we were living together.

Lillian had moved to Glasgow from a small Scottish town to study literature at university, like I had. I think this was why she was receptive to all the bullshit I spouted that first day and why we got on so well. She was also about to start her second year away from home and at a point in her new life and literary studies where she'd discovered MDMA and Anaïs Nin. She wanted to have fun, and for that fun to have more than a touch of jeopardy. As for a match made in heaven, we were never that, but we did provide something that each of us was looking for. Lillian wanted to need someone like me. And I needed to want someone like her. For the best part of a year, we listened to excessive amounts of Belle and Sebastian, danced, sang, fucked, and drank our way through our illusions of one another, until we both discovered who the other really was.

Looking back, I wouldn't go so far as to say I was happy. I don't think I've ever been *happy*. I *would* go so far as to say that I didn't trust happiness and thought it a condition to be wary of. That I considered it a luxury that divested you of the ability to see the world as it really was, and had convinced myself, not that happiness didn't exist, but that it didn't exist for someone like me. And yet when I did manage to stay sober long enough to focus properly on the world around me, on Lillian, I almost believed I could make it. That it might be possible to salvage something from this life. That love might reappear much as it had first disappeared, without me even noticing. Something unknowable in the empty air.

Lillian was eight years younger than me, and would wink, then say my name in this breathy voice before kissing me. I would pour strong drinks and tell her that one day I'd do something magnificent, and that when I did, she'd be right by my side. I adored everything about her. And knowing this, she adored everything about herself that I adored too. The way she danced, her unforgiving laugh, her filthy sideways glance from her brown, almond-shaped eyes. Even the way she sat on the toilet taking a piss, like a dew-weighted flower drooping on a stem.

For a while I seemed to have it all, in a manner of speaking. Okay, in a very loose manner of speaking. It was a pretty tawdry version of *it all*, but a version, nonetheless. I'd been in similar positions before, but they never worked out. No matter how I tried, it seemed I could never alter the outcome. It was like getting into your car, and for no apparent reason driving it straight into a wall, then a few months later getting into a different car and doing it all over again, *repeatedly*. For years I couldn't get my head around the logic of such catastrophic failures of understanding. After a while, having written off numerous relationships, I stopped trying to understand and resigned myself to the inevitability of each approaching crash. I even came to look forward to extracting myself from the wreckage. Yet this time I'd convinced myself that things might turn out differently. But they didn't turn out differently, they rarely do. In my experience, life has a habit of confirming negative assumptions far more readily than positive ones. This certainly proved to be the case on this occasion. Every other day we'd forswear each other, and on the days in between we'd declare our undying love for each other. It was fine with me

— this carousel of chaos and harmony was normal. A way of life learned in childhood and carried on through repetition into adulthood. But for Lillian it was only ever a ride she was on. I was her co-star in the indie movie playing out in her head. Her partner in the Conor Oberst song she liked to duet, while we staggered along the road, trying to flag down taxis that kept turning off their lights.

A year into our relationship, my belief that happiness was something only possible for other people, people who'd been raised differently from me, was borne out when I lost it all again. An afternoon, that's all it took. What does that tell you about life? What does that tell you about time?

•

3

The Examiner was a free weekly newspaper distributed in the south of Glasgow. *The weekly paper that delivers your daily news*, that was our tagline. To be honest, it was pushing it to call it a newspaper, since it never contained much news. And calling it *The Examiner* was laughable, since it never examined anything. For the most part it was a patchwork of advertisements and local interest stories that weren't even interesting to the locals. Write-ups on fetes, gardening competitions, community organised bake sales, squeezed between ads for criminal lawyers, Italian and Indian restaurants, nail bars and tanning salons, pawnbrokers, funeral directors, and private taxi rackets. The pillars of Glaswegian society. Then there were the classifieds, also known as the graveyard. If you were selling anything here, the chances were your life was on the slide. If it was your business you were advertising, it was probably already dead.

Then there were the actual obituaries, names of the recently deceased, accompanied by the bare bones of a biography and a heavily redacted eulogy. Twenty-five quid staccato death notices that read like lines of decoded Morse, followed by a page or two of local sport. Occasionally, there'd be reports of petty theft, public intoxication, assault, disorderly conduct, trespass, vandalism. So-called low-impact crimes that impacted massively on the victims. Perversely, our editor deemed the reporting of such incidents detrimental to the greater good of the community, and for the most part instructed us to avoid them.

You'd go to him with a report that a recently housed Syrian family's front door had been graffitied with anti-immigrant slogans and he'd ponder, then say, without even a hint of self-mockery, 'We'll leave that to the big boys.' By *the big boys* he was, of course, referring in a cringeworthy manner to the dailies, but the dailies weren't interested. Such incidents were so common that they were rarely written up. The next time you passed that house there'd be no curtains in the windows and all the rooms would be empty, and the family who'd lived there would have moved on.

The Examiner was one of those publications that you see the otherwise unemployable — euphemistically referred to in our office as *distribution agents* — hauling around the suburbs in large fluorescent orange bags, while in a state of utter stupor. For a few hours every week they stuff them through unwelcoming letter boxes or drop bundles of them at the entrances of apartment blocks and shops, before ditching the remainder down a railway embankment or in an industrial wheelie bin behind the pub where they've decided to call it quits for the day. You come across these poor souls sitting alone in dreary bars and quiet lounges in the arse end of towns and cities everywhere. Men and women in oversized high-vis jackets, always alone and hunched over barely touched pints. Woebegone, wracked by a suffering they can feel but can't grasp. Trying to figure out who they are and what the hell they're doing in the makeshift lives they're living.

Yeah, it wasn't much of a newspaper, and I wasn't much of a journalist. For the most part I was a cataloguer of events that weren't eventful. I wrote articles that people used to pad boxes when they were moving. That people of a certain generation lined their dresser drawers with or used to clean their windows. That men who lived alone took to the bathroom when they'd ran out of toilet paper. Really there was little separating me from the poor bastards who delivered *The Examiner*. And increasingly, just like my bewildered co-workers, I had no idea what the hell I was doing.

———

Our offices were on the south side of the Clyde, on the first floor of the Old India Building, an imposing, grimy, sandstone warehouse overlooking the Broomielaw docks. Less than a hundred years before, it had housed the headquarters of a prominent shipping agent. Now, surrounded by the huge steel endoskeletons of the new commercial buildings being built all around it, it contained a ragbag of marginal business ventures that squeezed out a living on its five tumbledown floors. Among the rows of locked, dusty rooms there was a tattooist, a clairvoyant, a head shop, an antiques dealer, a dubious import/export business, a pet shop that no longer sold pets, and an adult entertainment shop, all operating on the brink of legality or extinction. With *The Examiner* one of those heading towards extinction, the only legit business that was flourishing in the entire building was the bakery chain directly below us on the ground floor. As a result, our offices stank of reconstituted meat and hydrogenated vegetable fat, while every surface beneath the lowered ceiling was coated in a film of grease. It slowed everyone and everything down. Even the balls in the Newton's cradle on my desk seemed to have lost the will to swing. Not that this glutinous fallout prevented my colleagues from purchasing their lunch there. Or from having endless discussions each morning about the merits or otherwise of every piece of sweet and savoury crap they were going to consume that afternoon. It was a conversation depressing in both content and frequency. A low budget, high-fat remake of *Groundhog Day*.

Since I'd moved in with Lillian, the number of days I made it to the office had dropped below their already meagre level. When I did bother to go in, I usually got there around nine. The first thing I'd do was make a coffee, then I'd sit down at my desk and check to see if anything had happened that was worth following up on. Which is exactly what I did the morning I picked up my final assignment. The day things fell apart.

———

It was, on the face of it, an unremarkable job. An invite to a promotional event taking place in a church hall in Govanhill. I hadn't intended to drink, not at all. Then I picked a tattered playing card up off the pavement. The card was the seven of spades and it was midday — high noon in the land of holy trinkets and savaged hearts. The truth is, scoring runes is like scoring drugs. If you're determined to find them and know what you're looking for, you can find them anywhere.

The street leading to the church was narrow and the tenements on either side tall, creating a canyon-like vista. Apart from the occasional fluffy white cloud with nothing to do but drift and disappear, the strip of sky framed between the rooftops was clear and blue. The colour of Hail Marys and distant love — both invocation and response — it seemed to promise that there was someone waiting for me somewhere and that I should light out to find them.

Back on earth, the road gave off a fine dust and there was a yearning in the air, as if spring were chasing a warmth that had been stolen from it. An old guy with a long grey beard and wild hair shocking out of the sides of a baseball cap leaned out of his third-floor window in his black leather waistcoat and shouted down to me in a gruff, booming voice, 'Hey Señor, can you tell me where we're heading?'

On the pavement in front of his tenement there was the stripped chassis of an old Norton, and in the room behind him I could hear his words echoed in the crackle and scratch of a record that sounded like it was clattering out of cheap speakers. He looked like some Hells Angels prophet who'd gone to seed, wheelless and beggared in Govanhill. I looked up and shrugged, then pointed to the church and walked on, keeping my eyes fixed on its doors.

'That's right, ma man, fucking Armageddon, ye shower of bastards!' he yelled after me.

As I walked towards the ornate portal, perfectly centred at the end of the street, it felt like I was being led to my destination down a corridor of light. Somehow I'd transgressed the visible landscape and entered an architecture composed of sunlight, shadow, and dust, which had something of the pilgrimage about it. I could have been in mourning or Jerusalem. I could have wandered into someone's old home movie. I could have been anywhere.

The main doors were locked, so I entered via a fire exit that had been left open at the side of the building, then continued along a cold, dank, labyrinthine passage that led to the hall. Once inside, there was nothing to do but drink. To have done otherwise would have been sacrilege. I'd opened up to the day. Bore witness to the seven of spades, the prophet, and the wine. The kingdom, the power, and the glory.

You see, this is how we forgive ourselves our trespasses, our lapsed faith in life. With spiritual sleights of hand and praying for all we are worth.

I'd imagined sunlight through stained-glassed windows playing across chiselled stone walls. My very own holy slo-mo disco. Instead, the hall was cheerless, purely functional. An early Seventies add-on to the main church, with no stained glass and two rows of high windows covered with metal grills. Epiphany was tipping fast towards the slough of despond and desperate to avoid a wretched, lacklustre state of mind, I quickly drank another glass of wine and adjusted my expectations. Looked at from a different angle, the venue wasn't so disappointing. It was sober. No, not *sober*. More wine. It was sensible. *Ascetic*. The perfect counterpoint to the event. Saved from another trial and delivered from evil. Another goddamn amen.

What had been billed as a pleasant afternoon of light refreshments intended to promote ladies' hairdressing salons felt a little out of kilter from the start. A spirit of disharmony hung in the air, as if the venue desperately wanted to exorcise the event. You could sense it build between the contrasting elements within the hall. In the click-clacking of high heels across the wooden floors. In the spandex, glitter, and stramash of vivid pinks and greens and reds against the dark mustard-coloured walls. In the bouquets of liberally sprayed perfume overlapping the odour of yesterday's lentil soup and the dampness. In the dirty-mouthed talk and shrill laughter echoing up into the high rafters. Other than Christmas and when it was used by members of the local Freemasons Lodge to hold meetings, I can't imagine the place having ever known such adornment. But a box of rat-tailed tinsel and some men wearing white gloves and well-pressed girdles were nothing compared to twenty-odd half-cut Glaswegian hairdressers.

As well as myself, there was a photographer from *The Examiner* there, Roddy Bootle. Roddy had despised me ever since I'd told him his work was an endless series of banal snapshots. Today he was trailing the local councillor, who was smiling and marvelling at the enterprise of his constituents, while imagining how splendid his face was going to look in next week's newspaper. I talked to them both briefly, then excused myself, telling them I was intrigued by the undercurrents of the day and wanted to explore them further.

Before I moved on, Roddy made his thoughts on my journalistic approach clear.

'Undercurrents, my arse,' he said. 'You're so full of shite it's unbelievable.'

'That's your problem right there, Roddy. You don't believe enough, as a result you don't *see* enough. Not ideal for a photographer,' I responded.

'I've always thought that even if we believe in nothing, we have to believe in something,' the councillor interjected with a baffling rhetorical juxtaposition and an end-of-conversation smile.

What I believed as I gazed at the healthy supply of booze weighing down the folding trestle table and watched all these scissor-happy hairdressers size each other up, was that the councillor's beaming coupon wasn't going to be the highlight of the day. When it finally came, the breach itself wasn't unexpected, but the manner in which it arrived was. With the warm Prosecco and Pinot Grigio in full flow, there were the expected flashpoints. Needling developed between the owners of rival salons. Blatant attempts were made to woo prized staff. Rumours spread about unpaid bills, tips not being distributed, liquidation. There were bitchy asides between prima donna stylists. Sarcastic remarks regarding colouring disasters were thrown across the room. Someone vomited their party food into a waste-paper bin. But things really got going when the owner of Ruff Cutts, a Dusty Springfield lookalike in her fifties, took umbrage at certain comments made about her clientele.

The fact is, Dusty should never have been there in the first place, since she ran a dog-grooming salon. It was this aberration that kicked everything off. There had been a few jokes at her expense, and rather than take them in good humour, Dusty decided she'd fight her corner. Initially, she was content to stumble around proclaiming the technical superiority of those who cut dog hair over those who cut human hair. But when staff from one of the salons started whistling and tossing cocktail sausages for her to fetch, the situation deteriorated rapidly. She was bouncing from group to group like a ball hitting the bumpers in a pinball machine, spilling wine everywhere she went, when she finally hit the bullseye and the afternoon lapsed from absurdity to all-out violence. In a loud, foul-mouthed rant, Dusty accused a young woman, who'd stood her ground and stared Dusty down when barged into, of not only poaching her clients, but of seducing them.

The young woman looked momentarily stunned, before asking, 'Are you saying I fuck dogs?'

'That's exactly what I'm saying.'

'*What?*'

'You fucked them all. *My poor pooches.*'

'You're crazy.'

'I'm not. You did. They told me so.'

'Who told you so?'

'*The dogs*,' Dusty claimed, breathless and wide-eyed, like a child caught out in a ridiculous lie blaming it on the fairies at the bottom of her garden.

For a moment there was silence in the hall, then the young woman burst out laughing. Dusty responded by throwing a glass of wine in the young woman's face and the two of them started fighting. After initially getting the better of her adversary by spinning her around in a headlock, Dusty was overcome by the young woman's speed and agility. Losing her footing, she found herself pinned to the floor, being repeatedly slapped in the face. Several people stepped forward to pull them apart, but were furtively rebuffed by the loose crowd that had gathered around the two women, like in a fight in a schoolyard.

By now, Roddy was running around, snapping away, while the councillor looked on in horror, and I somehow found myself at the centre of those doing the rebuffing. When Dusty spat in the young woman's face, someone further back yelled, 'Shear the bitch!' Then someone passed me an object and urged me to give it to Betsy. I had no idea who Betsy was, but assumed she was the young woman. Without stopping to look at what I was holding or to think about what was happening, I held out the object and allowed her to take it from my hand. Wielding a set of battery powered clippers, Betsy went about shaving a considerable chunk off Dusty's considerable beehive right down to her scalp. When they finally pulled a grinning Betsy off Dusty and led her to the kitchen at the back of the hall, she winked and mouthed a kiss, then handed me the still vibrating clippers. Looking down at a ravaged and bloodied Dusty, who was refusing assistance to stand, I felt both ashamed and aroused, and had the absurd idea that this must have been how Lee Harvey Oswald felt as he stood with his rifle in his hands, gazing down from the Texas School Book Depository. After the police had arrested Dusty and Betsy and led them away, I looked at the undisputed evidence of mental illness laid out all around me and thought, God really does move in mysterious ways. The councillor had done a disappearing act, but an animated, grinning Roddy kept popping up wherever I went and going on about the money shots he'd taken.

'You're going to love them,' he said.

'No, I'm not,' I responded.

'Yes you will.'

'I won't.'

'You will.'

'I promise, I won't.'

'Oh, I promise, *you will*.'

'This is fucking stupid,' I said and headed for the trestle table.

To avoid fighting with Roddy I drank enough wine to start a fight with myself. Still troubled by the role I'd played in Dusty's shearing, I figured I was due a good self-inflicted beating. When they were all out of Prosecco and Pinot Grigio I left the church and walked unsteadily back out into the same street I'd walked along earlier. The sun was still up and out there somewhere, but it had moved on, swung westward with its shiny ways like a carnival departing town, leaving a tomb-like street in its wake. Lillian had said she'd cook dinner that evening, and I'd crossed my heart and hoped to die and promised to be there, but I didn't want to go home now, not yet. I wanted to push on and stay awake for as long as physically possible. What is it they say about the mad not wanting to sleep? It's because they're afraid of who they'll meet in their dreams. Luckily, I still had my seven of spades.

I'd written an article the year before about a derelict synagogue on the edge of Govanhill. One of only two Eastern European-style synagogues in the UK, it was being fought over by its custodians and a collection of Jewish anarchists. The former wanted to sell it off to developers, who planned to erect residential flats, the latter to reopen it as a place of worship. While researching its heritage, I'd met and for a brief time dated a girl I'd interviewed. Marisa was Russian and had moved to Glasgow to become a veterinarian. At least that's what she said at first. She soon altered her story and told me that, though she did love animals, in truth she'd fled here. That because of a situation she'd got herself involved in with the Bratva, she'd had no choice in the matter. At first I was intrigued by her, then I feared for her, *then I feared for myself.* Whenever I was with her I got the feeling that she wanted something from me. Something total, that involved all of me. That once given would be unrecoverable. She showed me some photographs of herself shooting watermelons with a Glock in a sun-drenched clearing in the Black Forest. She said she'd been given the gun to protect herself, while hiding out in a farm. There were other troubling intimations. That people may have been imprisoned because of her actions.

That individuals may have been tortured, individuals that she knew to be innocent of the transgressions they'd been accused of — because she was complicit in them. That someone may even have been murdered because of her. I should have known better than to get involved with her. Actually, I did know better, but did it anyway. My addiction to head-on collisions was deep-rooted by this point, and from the day we met I knew I had no option but to see this particular crash all the way to the scrapyard.

It turned out I was correct about her wanting something from me, though nothing as darkly romantic or fatal as I'd imagined or secretly hoped. She wanted me to lend her money. Two thousand pounds to pay a debt she said if she didn't settle could result in her murder. I gave her half the money and only heard from her again in a series of brief, staccato texts sent a minute or so apart a week later. *You are sweet*, she texted. *I could almost love you for your naivety*, she texted. *Oh God, yes, yes*, she texted. *I could have loved you*, she texted. *But your stupidness would have got in the way*, she texted. *Do not contact me again*, she texted. I thought, either she's trying to figure out exactly how she feels about me or she's texting me while snorting coke bought with the money I gave her. Knowing Marisa as little as I did, the second scenario was far more likely.

I did see her a couple of months later in a bar one evening. She was with a large group of people and when she saw me approach she drew her thumbnail slowly across her throat, then spoke to a guy who moved towards me with purpose, at which point I made a beeline for the door. I'd already been robbed of my money, and now I'd been robbed of the emotional hurt I was due, too. Further along the street I entered another bar and started a fight with someone, hoping the guy might batter the hurt back into me, which he duly did. Afterwards I went home and listened to *Bitches Brew* very loudly on my stereo. I lived in what was advertised as a studio flat. In truth it was a bedsit in a converted townhouse in Glasgow's West End. My neighbours on either side started banging on their walls, also my neighbours above and below on their floor and ceiling, respectively. I fought with them too, though only verbally, until I crashed out exhausted.

But all that was in the past. I was a changed man now, and I decided I would go and find Marisa. Not to demand my money back. To show her I was capable of forgiveness and great understanding. To somehow move myself closer to setting the world, or at least my world and Marisa's, to rights. This was my genuine intention.

I'd never been to her home and wasn't sure where to start looking for her. We'd always meet in cafés, but it was too late in the day to try those. I decided my best bet was to buy a bottle of tequila from an off-licence and walk the streets with my seven of spades, willing her or someone who knew her to appear.

I bought my tequila from an off-licence called the Land of Liquor, only it turned out it wasn't tequila, it was mescal, and there was a *gusano de maguey*, a pale moth larva, at the bottom of the bottle. As soon as I saw that godforsaken creature, I knew that I'd follow it through darkness and disharmony until I caught it. That I'd chase it all the way to the moon it would never reach.

I don't recall all the details of that evening. I spent some time wandering around trying to suck the larva from its golden circumfluence, but it kept floating up and away from me, as if in thrall to some celestial orientation even in death, whenever I tipped the bottle to my mouth. The details I do recall, spin and whirl around my mind like figures and objects caught in a tornado. Halfway down a lane I saw a woman in a white dress backed up against a chain-link fence by a man. Her pants lay discarded on the ground and her legs were wrapped around his waist, while they both clutched the wire. The fence secured a plot with a partly demolished house and they were going at it as if they were trying to fuck their way back inside, or purge themselves of something that dwelt among the ruins. For some reason, as unfathomable to me now as it was then, the rattling of the chain-link and the rhythm of their fucking reminded me of Prokofiev's *Troika*. As I stood watching, my heart fluttered excitedly for them. Then they slowed to the occasional half-hearted thrust, and now all I could hear were the little horse's bells in Robert Frost's 'Stopping by Woods on a Snowy Evening'. It was all a bit droll and ridiculous and sad, like all dispirited sex is, and I walked on, leaving them clinging forlornly to the galvanised fencing.

I saw cars circling the neighbourhood, cruising the streets. They would slow to a stop and a barely clad woman would emerge from a tenement close and get into the passenger seat, then the car would drive off.

I saw money change hands between two men, then a boy no older than seventeen follow one of the men down an alley.

I saw a man stride across a road and grab the lead from the hands of a child who was standing with his dog. He dragged the dog, with its belly flat to the ground and its legs and face locked in fear, back across the road then holding it down by its neck, rubbed its face into a pile of shit at the entrance to the tenement he'd exited. The child ran across the road, screaming and crying for the man to stop, but the man ignored him and beat the dog until it lay trembling and whimpering on the pavement. It all happened so quickly, the violence was so intense, that I couldn't move. I wasn't the only one, there were others who'd watched. Some also in fear and shock, one or two smiling nonchalantly. When it was over the boy picked up the dog's twitching body and cradling it in his arms, walked off sobbing. I approached him to offer help and he looked at me contemptuously and spat on the pavement near my feet. An hour or so later, I wound up in a house where everyone looked drugged to the edge of death.

But first I met a man selling jewellery on a small folding table set up at one end of a row of market stalls that were covered over and tied shut. In an accent I couldn't place, he told me his name was Omar Sharif, but that people called him the Sheriff, all of which I found hard to believe for a host of reasons. He had a tray of large plastic costume rings. About twenty-five gaudy pieces displayed on a large red velour pad that he was selling for two quid each. I asked him for ten.

'A man of fine taste,' the Sheriff beamed as I put a ring on each finger. Smelling the booze off me and clocking the bottle sticking out my coat pocket, he asked if there was anything else I'd like to buy beside rings. I asked him if he knew Marisa.

'You're looking for sex?'

'I'm looking for Marisa,' I said.

'Exactly, you want a girl.'

'Yes. I want to find a girl. A young woman. Marisa.'

'I know exactly who you want, follow me,' he said.

He wasn't Russian and he certainly wasn't Egyptian. At the time I believe I thought he might have been Romanian. In hindsight, I realise he was probably Scottish, putting on a mock Eastern European accent. Either way, I'm certain he had no idea who Marisa was and didn't care whether I found her or not. But I didn't think any of that then. I had my seven of spades and my mescal and moth larva and my plastic costume jewellery worn like the insignias of an alternative law — as if I'd just been deputised by some fugitive sheriff — and I believed I had a wrong to mend.

He closed his tray, then folded up his little table and put both into a blue Ikea bag. Without questioning where we were going, I followed him to a grand, dilapidated Victorian villa in Pollokshields. He banged on the storm doors and when no one answered he made a phone call and minutes later they were partially opened by a tall skinny guy who was wearing tight black jeans and a white vest, out of which poked a vulture-like neck and head. We sidled into the inner porch and after the doors were closed behind us we entered a long hallway, dimly lit by a few heavy-duty gripper lamps. The Sheriff said someone would need to be paid if he was to find what I wanted. I gave him a twenty-pound note and he left me and walked up a flight of stairs. The guy who'd let us in led me into a large room directly to our right that had an oval black-leather-studded bar in the near corner to my left and a red curtain drawn right across the centre of the room.

'Ye okay?' he enquired.

'Fine.'

'Ye look a bit fucked.'

'I'm fine.'

'What are ye after?'

'I'm looking for someone.'

'A girl?'

'No, a young woman.'

'Girl, young woman, what's the difference?'

'At least five years.'

'Right, whatever. And the Sheriff said he'd find a girl for ye, did he?' He asked, his head shaking with mirth.

'Yeah. But not just *any* girl.'

'Right, ye want a special girl.'

'She's a young woman.'

'A special young woman.'

'I never said she was special.'

'Okay, whatever, any fucking young woman. But he said he could do this for ye, did he, the Sheriff?'

'He did, yeah. Find a particular young woman.'

'How exactly do ye know the Sheriff?'

'I'm his deputy.'

'Wait, *his what?*'

'Deputy.'

He let out an involuntary snort. 'Fuck me gently,' he laughed, 'like the doig?'

'The what?' I asked.

'The *doig*, man. The *doig*.'

'What's a *doig?*'

'A dog man, *a doig*. *Deputy fucking Doig*.'

'You mean Deputy Dawg, but like Doig. *Deputy Doig*.'

'Aye, *exactly*.'

'Like *beigel* instead of bagel?'

'What the fuck is a *beigel*?'

'It's like a doig, only you can eat it.'

'What the fuck are ye talking about?'

'What the fuck are *you* talking about?'

'Forget it, ye fucking bampot. Here, help yersel to a drink, *Deputy Doig*,' he chuckled and nodded towards the bar. 'I've a feeling the Sheriff will be a long time,' he said, before leaving me on my own.

There was nothing to help myself to, but I found a plastic glass and drank several mescals. Music was coming from somewhere deep within the building, while occasional moans and snippets of conversation floated into the room from points unknown. There was a heavy presence of multiple bodies in the house, and yet a thick uneasy quietness, as if everyone were sinking or being forcibly submerged. This room was lit by gripper lamps too, I imagined the whole building was lit with them. The interior was murky and damp and had an eerie, aqueous light, like a house sinking in a dream. Huge chunks of plaster had fallen from the ceiling and walls, revealing what looked like the wooden frame of a massive old ship. I walked into the centre of the room and grabbed hold of the curtain and didn't let go until I'd floundered, popping it hook by hook from the rail, right across the ceiling. Its absence revealed a row of metal-framed single beds backed against a wall like in a dormitory. I lay down on one of them and thought of *Goldilocks*, then drifted off to sleep thinking about the Grimm's fairy tale *Hansel and Gretel*. Then I was *Alice in Wonderland* and I jumped to my feet. At one end of the wall there was a door and I opened it and began wandering through a series of interconnected, large, high-ceilinged rooms in the sprawling ground floor of the house. There were used condoms and empty beer bottles and nitrous oxide cylinders everywhere, as if there had recently been a party. The last door I tried opened onto a room where four men, three women, maybe more, were scattered in various positions across a double bed, two armchairs, the floor, and a settee. I flopped down into the settee, where a guy was slowly disappearing into the greasy cushions at the opposite end. A short, balding, white guy with a round, pockmarked face, said something I missed in a broad Glaswegian accent, while in another room I was sure I heard a baby crying. He may have simply been the only person who was still standing, but I got the distinct impression he was the host, as he walked around the room doing whatever he wished to whomever he wished. He put his hands up a woman's top, then down her pants, and she began twitching and jerking as if she were trying to escape him in her dreams. After she'd given up and stopped running, he moved on to a man who was passed out on the floor. He unzipped the man's trousers, pulled out the man's cock, then his own, and began to arouse and masturbate the man and himself. His left eye was scarred closed, but he stared at me with his right eye, while pleasuring himself and the unconscious man. As I watched him, I drank straight from the bottle of mescal and finally felt the larva rest on the tip of my tongue. I moved it around inside my mouth and winced as I bit down and popped its liquid guts into the back of my throat. I knew it wasn't hallucinogenic, but I'd hoped it might yet be transformative. At that moment the host licked his lips, then put his head down between the guy's thighs and finished him off in his mouth. I wanted to move, but for the second time that night I couldn't. Then I saw a sliver of light at the edge of the dirty blue curtain that was nailed to the wall near my shoulder. At the same time a buzzing noise started up in my head. I realised the buzzing was coming from behind the curtain and I looked closer and saw a huge bluebottle move around the edge of the curtain into the room, followed by a second bluebottle, and then a third. All three of them moved awkwardly from side to side like tiny gunslingers, drunk and bloated on blood and death. As they stood facing me down I realised I was woefully outnumbered and outgunned, and I wondered how the hell I was going to get out of there. I was ill with a sickness that dropped through my being, through the earth, through space, and I leant over the edge of the settee and vomited over the floor. Immediately a terrible fear entered me, the fear that if I didn't kill whatever was eating me up, then I would have no choice but to either kill myself or start killing other people. I stood up and lurched towards the door. The grinning host, sated on the fill he'd had of others, watched me through his heavy-lidded eye as I left.

I was staggering through room after room, becoming increasingly frantic, when finally, I burst out through the storm doors and ran into the middle of the street. The sky was covered with long scrolls of burning cloud that looked close enough to touch. But when I reached out to take hold of one, the entire sky began to unravel, and I started running again.

When I stopped to see where I was, I realised the streets were quiet and there was no one else around. I hoped it was morning, but my mobile phone was dead, so I couldn't tell if it was early morning or late evening. I walked until I found a main road where the shutters of shop fronts were being rolled up and traffic was flowing, but it was still too early for the pubs to be open. I was cold and shivering and didn't know where to go, so I walked into town and straight into House of Fraser. I remembered going in there once with my mum and dad when I was a child. We were still a family then, and I'd never forgotten how warm and comfortable and luxurious it felt in there, like some dream show home. My mum had wanted to buy make-up, and that's where I went now, straight to the make-up department. I stood looking around, wondering what to do next, when a young woman, whose true face it was impossible to see because of all the product she wore, approached me. Her eyes were kind though — even with all the make-up I could see that she had kind eyes.

'Do you need assistance?' she asked.

'Yes, yes, I need assistance,' I slurred, unaware of just how fucked I was until I tried to talk.

'And what exactly can I do for you?' she asked.

'Make me,' I tried to smile.

'Make you what?' she asked kindly.

'Make me *me*,' I said.

'What? Are you serious?'

'Yes.'

'The only thing I should make, is make you go home to your bed.'

'Please,' I pleaded, almost crying.

'You want me to give you a makeover?'

'Yes. Transform me.'

'Are you for real?'

'Unfortunately.'

'You're crazy.'

'Please.'

'You're drunk.'

'Just a little.'

'Just a little? *You're absolutely reeking.*'

'Please, just this once.'

'And then you'll go?'

'I will. I swear.'

She shook her head and looked at me warmly. 'Honestly, I must be bloody daft. Sit up here and I'll see what I can do.'

She worked quickly, but diligently. It took less than ten minutes. When she'd finished she took a step back and looked at what she'd created.

'How do I look?' I asked.

'Angelic,' she said.

'Really?' I asked.

'Yeah, in a scary sort of way.'

4

When I turned up at Lillian's days later I had my key in one hand and was clutching a bottle of red wine in the other. The security chain was on and she wouldn't let me in and would only talk through the gap. This time she didn't bother to ask where I'd been, because she didn't care anymore. Which was just as well, because I couldn't remember much of what occurred after House of Fraser. I recall passing through a series of pubs, like a worn thread through the eye of so many needles. There were parts of the city I didn't recognise, and rooms in flats and houses I didn't recognise. There were further cosmetic transformations. And perfumes and warm skin and mouths I was lost in. Yet none of my memories stitched together. Rather it was an unstitching. An agglomerate of subtractions. A series of absences. Of illusory moments falling away, one after the other.

I remember calling my work with one excuse for not being able to make it in, forgetting I'd done so, then hours later, calling again with a completely different excuse. I think this happened several times. On one occasion I had rabies, and on another I declared myself deceased.

I watched Lillian with a certain voyeuristic pleasure as she criss-crossed the hallway, walking from room to room with a bin bag, dismantling what remained of our relationship. When I heard the window in the living room slide open, then come down with a dull thud seconds later, I knew my belongings were on the pavement two floors below. I should have gone to collect them, but again I couldn't move. Watching her felt sickening and liberating in equal measure. When Lillian came back to the door, she tossed a copy of the novel I'd written over my head. I'd written it on her laptop and the only copy I had was the one cascading down the stairs. I began gathering up all the pages, and when I returned to her door, she slammed it shut.

She was twenty-one years old and kissed me like I'd never been kissed before. But now she told me from behind a locked door that she wasn't interested in kissing an old drunk who couldn't grow up or write for shit. To be fair, I could see where she was coming from. For both our sakes I should have walked away, but I couldn't for reasons that were too powerful to overcome at that moment. I knew how much I'd miss her. Her mouth, her breasts, the soft warm press of her skin, our impossible future. I knew, because her absence already hurt.

After a minute's silence I realised she wasn't in the hallway and I got down in front of the letter box and opened the flap. I could smell warmed croissants, freshly brewed coffee, and pressing my face hard against the cold metal rim of the letter box, I was able to see just beyond the edge of the kitchen doorway. The kitchen had large, east-facing sash windows, through which the morning light spilled into the hallway as if from an open treasure chest filled with gold. I could hear her moving around in there, but I couldn't see her.

'Please let me in,' I called into the empty hallway. 'I just want to be inside with you, sitting at the kitchen table. Please, Lillian, let me explain.'

'Too late,' she called back.

'But you don't know the things I've seen.'

'I don't want to know.'

'Such awful things happening to people.'

'Don't tell me any of your shit. I don't want to hear it.'

'I saw a couple fucking in the street, well almost, they were down a lane. And a dog. A poor, poor, beaten dog.'

'No more. I'm sick of you. Sick of all the crap you bring into my life.'

'There was a depraved, one-eyed man. I couldn't do anything to stop him. I couldn't stop any of it.'

'You can't do anything about any of it because *you are it*. It's all you.'

'What is?'

'The darkness. It's you. It follows you everywhere. *You are the darkness*.'

'Please, Lillian. I know you've had enough. I have too. I swear. Please, please let me in.'

'Fuck off.'

I started sobbing and reciting fragments of poems I'd written. That's when she said she was going to call the police or her brother if I didn't leave. That all my shit was about to catch up with me. Two sonnets, an elegy, a few haikus, and some free verse later, she made good on her threat. I was thankful that at least she hadn't called the police. It was Friday and the courts were closed until Monday. In another life I'd have been handcuffed and flung into a cage in the back of a van and left in a police cell all weekend and that would have broken me completely. Instead, her brother turned up with two bandmates from the tribute group he was in, It's Naw Patrol.

'Do something with him,' she said to them through the gap in the door.

I was down on my hands and knees, gazing up at them.

'It was only poetry,' I said.

'Look at the fucking nick of yourself mate, you're a mess,' Jimmy the drummer said.

'That seems to be the gathering consensus,' I smiled.

'He stinks worse than a dog,' Lillian added, sniffing through the gap.

'He is a fucking dog,' her brother affirmed.

'Why don't we all go inside and discuss it over a drink?' I suggested, proffering the bottle of wine I'd been clutching.

'Fuck you, shithead,' he said.

'What if I lay here, then? If I just lay here, what would you do then?' I smiled up at him.

'You know, I always hoped you'd just fuck off and die somewhere,' he responded.

'And every time you sang that fucking ridiculous song I felt like lying down in the middle of the road and doing exactly that.'

At this he nodded to his bandmates that it was time to get this over with, and they got hold of my arms and legs and threw me down a flight of stairs.

The bottle smashed when I landed, covering my greatcoat and the white shirt I was wearing in wine, but I'd kept hold of the manuscript and somehow I wasn't cut by the broken glass. Miraculously, I was relatively unhurt from the fall, but I did manage to punch myself full in the face, which hurt like hell and sent blood pouring from my nose. Lying in the close below I heard laughing and music as Lillian let her brother and his bandmates into the flat. For some reason I still thought there was a chance she'd come down and take me back. Perhaps I thought there was something left of the spirit she'd shown the afternoon we met. That she'd relent and take one last chance on me. But there was nothing left, she didn't relent. I could understand her exasperation with all the madness I'd brought into her life, and the poetry was so bad it certainly merited a little violence. Still, I never thought the humiliation was necessary.

As soon as I was out on the street I looked through the bin bags and found a rucksack which I stuffed with a few essentials. Some clothes, my passport, my old transistor radio, and the first book I'd bought after moving to Glasgow. A copy of Rilke's *Duino Elegies* that I picked up in Voltaire and Rousseau. Everything else I decided to get rid of. I was going to draw a line in the sand, make a clean break, start all over again.

When I dropped the remainder of my belongings in the doorway of a charity shop further up the street the three staff members inside all stopped what they were doing and watched, open-mouthed and horrified, as I smiled and waved at them. I knew I didn't look great, but I didn't think I looked that bad. Wondering what they saw that was so dreadful, I stepped to the side and looked at my reflection in a dressing mirror in the window display. When I did I was almost as shocked as they were. I looked like a bludgeoned drag queen. As well as being covered in blood and wine, huge false eyelashes that looked like peacock feathers were falling off my ochre and gold eyelids. My cheeks were rouged, and I had dark glittery blue lipstick spread all over my mouth and jaw. I'd set out from Frasers looking like Elizabeth Taylor in *Cleopatra* and wound up days later somewhere between Baby Jane and a birthday cake that had been left out in the rain. I started laughing a little hysterically, and if the staff had looked shocked before, now they looked genuinely scared. One of them rushed to the door, locked it, then pulled the blind down. I was laughing like a full-blown madman, but I didn't care, not about how I looked or anything else. Because this was the day I was going to start all over again.

I walked along Argyle Street, then cut up onto Byres Road and headed for the Botanic Gardens. I had one more thing to discard. Choosing a bench by an old ash tree, I sat down and began throwing the three hundred or so pages of my manuscript up into the air. A few caught the breeze and fluttered off through the park. The rest — like captive birds unsure what to do after being unexpectedly released — lit on the branches of the tree or lay on the ground around the bench and my feet. On my way to the park, I'd envisioned this grand gesture. A cathartic, life-changing event. Instead, the overwhelming feeling was a mixture of entropy and emptiness. Afraid I'd be done for littering and feeling lousy at the thought of leaving someone else to clean up the mess I'd made, I began to pick the pages back up off the ground and out of the ash tree. But there were too many of them and the breeze had picked up and they were fluttering off in every direction, so I gave up and stuffed the pages I'd gathered into a nearby bin. I'd thrown it all away again, moved further around the bend to stumble off through God only knew how many more bars, and I was okay with that. As far as I was concerned I was back exactly where I belonged.

Everyone self-mythologises a little in life, addicts more than most, especially alcoholics. It's a habit hardwired with the belief that we're on a mission from

God. I've sat in some of the worst dives in Glasgow alongside some of the most depraved people you could ever have the misfortune to meet. Characters capable of carrying out the most despicable acts. Yet I'm certain that secretly every last one of them believed they were the prodigal son at one time or another. I was no different. I told myself things hadn't turned out so badly. That it was all part of a bigger plan.

In the end, it wasn't because Lillian was younger or because we drank too much. Though she was and we did. Or that our kisses began to fail each other's lips. Even when we fought, and towards the end we fought all the time, we always wanted each other more than ever afterwards. And it wasn't a matter of wanting different things from life. It wasn't even the dark places I went to. Lillian was right, it was the darkness I carried deep inside.

5

My first day back at work following the Govanhill debacle turned out to be my last. As soon as I entered our office I knew something was wrong. The first two colleagues I smiled at shook their heads then turned away, the third looked right through me as if I weren't there. When I sat down at my cubicle I discovered numerous Post-it notes, all exhorting me, with a combination of capitals and exclamation marks, to talk to the editor. Expecting as much, I was preparing to walk into his office and take what was coming, when I noticed the photograph leaning against my ball-clackers. It was of me at the Govanhill event, a glass of wine in one hand and in the other a set of clippers I was in the process of passing to Betsy. I picked it up and read the inscription on the back in red ink, *The money shot*, was all it said. Beneath this there was a smiley face and the initials, *RB*.

I knew there was little chance of coming back from this. There was even less chance of me facing the editor without assistance. Thankfully, it was Monday, and Monday was new stock day at Donny's.

Donny's head shop was on the top floor. On the way up to see him I stopped off at Suzy's to ask if she wanted to join me. When I walked in, she was talking to a woman inside the purple-curtained booth where she did her readings. She must have already established a connection with the other side, as the woman had only just finished sobbing and between occasional chest-heaving sighs, was now snivelling quietly like a child who'd been told off.

'It's been five years,' the woman whimpered.

'He says not to keep the past, to let it go. Have you been keeping the past?'

'Keeping the past?'

'From before, holding on to ...'

'Things?'

'Yes. Things.'

'Yes.'

'You've let go of some of his belongings, haven't you, but not everything? There are things you won't let go of, that's what he's telling me.'

'Yes, that's true.'

'His hobby?' Suzy ventured.

'Yes.'

'It wasn't just a hobby though ...'

'No.'

'It was his passion, wasn't it?' Suzy was clearly in full flow now, reading the woman's every movement and expression.

'Yes, his instruments.'

'Oh my, he's smiling. He loved his instruments, didn't he?'

'*Yes*,' the woman said with a hint of fear in her voice, as if the person they'd reached might appear any second.

'And he still does. But he says he doesn't need them now, not where he is. He says heaven is full of music.'

'*He's in heaven?*' The woman gasped.

'Yes, there's light all around him, so much light. He's in the good place.'

'But you loved your instruments, I can't get rid of them,' the woman said a little frantically, and I imagined her glancing from side to side and then behind to see if she could catch a glimpse of the departed.

'The tin whistle. He's saying keep the tin whistle to remember him by, but nothing else.'

The woman went quiet and didn't respond.

'Maybe it's a recorder or a bugle, a wind instrument of some sort?' Suzy continued, feeling her way through the fog of her client's emotions.

'They're all percussion instruments, he loved percussion,' the lady said, then stopped snivelling.

'No, wait. It's not a tin whistle. I hear bells.'

No response.

'No, not bells. It was like bells, but not bells. It's a a a t-t-t-tria …'

'*Yes.*'

'T-t-t-riaanng …'

'*Triangle!*' the woman exclaimed.

'*Yes.* Did he have a triangle?'

'It was the first instrument we bought him,' the woman blurted and started sobbing again.

'That's it. He says you should keep the triangle, but to give the rest to charity.'

'That's Robbie, that's exactly what Robbie would say to do.'

'He doesn't want you crying every time you see his instruments. He wants other people to have them now. He wants them to bring happiness, not sadness. He says, "Mummy, don't worry about me. Mummy, in heaven everything is music."'

At this, the woman started outright wailing — 'My son! My son! My only son!' — while Suzy pushed on towards her finale.

'When he talks, it's music. When he moves, it's music. Even when he thinks, it's music. He says he has all the beautiful music he'll ever need now. Just keep the triangle, keep that, and on his birthday each year hit it once for every year he had on earth.'

'Thank you,' the woman gushed. 'Oh, thank you so much, thank you.'

When they exited the booth, Suzy saw me and smiled. 'Please, sir, take a seat and I'll be with you in a few minutes.' Then she turned back to the woman. 'Would you still like your spirit portrait?' she asked her.

'Yes, if that's okay?'

'Of course. I think it'd be good for you to see all the love you have around you.'

For a tenner Suzy would give you a spirit portrait. She had a polaroid camera in a box with a light bulb and a transparent, coloured, spinning disk. She'd take your photograph, then explain who and what all the coloured blobs around your face and body were — the spirts of relatives, guardian angels, energies, etc. Carrying her spirit portrait in a green velveteen sleeve, for which she'd paid an extra fiver, the woman walked out, snivelling gently with a becalmed, happy expression on her face.

'How can you sell that crap to people?' I asked Suzy once she'd closed the door behind her.

'Because I believe in it.'

'You believe in snake oil and bullshit?'

'I believe in hope.'

'False hope.'

'There's no such thing as false hope to the hopeless.'

'There's no such thing as fucking spirit portraits.'

'Really? Are you sure of that? Did you know this building is four hundred years old and one of only fourteen power points on earth that can ground the vibrational frequencies coming in from extraterrestrial sources?'

'No.'

'Why else do you think I am here?'

'Because it's falling apart and the rent's cheap.'

'No, *for the vibrations*.'

'Listen, I was going to drop in to see Donny, maybe go to Fung's for lunch — do you want to join us? They give you fortune cookies. *For free*.'

'I see dark clouds,' Suzy said.

'I see egg foo yung.'

'I see tragedy and disaster.'

———

When we walked into Donny's he was leaning over the counter on his elbows, staring into the middle of the room.

'Hey, Donny. Donny, are you there? Can you hear me?' I asked.

It took him some time to register our presence, and even when he did it was like he was only partly conscious of it. He wore a luminous, dreamy expression that was gradually darkening to one of sorrow, as if he were witnessing the disappearance of a remarkable vision.

'Hey,' he said, lifting his head and regarding us with eyes heavy with tears that hadn't dropped. Collectively they probably wouldn't have filled an espresso spoon, yet emotionally they were weighted like infinity pools. 'I was just thinking about the first time I met Lee.'

'Jesus, maybe you're right about this place. Heavy vibes,' I whispered to Suzy. 'Are you okay Donny?' I asked.

'Yeah. I'm okay,' he said, blinking reservoirs of sorrow back inside.

'You don't look okay,' Suzy said.

'It's Lee, he's in hospital.'

Lee was Donny's on-off lover. Donny wouldn't hear from him for months, then without warning he'd blow back in full of passion and promises, before drifting away again as indifferent as tumbleweed.

'Is it serious?' Suzy asked.

'The doctors say he won't walk again.'

'Wow,' I said.

'Wow? *WOW*? Oh yeah, it's amazing. Fantastic. *Fucking wow*. For fuck's sake, he hasn't won the lottery — *he's paralysed*.'

'Sorry, I didn't mean to sound insensitive.'

'Promise you'll never consider a career in counselling.'

'I won't. I promise.'

'Good.'

'It's just a bit shocking,' I said.

'*More than a bit*,' Suzy added.

'Yeah, more than a bit,' I concurred.

'How about a big bit?' Donny asked, sarcastically.

'Well, yeah. Exactly. Really big,' I replied.

'What happened, if you don't mind me asking?' Suzy interrupted.

'Jesus, you can be a moron sometimes, do you know that?' Donny said to me.

'Yes, I know that.'

'As long as you're aware of it.'

'I'm aware of it.'

'The police clocked him speeding on the M8 and when they tried to get him to pull over, he fled.'

'He crashed?'

'No, he pulled up on the hard shoulder and got out and ran.'

'Did he have a reason to run?' I asked.

'He had an ounce of weed on him. That was it — not even enough to be done with intent to supply. But he was coming off a three-day speed binge and got totally spooked.'

'I'm sorry to hear that, Donny. I know how much he means to you,' Suzy said.

'Did a car hit him?' I asked.

'No, he stripped and jumped off a bridge.'

'He tripped and jumped?'

'No. Stripped and jumped. Totally starkers.'

'Why did he take off his clothes?'

'He thought he was jumping into a river.'

'He wasn't?'

'It was a railway bridge.'

'Holy shit. *Oh my God*,' I corrected myself.

'I love him, you know.'

'Hey, of course you do. And even if he can't walk, he's still Lee.'

'You probably think I'm stupid for saying I love him, don't you? I know he's a mess. But I knew him before he was fucked up. He was so gentle. Even now, when he's straight, there's so much kindness in him, you just wouldn't believe it.'

'Oh, I can believe it, Donny,' Suzy said.

'It could have been worse,' I smiled, consolingly.

'How?'

'He could have been hit by a train.'

'Yeah. I suppose. I got this shit in yesterday, from Bulgaria,' Donny said, casually changing the topic, as if he'd suddenly assumed a different persona and forgotten all about the conversation we'd been having. He held up what looked like a tiny white statue, roughly the size of a small grape, of a baby wearing a helmet and carrying a rifle.

'That looks like a tiny statue of a baby wearing a helmet and carrying a gun,' Suzy said.

'It is a baby wearing a helmet and carrying a gun,' Donny responded, before putting it in his mouth and crunching it. 'Do either of you want to try one and tell me what you think?' He asked, holding out a bowl filled with them.

'Is it legal?' Suzy asked.

'For now, yes.'

'I don't know if I should,' Suzy replied.

'Certainly,' I said.

'Careful, these fuckers come out fighting,' Donny warned as I bit the head off a tiny soldier.

'Is that the first you've taken?' Suzy asked.

'It's my tenth since yesterday.'

'We were going to ask if you wanted to get lunch at Fung's?' I said, tossing the remainder of the little soldier into my mouth, while wondering if Suzy really did know things that the rest of us didn't.

'Chinese? Sure. At least I'll always know where he is now,' Donny said.

'Always know where who is?' I said, picking up a handful of soldiers and passing some to Suzy.

'Lee.'

'How's that?' Suzy asked, absent-mindedly swallowing one of the soldiers.

'He can't walk,' he smiled dolefully.

Fung's was on the ground floor of the building directly opposite ours. Previously a discount bed shop, it was a large, rectangular space that looked set up to resemble what someone thought a Chinese restaurant should look like circa 1970. It had been open a couple of years, but still had a vacant quality. If you looked in during trading hours, it looked like a mise-en-scène set up for some elaborate sting. And if you walked passed by and looked in when it was closed, you might assume it was never opening again.

The ceiling was covered in square, polystyrene tiles, and there was a red carpet and soft red lighting, and white linen tablecloths draped across round banqueting tables with red napkins folded and shaped to resemble swans at each place setting. The dining chairs were high-backed and ornately carved in dark wood, and the walls were covered in red dragon-themed wallpaper. Paintings depicting oriental-style mountain landscapes adorned the walls, while in the centre of the room an assortment of goldfish swam in the neon-blue water of a large aquarium. However, by far Fung's most impressive prop was the huge, multicoloured paper dragon that hung from the ceiling and snaked across the room.

I wouldn't say I ate there regularly, but regularly enough to be accorded the elaborate, over-friendly charade of being considered a valued customer by its owner, Jimmy Fung, who referred to me as *Mister Paper Man*. I was never sure if this was a genuine term of endearment or a thinly veiled slight.

Jimmy sat us next to the window at a table that could have comfortably sat ten and we began to peruse the extensive menu. Ordering seemed to take forever as we kept forgetting what we'd decided to have. On the occasions when we managed to make a collective decision and nail it down, we'd call the waiter over and order that one dish. We continued in this manner for a considerable time, so that our entire lunch was ordered piecemeal. In between all the confusion and indecision, Donny kept feeding us soldiers, and bottles of white wine, beers, and baskets of prawn crackers kept appearing. By the time we'd completed our order, we were so confused we'd forgotten what we'd chosen. Not that I cared. By this point I'd drunk so much and eaten so many prawn crackers, I wasn't hungry anyway.

—

Our food had taken an inordinately long time to order, but when it did finally start arriving, it seemed to take longer for it to stop coming than it had for it to start. The three of us looked on open-mouthed while the waiter put plate after plate down on our table, then returned to the kitchen for more — our heads swinging continually from right to left as if we were watching a tennis match. When he finally stopped going back and forth and walked instead to the bar to take care of something else, we sat for several minutes in stunned silence staring at what was set before us.

'I don't feel right,' Suzy finally said.

'No?' Donny asked matter-of-factly.

'I don't feel right at all.'

'Not right at all how?' he continued.

'Like something is definitely wrong.'

'My hands smell like old fish,' I interjected.

'Can you be more precise?'

'Like old plastic fish.'

'I was talking to Suzy.'

'I think it's the prawn crackers.'

'No one is talking to you.'

'Like something is very, very wrong,' Suzy said.

'And I ask you once more, wrong how?'

'Like, oh my god, *what is all that*?'

'All what?'

'*Th-th-th-that*,' she said, pointing at the table. 'Oh, dear mother of God,' she continued, blessing herself then standing and backing away from it, as if whatever she saw was alive and threatening her. I hadn't stopped looking at the table — none of us had since the food had arrived — but now that Suzy had started freaking out, as if for the first time I saw what she saw. There before us, covering every inch of the huge round table, was a steaming, quivering, glistening, pungent mass of food, the like of which I'd never seen before. Not only in volume, but in variety too. Some of it looked straightforward enough. Starters of dim sum, spare ribs, spring rolls, prawn satay, chicken satay, chicken wings, prawn cocktails. Mains of sweet-and-sour chicken, chicken with green pepper and black bean sauce, prawn curry, chicken curry, aromatic crispy duck, fillet of beef in Mandarin sauce, Szechuan chicken, salt and chilli chicken, prawns with spring onion in oyster sauce. Numerous soups, sides, and sundries. And then there were things on the table I'd never seen before, and having seen them, dearly wished I hadn't.

We'd not only forgotten what we'd ordered each time we'd called the waiter over, we were so fucked we'd forgotten we'd ordered at all and had kept ordering more.

'Where did all *that* come from?' Suzy yelled, then suddenly threw up, catching most of it in her cupped hands.

'I've no idea. My hands really do stink, though,' I reiterated.

'I've no idea either. Would you like a glass for that?' Donny asked calmly, indicating the vomit in Suzy's hands.

'Oh no, oh no, oh no, oh no,' Suzy was whispering, over and over. 'I need to get out of here.'

'Where to?' Donny asked. 'They'll come after you.'

'You'll never make it out alive,' I said.

'You two are fucking nuts,' Suzy said.

'You foresaw your own doom,' I smiled.

'I need an escape plan,' she said, looking around, panic-stricken. She glanced outside and must have figured out a getaway, because she immediately started running towards the exit with her arms stretched out in front of her, still cupping the vomit. When she reached the doors, she threw a shoulder against them and barged outside.

The other fifteen or so diners who were in the restaurant had all turned to see what the commotion was, as had Jimmy and the two waiters who were standing at the bar. The window onto the street ran all the way along the length of the building, just above waist height, and we were able to observe Suzy after she'd exited. As soon as she got outside she flung her vomit over her left shoulder, then started bounding along the pavement. When she reached the far end, she stopped where a large and powerful-looking motorbike was parked. She was only four or five feet away now and she glanced in at us, then down at the table. Whatever she saw must have terrified her, as she was screaming at the top of her lungs when she mounted the motorbike to make her getaway. She was up on the seat, pumping the starter pedal over and over and revving the throttle, then in a blink of an eye she was gone. Disappeared clean out of sight.

Jimmy was at the table now, looking very anxious. 'Oh my god, what's wrong with that woman?' He asked.

'*What's wrong?*' Donny replied, dumbfounded.

'Yes, what's wrong with that woman?'

'Isn't it obvious?'

'No?'

'Are you the manager of this restaurant?'

'Yes.'

'Are we your customers?'

'Yes. Yes.'

'Then isn't it clear to you what's wrong?'

'No. No. No.'

'This,' Donny said with a grand sweep of his hand across the table, 'this is wrong.'

'What? What's wrong?'

'All this,' Donny reiterated, flinging both hands towards the table and opening his arms wide, to indicate everything that was set before us.

'The food?'

'Yes. *Yes*, the food.'

'Something's wrong with the food?'

'Yes, something's wrong with the food.'

'What?'

'*Where did it all come from?*'

'You order it,' Jimmy replied, visibly nervous now.

'No, we didn't.'

'Yes, you all order and keep ordering.'

'No.'

'Yes.'

'*We didn't.*'

'*You did.*'

'I don't remember ordering it either, Donny, but we must have. Maybe we were planning on feeding all those soldiers,' I said, grinning.

'Have you already forgotten that you're a moron?'

'Donny, you're wasted. I'm wasted. Suzy is wasted. We are all fucking wasted.'

'The entire world might well be wasted, but I am not. I know injustice when I see it. Take advantage of the white man, is that it?'

'What?'

'I heard all of you whispering over there. I know your game. I'll give you *what's fucking wrong.*'

'What you say?'

'What *did* you say?' I asked Donny nervously, sensing another shift in personae and that a very bad situation was about to get much worse.

'I'll give him something fucking wrong.'

'Take it easy, Donny. There's no need for that,' I said.

'You give me something fucking wrong?' Jimmy said with a quizzical look on his face.

'Fucking yes. I'll raise this bastarding hellhole to the ground!' Donny yelled.

'What? What? *What?*' Jimmy exclaimed.

'Calm the fuck down, Donny,' I said, smiling with a freakish tranquillity.

'You pay, you pay fucking now and fuck off!' Jimmy yelled.

'No pay, no fucking pay, no way fucking pay,' Donny responded, swinging wildly from mock-Chinese to mock-Italian, to mock-Pakistani, by way of the

Welsh valleys. His eyes were doing strange and wild things. I looked at him and saw a mugshot of Charles Manson. I saw disaster.

'No need for that now, Donny. No need for that at all. That's totally out of order, *totally*. Jimmy, I'm very sorry. I really am so, so sorry,' I reiterated. 'This gentleman has had some bad news regarding a loved one. He doesn't know what he's saying.'

'Yes, I fucking do.'

'No, you *fucking* don't. Donny. Apologise to Jimmy. Get down on your hands and knees and say you're sorry right now.'

'No way. *I've got fire in my soul*,' Donny suddenly declared, as if yet another shift in persona had occurred.

'*What?*' Both myself and Jimmy said in unison now.

'I've got fire in my soul,' Donny repeated a little louder this time.

'You fucking crazy in the head,' Jimmy said, smiling in disbelief.

'*Fire, I've got fire in my soul*,' Donny reiterated even more loudly.

'I'm sure you have, Donny,' I said, still trying to calm the situation. 'Now take it easy.'

'I've got fire!' he shouted with his arms raised aloft and his clenched fists punching the air. '*Fire! Fire! Fire!*'

'*I'll pay!*' I exclaimed, frantically pulling my wallet out of my trouser pocket, sending everything in it flying and spilling across the floor. At the same time, I watched something silvery and jellied slither and shudder across the table, and heard it drop to the floor with a wet slap, then slurp off.

'*FIRE! FIRE! FIRE!*' Donny was yelling, while holding a Bic lighter aloft just below the head of the dragon. The flint sparked, a flame licked the air, and immediately a ring of fire shot around the room, devouring the paper beast as it went.

Jimmy turned towards the entrance to the kitchen and started screaming, '*Zhang Yong! Zhang Yong! Kill this motherfucker!*'

Believing Fung's was about to go up in flames, the other diners started panicking and running for the exits. The double doors to the kitchen swung open and a young, stocky-looking guy in chef's whites wielding a meat cleaver came bounding towards our table. This must have been Zhang Yong. Whoever it was, Donny saw him coming and bolted for the door. Yelling profanities in English and Mandarin, the chef gave chase and followed him out.

The paper stretched around the wire carcass of the dragon must have been particularly thin, as it flared and crackled around the room in a flash without doing further damage. The restaurant had cleared as quickly as the dragon had vanished, leaving only myself and Jimmy staring at each other in horror and astonishment. I didn't know what to say, so I got down on my hands and knees and started crawling around the floor, looking for cash or a debit or credit card to offer Jimmy. When I finally found a card, I stayed down there and crawled round in front of him.

'I'm so sorry, Jimmy. Please forgive us,' I said, kissing his shoes, then lying prostrate at his feet with my face in the serpentine weave of a carpet that was writhing and hissing all around me. I got to my knees and for the first time, looked at what I was holding. All I'd managed to find was a supermarket loyalty card. 'Do you take grocery points?' I smiled.

I stumbled onto the street and into a day that had grown unbearably hot and bright. Having consumed the dragon, it seemed the fire was now burning around the circumference of the world. I crouched down on my haunches and surveyed the chaos, while fire engines wailed their way towards us like unstoppable forces of nature. A group of suited men stood drinking the pints they'd ran out with. Others picked food off the plates they'd lifted. To my left, moaning softly like a dying animal, Suzy lay trapped beneath a Harley-Davidson. Neil Young was singing 'Unknown Legend' in my head and further down the road I could see Zhang Yong, his meat cleaver held aloft and glinting in the sun, pursuing Donny, who was about to disappear into a shimmering, high-pitched blip in the distance. I was trying to pull the threads running through all this back together, when I saw my editor, Richard Snodgrass, exit the bakery with a bun of some sort sticking out his mouth.

Richard crossed the road and strode towards me in a series of erratic spasms like an enraged headmaster. A not-so-secret drinker, he had the exaggerated, over-eager manner that all in-denial alcoholics have. You can tell them a mile off. Their cheeks a little too ruddy. Always trying too hard at precision of movement and thought. Overcompensating to conceal the fact that they barely have a handle on their motor skills, let alone anything else that's going on in their lives. He wasn't a bad man, but I couldn't help disliking him for what I saw as his cowardice on all fronts. Everyone knew he kept a bottle of vodka beneath his car seat, another in his desk drawer, and a permanently topped-up hip flask. If he'd only been honest, instead of always trying to appear the sanest person in the room. I'd always felt that what made an alcoholic deplorable wasn't so much their addiction, but their shame of their addiction. That they were unequal to the tragedy of their affliction, and as a result, were dispossessed of the grace needed to either seek help, or stick with it and see it through, whatever the outcome.

'What on earth happened here?' Robert asked, taking a bite of what I now saw was a Yum Yum.

'Whatever happened, it didn't happen on earth,' I responded.

'What?'

'It happened somewhere else.'

'Where?'

'In here,' I replied, tapping my forehead with my index finger.

'What is wrong with you? Really, what on earth is wrong with you?'

'But are we on earth?'

'What? Yes, of course we are.'

'Are you sure?'

'Yes.'

'Positive?'

'*Yes, yes*,' Richard affirmed, overemphatically, as if he weren't sure at all.

'Did you know our building is fourteen hundred years old and one of only seven points in the universe that can ground out the vibrational frequencies coming at us from heavenly sources?'

'What?'

'Crazy. I know.'

'What? What do you know? The building isn't even three hundred years old.'

'Still.'

'Still what?'

'What if it was?'

'Okay, I'm not going to stand here discussing this nonsense with you.'

'I understand.'

'I did want to talk to you about other matters. I think you should take time off. You can't go on the way you are. I don't think you're well.'

'Sure.'

'Take a fortnight of sick leave.'

'No problem.'

'Better yet, take a month off.'

'Are those bugs crawling out of your pores real?'

'Take extended sick leave. Wait a few months, then we'll talk.'

'The bats are in the belfry, our love is on the moon,' I began to sing.

'*You're unhinged man,*' he half-yelled.

'If you insist,' I smiled, and continued singing. 'Where are the dogs that bit me, that blessed silver spoon, that blessed silver spoon ... ?'

'I do. I insist. On both counts. *I definitely insist.*'

6

There was a ringing sound, and my eyelids were opening and closing like butterfly wings, letting in glimpses of a morning that I didn't want to awake to. The light was sombre and aqueous. I was trying to let in just enough of it so I could swim back down into my dreams. Eventually the ringing stopped and after several minutes I managed to drift back to sleep, where I dreamt I was cast adrift in a small rowing boat, surrounded by a vast expanse of sea. There were dark storm clouds on the horizon and I could hear the distant hiss of rain. As the storm drew closer, the sound of the rain grew louder and louder, like pebbles, then stones battering a tin roof. I tried to ignore it, but when it rose to a deafening crescendo, I was thrown back into the world. Compelled to break through the membrane of another day, like a buoy cut loose from a sunken ship rising up through the depths to the surface of the ocean.

Heaving myself up, I swung my feet out of bed, found the floor, and staggered half-asleep towards the front door. When I opened it and there was no one there, I realised it was the phone that was ringing. I walked into the living room and picked up the receiver just as it stopped. I stood looking out of my living-room window, listening to the dialling tone, as several huge grey clouds shaped like gravestones drifted across the sky. My head was pounding, and I had a terrible thirst. I walked into the kitchen and stood at the sink, filling, then drinking, pints of water from the tap. After the fourth pint I started gagging and couldn't breathe. Fourteen floors off the ground and I felt like a drowning man. The sensation of drowning was compounded by the feeling of gravity sickness that was ever present on the upper floors of the high-rise. Desperate to lie down, I walked back into the living room and stretched out on the floor, parallel to the horizon, hoping this might redress the forces that were unbalancing me. I reached up and took the phone off the coffee table and sat it on my chest. For a few minutes, the reassuring weight of it slowed my heart and steadied my breath, then it started ringing again and I answered it with a start.

'*Hello.*'

'Hi son, it's me. Sorry to keep calling, but I need to talk to you,' a woman's voice said.

'Who is this?' I asked.

'It's your aunt.'

'How did you get my number?'

'I called your work.'

'They gave it to you?'

'Am I talking to you?'

'They should have called me first.'

'They did, but you never answered. I told them it was urgent.'

'How did you know where I worked?'

'I googled you.'

Mags was my father's sister. She was one of those people who only ever called to give you unwelcome news. She might call on some other pretext, but within seconds she'd be telling you about someone whose dog had been run over, or about someone who'd got married and then the day after their wedding had been told they had a terminal illness. She had the remarkable ability of being able to seamlessly weave misfortune into the most mundane stories as if it were the most normal thing in the world. She'd be telling you where to buy a cheap clothes line, which would remind her that Billy — you know Billy Stevenson? — well, they found him on the end of a rope last week. Garage.

Topped himself. Son's tenth birthday party going on in the house. Terrible thing it was.

It didn't matter that you had no idea who Billy Stevenson was and didn't need a clothes line. Most of the time you'd never heard of any of the people who'd been disfigured or had died, let alone knew them. I'd not spoken to her since I was sixteen, when she phoned the home of a friend I was staying with to tell me that my mother had disappeared and that she had a bad feeling about it. That her bones were telling her that my mother wasn't coming back.

'It's been a long time, Mags. What do you want?' I asked her.

'It's your dad,' she said after a dramatic and deliberately measured pause.

'Yeah?'

'He's back.'

'Why?'

'He's dying.'

'Dying?'

'Aye, *really dying*.'

'Is there any other kind of dying?'

'Well, there's the kind when you've a long time to go and the kind when you've not so long to go.'

'Which kind is he?'

'The not-long kind.'

'How long do the doctors think he has?'

'They're not sure, several months. If you ask me though, probably only weeks.'

'I'm not asking you,' I said.

'Okay, but I don't think it'll be long, not long at all.'

'What's he dying of?'

'Old age.'

'What does that mean? People don't die of old age.'

'No, but they die with what comes with it. He had cancer.'

'I didn't know.'

'Why would you? You've not seen him for a long time.'

'Over twenty years.'

'Well, there you go. I only found out recently myself. They caught it in time to treat it, but it took a lot out of him. His girlfriend left him during his treatment and since then he's been on his own. He's had pneumonia, some bad falls. He can't swallow properly …'

'Okay, okay. I get the picture.'

'Not to mention his mind going.'

'Is he in hospital?'

'No, he's in a maisonette.'

'What?'

'Yeah. It's on the outskirts of town. A nurse is supposed to visit him every morning and evening, but she doesn't always make it. He spends most of his time alone out there. I go across as often as I can, but he shouldn't be there, not now. One afternoon when I went over, he was sitting in the living room in the dark with the curtains closed. He'd been there since the previous evening. Hadn't a clue what was going on.'

'I know that feeling.'

'Come on, son. He'd urinated himself and was dehydrated.'

'It's sad, but what can I do?'

'You could visit him.'

'Has he asked for me?'

'He's mentioned your name.'

'Has he said he wants to see me?'

'Like I say, a lot of the time he has no idea where he is.'

'Has he though, asked for me?'

'Not directly.'

'You mean not at all.'

'You will try to visit him, won't you?'

'I don't know. I'll see.'

'Please.'

'I need to go.'

'But you haven't told me how you are.'

'There's nothing to tell.'

'Isn't there? How's your job going?'

'It's going. But you probably already know that.'

'I'd love to talk to you.'

'You just did,' I said and hung up.

Directly opposite the bus station, on the other side of the street, there was an off-licence I'd been in several times before. I crossed the road and stood looking in through the shopfront. It wasn't part of a chain or somewhere you'd go to buy an expensive bottle of wine. The surface of the window was overcrowded with large, star-shaped fluorescent price cards advertising their latest deals, and there were three neon signs. Two of them, one blue and one green, advertised beers they didn't stock. The third was red and buzzed and blinked *Merry Christmas* every day of the year.

In the window display a golden Maneki Neko, its raised left paw swinging in a continual beckoning gesture, sat in a little wooden rowing boat amid a sea of bottles. Someone else must have stood where I was now watching it beckon them too, because they'd written *not waving but drinking :)* with a black marker on the windowpane.

A metal grille ran the full length of the shop from the countertop to the ceiling. I wasn't sure whether it was there to protect the staff from the customers, or the customers from the staff. When I entered, the guy sitting behind the till looked up from his phone and watched me peer through the grille at all the different bottles on the shelves. There were so many I didn't know which one to choose. For a while I stood there looking at them like I was gazing at the stars or trying to figure out a complex equation on a school blackboard. After a couple of minutes, the guy put his phone down and stood up.

'What are you after?' he asked, looking at me and then back at the bottles, as if he was going to formally introduce me to whichever one I chose.

'I don't know,' I told him.

'What do you normally drink?'

'Whatever does the job.'

'What job?'

'Takes me where I need to go.'

'And where's that?'

'Today, to see my father.'

I'm not sure when I started mixing alcohol with alchemy, conflating the one with the other. Where I got the idea that drinks are like magic potions. That certain drinks are better for certain tasks. Every addict knows that in the end it all does the same thing, leaves you whispering to ghosts and begging bone conjurers for redemption. Yet every time I stood in an off-licence or in front of a gantry in a bar, insight went out the window, and after deciding where I wanted to go, I'd ponder which drink would be best suited to take me there. On one occasion, already drunk and determined to walk from Glasgow to Edinburgh along the Union and Forth & Clyde canals to read a poem at the top of Arthur's Seat one evening, I convinced myself a shot glass filled with a mix of white spirit and vanilla essence would do the trick to get me there. I drank several, made it as far as the Maryhill Locks, about three and a half miles from where I'd set out, and ended up spending two nights in the psych unit in Gartnavel Royal Hospital, then several days in the detox unit. Never made a blind bit of difference to me though. Ignoring the years of self-inflicted wounds, the humiliations, the near-death experiences, I kept searching for that magic bullet and playing Russian roulette with the bottle. Believing if I chose correctly, the next drink might provide the click that blew all the shit out of my head, wiped my mind clean, and led me to salvation.

'Whisky, I'll take a bottle of whisky,' I told him.

'A malt?'

'No, a blend.'

'Which one?'

'The cheapest you have,' I told him. I wanted it to burn me when I drank it.

Half an hour later, I sat down at the rear of the next bus going to my home town just as the engine roared and its huge metal body rattled and shuddered into life on the concourse. Outside there was sunshine everywhere. A landscape obliterated by light. A burning blue day filled with a terrible distance that made it seem as if the entire city could disappear at any moment.

I unscrewed the cap from the whisky and took a long drink and leant my head against the window. The light and the whisky merged with the vibrations of the bus into a river of memory that worked its way inside me and flowed through my body. I could feel it drift into my bones, loosen my spirit, and as I lifted the bottle to my lips again, take the pennies from my eyes.

The last time I'd travelled back to my home town on a bus I was with my father. I was eight years old and had been staying with him since my parents had separated several months earlier. My father was a cabaret singer and we'd moved to the north of England, where his agent had connections in the local entertainment industry. He'd be out singing most nights of the week and would take me along to his gigs. Occasionally, they'd be in the chintzy lounge of some no-star hotel, but mostly he played welfare and social clubs. Places filled with men and women who worked hard in tough jobs they loved and hated in equal measure. Who'd lived lives that had broken their bones and their hearts, but who were too strong and proud to imagine there were events just around the corner that would break their spirits.

My father seemed to love the challenge of singing in these places. Hard gigs, in hard venues, with hard people, who didn't take any shite from anyone, but who, if they took to you, were among the kindest people you'd ever meet.

I remember the haze of smoke and sweet perfume and cheap aftershave and innuendos that hung in the air. A distillation of promises kept and broken. Of rough sex and tears and hidden tenderness. I remember the physicality of the politics and the smell of booze and sweat and nicotine that clung to the carpets. And all of it intoxicating and strangely comforting.

Most nights my father would give me a half pint of cola and a packet of crisps and sit me at a table of women in their mid-forties to late fifties, who'd just finished a game of bingo. Such women were his preferred guardians for me. Proud to be charged by my father with watching over his boy, these were usually married women who knew intimately all the dark zones of life. Who communicated very little with words, but spoke so graciously with their eyes. Those soft dark looks that said, you are safe and cherished. Unquestioned nurture, and tacit agreements, signed with fleeting looks. A maternal concord to not ask where my mum was. Strong women touched with a rough holiness. Secret practitioners of countless superstitions and intimate desires known only to themselves. Women just as capable of mending torn hearts as torn school and work clothes. Women I wished were my mothers.

I remember how nervous I'd be for my father before he went on stage. There'd usually be some tattooed Neanderthal or gobby cakehole, who would comment about the fucking cheek of the fucking convener booking a fucking Jock, when we have better singers in Blackburn and even in fucking *Burnley* for fuck's sake.

But I never needed to worry. By the end of opening with 'Forever in Blue Jeans', everyone would be clapping and agreeing that he was different class. And he was, he was the real thing. A born entertainer with the voice to match. By the time he closed his set with 'In the Ghetto', then 'Ring of Fire', the entire place would be rocking. Everyone up on their feet, singing and laughing and crying, and demanding *more*, *more*, *more*. Even the Neanderthal would be forced to admit that he wasn't bad for a fucking Jock and would be the first to approach my dad after his set to tell him how great he was and to buy him a drink.

I'd be so proud and so sad afterwards. Those first few moments when he came down off the stage and walked towards our table were the closest I ever felt to him, and the furthest away. The look in his eyes was so strange. It was difficult to tell if it was a lack of recognition of who I was or a sudden realisation.

From the little I remembered, it hadn't always been like that between us. Something had changed. At some point before we left Scotland there'd been a shift in the order of things. Doubt and anger entered. After moving south, the confusion only increased. As if trying to protect me and stay close to me had intensified whatever was pushing him away.

It would be late once he'd packed all his gear in the car and we'd start the drive back to our flat. He'd put a Glen Campbell cartridge in the old 8-track car stereo, which was a relic even then, and wrapped in a travel blanket, and cocooned in the night, we'd listen to 'Galveston' through speakers that crackled like embers in a dying campfire. Moving over the road with a rare, reassuring sense of momentum as the stars glittered in the cold black sky, I'd fall asleep. And for a brief spell, the past few years would disappear, and we'd drive towards a different future than the one awaiting us. A future that arrived faster than I could have imagined.

One evening my father and mother had an argument over the phone, which in itself was nothing new. But the next morning at breakfast and for the next several days he wouldn't look at me, except when he thought I wasn't looking. I'd catch him studying me in a mirror or in the reflection of a window or from across the room and he'd quickly look the other away. A week later he told me that we had to go home and that we'd be leaving the following morning.

At the time I wondered why we were leaving in such a hurry without our things. You never do question such things when you're a child. You just do what's asked of you or what your told to do. You take it for granted that everything is for the best. And if it's not, well, you don't find that out until years later. Until it's too late to do anything about it, and you're left living the rest of your life with the consequences of decisions you had no control over.

—

Ours was the first bus to depart that morning and I was still wearing my pyjama top beneath my blue parka and was barely awake as we pulled out of Blackburn Bus Station. A washed-out dawn seeped into the day through a pale-yellow fissure stretched between the land and a coal black sweep of cloud smudged like graphite across the sky. Not a word was uttered as we navigated the deserted streets, moving methodically through the gears, and the sad melancholy drift of all industrial towns viewed from a bus window at 6 a.m. Picking up speed as we progressed towards the outskirts, it felt like we were deserters fleeing an area under quarantine. I didn't know anyone in the town, and yet I felt a terrible sense of guilt for those we'd left behind. I don't think I was the only one to feel it. The further we travelled, the chattier and more excitable the other passengers on the bus became, like they couldn't believe they were actually going to make it out of there alive. Twenty minutes later, when we swung onto the M6 at speed and started heading north, everyone seemed to breathe a collective sigh of relief and settle down into the journey.

My father read a book and I looked out the window, determined to count all the lamp posts we passed on our way to Scotland. I kept trying, but I never made it beyond fifty. My gaze would shift to roadkill on the hard shoulder, or a bird of prey hovering above a field, or a lamp post would be erased by a shaft of light breaking through the clouds and I'd lose count and need to start all over again.

After a few hours, most of the other passengers started rummaging around in their bags, unpacking the food they'd brought. I hadn't eaten since the previous evening and the warm floral clouds of tea and soup steaming from flasks and the noise of bags of crisps being torn open and sandwiches being unwrapped made my stomach ache. We didn't have any food. Other than the clothes we were wearing and the paperback my father was carrying, we didn't have anything else with us at all.

'Do you want something to eat?' my father asked as I strained and fidgeted in my seat.

'Yeah, I'm starving,' I told him.

'We're due to stop soon. I'll get you something then. What would you like?'

'Pizza.'

'*Pizza?*'

'Yeah.'

'What sort of pizza?'

'Ham and pineapple.'

'Hawaiian pizza, for breakfast?'

'Uh-huh,' I beamed.

'Hawaiian pizza it is, then,' he smiled.

Ten minutes later we drifted up off a slip road and began to make our way through the centre of a small town. The driver announced over the tannoy that we'd be stopping for a thirty-minute break, and that the passengers were free to come and go as they pleased, provided they were back on the bus in time to leave. My father said he'd spotted a takeaway place that sold pizza and that I was to stay in my seat and not to move before he got back, no matter what.

It was an old bus station and dingy and cheerless inside. A few strip lights snapped and flickered beneath the corrugated iron roof, and a cold breeze tinged with petrol and oil drifted in through the open door of the bus. I sat in the half-light of the interior, watching the red digits of the LCD clock above the driver's seat tumble without purpose or meaning into the future, while the passengers filed past me off the bus. The numbers glowed the same soft red as the little votive candles that burned in the church we used to attend on Sunday evenings, and I felt a sadness like the one I'd feel at the end of Mass. Everyone else would leave, but I'd be told to stay to recite my Hail Marys and Our Fathers for the sins I didn't even know I'd committed.

Some of the passengers went into the terminal to buy a magazine at the news stand or to use the toilet. Others stood by the side of the bus, stretching their legs or smoking. After twenty minutes, most of the passengers were back on board, packing away their things. After thirty minutes, a few stragglers hurried on, smiling and apologising as they passed the driver. Then there was only one guy still out there, standing next to the door of the bus, smoking a cigarette, frantically sucking on it like he was trying to deflate all his troubles. The driver told him to get a move on and he took a long last drag and then he was on the bus and in his seat too. But still no sign of my father.

After several minutes of continually checking his watch, then the little chrome tally counter he was holding — willing another digit to appear in the display — the driver edged the bus forward until its bumper protruded just beyond the entrance to the station. He kept straining his body over the steering wheel, trying to look up and down the street as far as he could. It was raining a little and like a human metronome, between each sweep of the windscreen wipers he'd look left, then right, and when the rain covered the window again, he'd glance back at me.

He was becoming increasingly agitated, and after a few minutes he slapped the steering wheel with both hands, then cut the engine and got off the bus and walked out of the station. He stood looking up and down the road, while all around me the passengers voiced their unhappiness at not having departed. When the drizzle suddenly became a deluge, he ran back onto the bus and sat down and hit the ignition. Everyone knew the cause of the delay and someone near the back shouted to the driver to call the police. Someone else suggested that I should get off and wait for my father at lost property. Another person said they should call an adoption agency, then started laughing. Speaking over the tannoy, the driver told the passengers that he wasn't allowed to let me off on my own, but that he'd only wait two more minutes, then he'd leave.

I was an eight-year-old boy who'd grown up hard and never called my father *Daddy* or any of that shit, but now I was crying like a baby and wanted my mum and for the three of us to be together, instead of being on this bus on my own with no idea what was going to happen to me. I felt dizzy and sick, as if I'd just understood for the first time in my life that the earth was spinning at a thousand miles per hour and that I was spinning with it. I felt like everything around me was losing its mooring, and I wanted to drop to my knees and hold on to the world and everything dear to me that was on it. The tears were streaming down my face and I was whispering, imploring God to bring my father back. And then we began to pull out of the bus station and I tore myself from my seat and ran to the driver, begging him not to leave. I was terrified and crying uncontrollably, but he wouldn't stop to wait for my father or to let me off. He said there was nothing he could do about it, that he had to stick to the schedule. Then we turned onto the road and the driver was swearing at me, saying it was my father's own fucking fault and that the authorities would deal with both of us later.

We were out on the street now and he had his foot on the accelerator and the bus was picking up speed again. Through a fog of tears and sighs and with my chest heaving, I kept repeating, '*But we can't leave my daddy, please, my daddy, my daddy.*' Then there was a banging on the door and my father was sprinting alongside the bus in the torrential rain, thumping the door with the palm of his hand. I was sure he was going to slip and stumble under the wheels and I was screaming for the driver to stop and finally he did.

My father clambered up the steps, cursing the driver and anyone else who glanced at him as he walked back to his seat. But when he sat down, he looked crushed. He was breathless and ashen, his wet shirt sticking to him like a shameful second skin. I felt awful for him and wanted to yell at the passengers to stop commenting and tutting and looking at us.

'I did order your pizza, it just took them too bloody long to cook it,' he said, without turning to look at me. 'I promise I'll get you whatever you want when we get off the bus back home.'

I knew he was lying about the pizza, because I could smell the whisky on his breath. Not that I cared. He was beside me again, that's all that mattered.

'I'm not even hungry. I hate pizza anyway,' I smiled at him.

He didn't respond to my childish camaraderie. He was somewhere else now, deep inside his shame and anger. Looking at him, I wanted to start crying all over again, but I didn't. I swallowed the sorrow fluttering in my chest and narrowed my eyes as much as I could to keep my tears in check, because I knew that if I started crying, his shame would disappear and there would only be anger.

He fell asleep after fifty lamp posts and I switched my gaze to the beads of rainwater streaking across the window, imagining they were tiny mercurial comets that chimed like glass bells and died whenever they collided with one another. For miles I listened to them toll. Losing myself in them, dying over and over again. Outside, the world didn't notice the bus passing through it or care about what had happened onboard. We drove on and life passed by like scenes from a movie I would never play a part in. I was driving away from what was left of my childhood and I knew there was no way back.

When we approached my mum's house that evening, my father told me he'd wait around the corner, so that I could surprise her when she came to the door. I rang the bell and kept ringing, but no one answered. After five minutes I went back to get my father, but he'd gone. I walked back to my mum's and sat on the front step, waiting for either of them to return. My mum was the first to show up. It was dark and she was drunk and with a guy I'd never seen before. I still hadn't eaten, so she made me buttered bread with sugar sprinkled on it and milky tea, which I drank on my own in the kitchen, while she sat with the guy in the dining room. Her visitor seemed aggravated by my presence, and I was hoping he'd get up and leave. The kitchen door was ajar and I watched them through the narrow gap. For a moment it looked as though he was about to go, then my mother started kissing him and unbuckled his trousers. Then her hand was moving up and down between his legs and he was gazing up at the ceiling and moaning. I stepped away from the door, then crossed to the sink and gazed out the window. I wanted to look as far away as possible, but the fluorescent strip light made a mirror of the window, and all I could see was the garish reflection of the kitchen and my face floating in the midst of it. A few minutes later, my mother bustled in. Flushed and sweating, she picked a dishtowel up off the counter and wiped and dabbed the corners of her mouth, then she told me to get up to bed and said we'd talk in the morning.

I still had my pyjama top on, so I didn't need to change. I took my jacket and trousers off and curled up into a ball in the bed in my old room that had been whitewashed since I was last there. Lying between cold sheets in the dark, I felt like the loneliest person in the world, and it occurred to me for the first time how tiny and insignificant my existence was. At such junctures people often say they realised *right then* that God did not exist and that there was no love in the world. You know, moments of stone-cold revelation generated by trauma. But I don't believe them. If they're writing from experience, then they're either lying, or applying a shitload of hindsight. If they're writing from someone else's perspective, then they're taking liberties. Right then you're so deep inside yourself you might as well be in outer space. The truth is, you don't think such thoughts. Such thoughts just aren't there to be thought. God and love do not exist where you are then. There's only loneliness. And maybe something like — I'm going to die one day and there's nothing I can do about it.

If I could have affixed that night any meaningful sense of revelation whatsoever, it would have been of a desultory nature. Even loneliness loses its shine when you realise that you are not in fact the loneliest person in the world, only one of many. All you're left with then is your run-of-the-mill aloneness and the mundane revelation that there's no way home. That regardless of where you are or who you are with, you will always be alone and moving further away from where you started and nowhere near where you hoped you'd be.

When I got up the next day the guy from the night before had gone. There were others, but I never saw him again. It turned out my father hadn't phoned ahead to say I was coming or bothered to check beforehand to see if my mother would be home. She was certainly surprised to see me, just not in the way I'd expected.

My father called one evening around a week or so later. He was drunk and rambling about things I had no idea of. He said there was something he needed to tell me.

'The Devil, it's the Devil,' he said, slurring his words down the line.

'What are you saying?'

'The Devil ...'

'The Devil?'

'Yes. He's real. I know him.'

'*What?*' I asked, terrified.

'I can't talk to you now.'

'Dad, please,' I begged him, 'what do you mean?'

'We can't talk while you're at your mum's.'

He told me to be at the phone box at the bottom of the housing estate in an hour, that he'd tell me everything then, then he hung up. I was nauseous and confused when I got off the phone and kept needing to go to the toilet to pee whenever I went to leave. The sky was dark by the time I'd got out and walked down through the estate. From a distance, I could see the pale glow of the yellow light inside the phone box, and as I got closer, I could hear it ringing. I started running towards it, but it stopped just as I made it to the door. I waited half the night for him to call back, but he never did.

I awoke with someone gently shaking my arm and looked up to see the bus driver standing beside me.

'Are you all right?' he asked.

'Yeah, I think so,' I told him.

'It looks like you got through a fair bit of that,' he said, pointing to the bottle of whisky on the seat beside me.

To the side of the driver, framed by the window, the sky was a picture postcard of a summer evening. It was cool and calm and there were no clouds, only the criss-crossing contrails of jetliners breaking up and drifting across the sky in a series of fiery rags. It felt like the evening was exhaling and letting go of everything the day had been holding on to.

'Where am I?' I asked the driver.

'You missed all the stops and went right round mate, you're back in Glasgow.'

The words scratched into the lamp post, the beckoning cat and the message on the off-licence window — I was always noticing such things. I mean, every time I had a good intention or was determined to see something through to its conclusion, something unexpected would intervene and derail me. I tried to tell myself it was coincidence, but it happened so often I began to wonder if maybe it wasn't coincidence, but fate. Then again, there are random correspondences, obscure symbols, arcane words and riddles, cries for help written everywhere. And if you stop to read each one, you'll always see what you want to see, miss what you want to miss, and avoid going where you have to go.

7

It was 6 a.m. and I found myself hostage to a drug-induced epiphany. I had a friend's funeral to attend and believed I had no choice but to go dressed in a suit and shirt, or else naked. After taking a small dose of LSD and drinking into the early hours I'd convinced myself that to show up wearing anything less or more would be downright unholy and result in the dogs of hell being unleashed upon my soul. I'd also been baptised in a bathtub filled with cold water by Peter Falk, watched the Sacred Heart float down out of the sky towards the high-rise, and fallen tragically in love with the guilt of the world, with the unconstrained, blissful affliction of a lapsed Catholic. And all while listening to Elvis Presley sing 'Amazing Grace' on a loop.

In hindsight, maybe it wasn't such a small dose.

Dressed in nothing but the light of the dawn and cowboy boots, I was kicking empty beer bottles from room to room, wondering where I'd get the appropriate funerary attire, when I remembered there was a wardrobe and a dresser with men's clothes in a flat on the sixteenth floor. The widow who'd lived there had left all her husband's belongings behind when she moved out. I'd already taken a set of lawn bowls, a pool cue, some cufflinks, and a box of paperback Western novels. I didn't think he'd mind if I added a suit.

The last time I was there, I'd left the bedroom window open. When

I returned, the room was covered in bird shit. It was everywhere. The door of the old mahogany wardrobe had swung open and a quick glance inside confirmed that its interior and contents were likewise caked in guano. I checked the dresser and found a dead crow in the top drawer. It had a scrap of tinfoil in its beak that it must have squeezed itself in there to retrieve. The whole unit had been overrun with mildew, and black dots and swirls of dampness had sprung from behind it and spread up the wall and across the ceiling like the map of a constantly expanding universe.

I'd given up on finding anything to wear and was about to leave when I noticed something stuffed under the wardrobe. Toeing at the bundle, I managed to reveal a corner and pulled out a garment bag. When I held it up and unzipped it, I couldn't believe what I found inside. A gold velvet suit and a ruby-red shirt. I tried them on and checked myself in the mirror fixed to the back of the wardrobe door. The suit was so creased it looked like an unfolded piece of origami and everything was damp, but both the suit and shirt fit perfectly. Still, I didn't feel comfortable wearing them. It wasn't the tailoring or the damp material clinging to my skin. It was the polaroid I found in the inside pocket of the suit jacket that made me feel uneasy. Like I was dressed in a dead man's dream I'd stolen from his grave.

In the polaroid a young couple were standing beneath the red signage of The Doublet Bar in the West End. They were laughing and holding each other around the waist with one arm and waving at the camera with the other. The guy, sporting a four-inch, jet-black pompadour, was dressed in the suit and shirt I was now wearing. The woman, in a white mini dress. The intervening years hadn't been kind, but it was definitely the elderly couple who'd lived in the flat. Both looking straight at the camera, their eyes alive with the desire to start chasing their future together.

On the white strip beneath the image someone had written in smudged blue ballpoint *Burning Love*. But nothing burned now. All the colours in the polaroid had yellowed and the fading image resonated with the sadness of an unanswered, long-distance phone call.

I thought about them growing old together in these few small rooms, so high up and far away from the world. About the man dying and his wife returning alone from his funeral. I'd occasionally see them in the Satellite having a couple of drinks, but after he died I never saw her in there again. I never saw her out at all. She must have been on her own up there for months, listening to the wind cry through the letter box, watching shadows stretch across the walls. My money was on her being in a coffin just like her husband when she finally exited — sooner rather than later. Instead, when the building was condemned and she was offered resettlement money and a new place to live, she up and left straight away. Walked out, went down in the lift for the last time, leaving all her husband's things behind. Though on the face of it an unremarkable act, it struck me as such a violent abandonment of memories. Perhaps she'd forgotten the man they belonged to. Maybe she couldn't stand her husband by the end, had never really liked him. Or perhaps his things were just too heavy to carry. I'd never spoken to the woman or her husband, but as I walked through what remained of their home, my heart broke for them. The dust motes drifting through the morning light and settling over everything like spent glitter seemed to mirror the mundane drift of their lives. While the dampness and the mould marked the bleeding out of their dreams. I got the feeling this was a flat that had died a little more as the couple themselves had slowly died inside.

I'd left 'Amazing Grace' looping at full volume on my stereo, and all this time I could hear it echoing up through the lift shafts and the stairwells and drifting out into the surrounding streets like the soundtrack to a movie only I would ever see. A Glaswegian reimagining of *Lonely are the Brave*, adapted from one of the paperbacks I'd taken from the flat the last time I was here. Leaning the polaroid against a china figurine of a rearing horse on the windowsill, I looked out over the city as a narrow bank of red cloud, burning like the contrail of a napalm attack, dispersed in a scattering of torn embers above the horizon. I watched the last pale echo of the morning star disappear into the papery blue sky, then thanked the man for everything I'd taken. When

I turned to go, I stopped briefly and looked at my reflection in the mirror. Elvis — the man whose suit I was wearing, and the man in me — may have left the building, but in the glorious desolation of that moment, I felt a little of all our spirits live on in the high rise.

The last time I'd seen Johnny was in the Waterloo pub on Argyle Street. He'd gained a lot of weight, shaved his head, and was wearing sparkly blue eyeshadow. He looked like a short, fat, Michael Stipe. The first thing he told me was that he'd turned a corner.

'No more booze or drugs, no more rent boys. I'm tired of shitting myself in public. It has to stop,' he said.

Then he asked me to buy him a drink. An hour later he was knocking back straight vodkas and chatting to a pretty young man from London.

'Don't judge me,' he said, after returning from the men's room with his new friend.

'I wouldn't,' I told him.

'What's that line you always come out with when you're drunk?'

'How would I remember?'

'We learn by going where we have to go,' he smiled.

Two days later Johnny was found slumped over on a bench in Glasgow Green bleeding from a deep trauma to his head. He died in the ambulance on the way to hospital.

Before catching the train to Johnny's home town, I stopped in at the Satellite to have a drink in his memory. The Satellite was my local and the only business still trading in the Trinity, the derelict shopping precinct that once served the surrounding tower blocks. Flat-roofed and windowless, the Satellite was a bunker-like structure that wouldn't have looked out of place on some inhospitable headland or beach during World War II. The clientele was a mix of serious drinkers, stragglers from the previous night's parties, and the occasional blow-in. Combatants and casualties of battles that were raging in their heads. Evacuees from their own lives. Once the hub of the community, it had left the earth's orbit and was drifting through space. The perfect place to lose track of the world, while convincing yourself that one day you'd go back to it.

Bathed in the late morning sun, the Trinity looked like it had been painted eighteen-carat gold. Its concrete walls, pillars, stairwells, and walkways glowing like some post-apocalyptic El Dorado on the scarred landscape. A broken vision as commensurate to humankind's capacity for wonder as there had ever been. Outside the Satellite, sunlight was spilling over the roof and down its weathered front, so that the cracked, grey slabs of the pavement felt warmed. I stood for a moment, bathed in that blessed heat and light, then entered the Satellite. Inside was a complete contrast. It was dimly lit and smelled of cold, wet earth. I took a seat at the bar and ordered a pint. Sitting next to me was a guy in his early twenties, who was staring at his hands. He looked mesmerised by them and kept turning them over and scrutinising them.

'Man, hands are strange,' he finally said, holding his in front of his face. He wasn't looking at me, but he was talking to me. 'Know whit ah mean? Sometimes ye look at them and wonder who they belong tae. Have ye ever thought about the millions of times you've used them? Aw the hings you've done wi them? Beautiful hings, terrible hings. Hands. Fucking *hauns* man, *fucking amazing*.' He turned to face me. '*Right?*'

'Sure,' I told him.

'Naw, a man cannae hide fae his ain hands, or fae whit he's done wi them.'

'Nope.'

'Unless the cunt chops them aff and runs away fae them.'

'You could only run from one of them.'

'Whit?'

'You'd have a tough time chopping off both.'

He proceeded to mimic chopping off his hands. 'Fuck, ah see whit ye mean. Aye, you'd need to get some other cunt tae gie ye *a fucking hand*,' he said, and started slapping the bar in a fit of laughter.

'Gets fucking complicated,' I said, laughing along with him.

'Very. Do ye want a pill?'

'What type of pill?'

'A blue yin, they're great. Ahve been flying like a fucking eagle aw night man.'

'I shouldn't. I've plans for the day.'

'Fuck plans, man. Who needs plans when you've got hands?' he said with a broad smile, while looking me up and down. 'By the way, ah fucking like yer style, bro.'

'I'm going to a funeral, only God knows where in Coatbridge, wearing clothes I took from a dead man's flat. I don't have any style.'

'Ye stole fae a deid cunt?'

'I suppose so, yeah.'

'Pure *arrivederci* like?'

'Gone. Departed. No more.'

'That's two deid cunts then. The wan wi the coffin. And the wan wi nae suit.'

'True.'

'Some heavy shite, man.'

'Indeed.'

'Aw the mair reason tae drop a pill.'

'You think so?'

'Aye.'

'Why?'

'It'll help ye find it.'

'The funeral?'

'Naw, *yer style.*'

I ordered another beer and washed down the blue pill. On a small wooden dance floor in a corner of the bar, a couple were embracing, but not dancing. In fact, they weren't moving at all. I put money in the jukebox, selected some songs, and like automatons reactivated by music, they started moving as soon as the beat kicked in.

I stood on the edge of the dance floor, watching them sway and kiss. They were sweating, and dark streaks of mascara ran from the woman's eyes, staining both their cheeks with Rorschach-like blots where they'd touched. Cocooned in a chemical silence, I stepped towards them and started swaying with them. From nowhere a young woman appeared and started talking to me. I couldn't hear what she was saying, but I could read her lips.

'Don't worry. You'll be okay. I'm on your side,' she told me.

'Really, I didn't know there were any sides left to take,' I answered.

The music burst back in, and I felt the drug kick and pulse through my body in powerful, synaptic bursts. I moved closer to her and she put her hands between my legs. Caught between a mirror behind the bar and the mirror on the opposite wall, I watched our reflections crash into infinity. Borne together and torn apart — unsure which side of the mirror I was on — for a while I lost hold of where I was and what I was doing.

When I came back to myself I was standing at the bar with no idea how much time had passed. I looked around the Satellite and couldn't see Hands or the swaying couple. Only the damaged young woman was still there. She was dancing on her own with her dress partly unbuttoned and a red shirt draped over her shoulders. I felt like I'd violated someone, or been violated, or both. The barman grinned and when he turned away his grin hung in the air like a scar. I finished my drink and headed for the door. When I stepped outside it was late afternoon, the sky was still clear and blue, but there was a sprinkling of snow on the ground now. I shivered, then realised I had no shirt on beneath my jacket. I closed my eyes and felt the earth fall away beneath my feet. When I opened them, I saw that it hadn't been snowing at all. In a flat high up in the nearest high-rise, someone was leaning out their window screaming, '*Fuck you, bastard!*' and tipping bags filled with confetti out into the air.

—

I ran onto what I soon discovered was the wrong train and stood looking around the carriage for a seat. A moment later the train started moving. Then the station started moving. Then I was moving. Suddenly, everything was moving. In the tunnel, I saw my face reflected in the window like an apparition and wondered if I was dead and going to my own funeral. Pulsing into the light, I watched as buildings stretched and snapped away like objects being sucked into a black hole. Once free of the city, the train began to pick up speed and I lurched down the aisle, pulling handfuls of confetti from my pockets. Outside, the scenery clicked rapidly away like a prolonged burst of photographs on a digital camera. I found a seat and began to wonder at the vast difference of the speed of things passing directly outside the window compared to things far off in the distance, which hardly seemed to move at all. I was sure there was a transferable life lesson in there somewhere, but I was too preoccupied with my sudden need to defecate to be able to concentrate on figuring out what it might be. There were no toilets on the train, so I jumped off at the next station and ran to the men's room and sat down just as it all happened. Afterwards, I felt hollowed out, empty, a ghost in the process of wearing out its shadow. I cleaned myself up and looked in the mirror. I looked like a pimp from a Seventies movie. No, I looked like a pimp from a Seventies movie who'd been pimped. I pulled the quarter bottle of vodka I'd bought on the way to the station from my jacket pocket and took a drink. It seemed I had finally found my style.

When I asked the guy at the ticket office where we were, he looked at me, shook his head, then muttered something beneath his breath.

'Where did you say?'

He repeated the name of the station, sneeringly, then conducted the rest of the conversation while looking down at his mobile phone. I had no idea where I was.

'Are we far from Coatbridge?'

'No.'

'When's the next train due?'

'Thirty minutes.'

'Does that stop at Coatbridge?'

'No.'

'There are other trains though?'

'Aye.'

'Any to Coatbridge?'

'Not direct.'

'Is there any other way to get to Coatbridge from here?'

'Taxi.'

'Does it take long?'

'Don't know.'

'Where can I get one?'

'Outside.'

I left the station and slumped into the back seat of the only taxi.

'Where to?' the driver asked.

'Coatbridge. The ticket guy said it wasn't far.'

'It's not.'

'He wasn't a total creep then.'

'Mind what you're fucking saying, that's Tommy, the station manager.'

'Apologies, is he a friend of yours?'

Just then the driver's mobile started ringing and he took the call, 'Hello? … In the back seat … Aye, total pansy, don't worry … Okay, speak later.' He put down his mobile, dislodged a glob of mucus from the back of his throat, then rolled down his window and spat it out. 'He's my brother-in-law.'

As we drove away from the station he scrutinised me in the mirror. He had one eye on the road and the other on me, like a lizard watching its prey.

'What are you doing here, if you're going to Coatbridge? Can you no read?' He grinned.

My chemical state was jarring with my physical state. Funeral aside, I should have felt good, but I didn't, not at all. There were far too many bad vibes in the air.

'I needed a shit. This sounded like the perfect place to have one,' I told him.

'Cheeky bastard, get out my fucking taxi,' he yelled, before swerving off the road and throwing me out at a lay-by.

It was a warm evening and for the first time that day I felt at peace. For a while I sat staring at the cracks in the pavement, seeing ancient, sacred geoglyphs, and talking to people who weren't there. I lay on my side with my face among the weeds and grass and said hello to ants, beetles, wood lice, wasps, and spiders without fear or favour. Not far off, a kestrel hovered above a field. After a minute, it disappeared. Its motionless head, dropping suddenly like a small stone, its body tilting after it like a dowsing rod. I remembered I was supposed to be at Johnny's funeral and stood up and took a good look around to get my bearings. A few miles to the west, the sun was going down behind an industrial plant brooding silently on the horizon. While in the east, a massive column of cumulus, glowing atomic orange in the dying light, unfurled like a mushroom cloud above a small town. I was lost and about to start walking across the fields towards the apocalypse, when I looked down the road and saw the headlights of a bus coming towards me and realised I was at a bus stop.

'Do you go into Coatbridge?' I asked the driver as I stumbled onboard.

'Aye, to the bus station.'

'Great.'

I sat on one of the brown, two-tone moquette seats and floated in the dreamy yellow glow of the interior, while the remains of the day smouldered beneath the burning sky. In the seat in front of mine there was a woman surrounded by bags filled with groceries. She looked tired, forlorn. I leaned across the back of her seat and offered her a drink of vodka, which she declined. I decided I'd cheer her up with a poem and began reciting 'Do not go gentle into that good night'. But the only lines I could remember were, 'Do not go gentle into that good night, rage, rage against the dying of the light.' As magnificent as those lines are, no matter how much gusto I put into them — and I really flung my weight behind each word with the finest Welsh accent I could muster — there's only so often you can proclaim the same two lines over and over. As the woman began ferrying her bags to a different seat, I launched instead into a rousing version of 'Rhinestone Cowboy', followed by a poignant rendition of 'Danny Boy'. The bus didn't go all the way into Coatbridge for me. I got as far as the outskirts of the town, where the driver escorted me off the bus opposite a roundabout.

The roundabout looked like an oasis of calm amid the chaos of neon timelines drawn by the evening traffic, and I veered and weaved my way through the cars and slumped down against the signpost in the centre of the island. Motorists sounded their horns and yelled abuse. A teenage girl leaned out of the passenger window of a car and threw a bottle of lemon Hooch at me. After it grazed the side of my head I picked it up and finished what was left, then I finished the vodka and lay back gazing up at the few grubby stars I could see twinkling beyond the light pollution.

When I woke up I was on a stretcher being carried into an ambulance.

'Can you hear me?' a stern-looking paramedic was yelling at me.

'Yes, I can hear you. What the fuck is going on?' I yelled back.

'You collapsed on the roundabout.'

'I didn't collapse. I fell asleep.'

'I'll be the judge of that,' she continued yelling.

A friendlier-looking paramedic appeared beside her.

'Why is she shouting at me?' I yelled at him.

'She worked on an air ambulance for years. *Helicopters, they're loud*,' he yelled now, too.

'Listen, I've a funeral to go to,' I told him calmly, as I tried to take stock of the situation.

'Not now *cowboy*,' he said, smiling down at my cowboy boots, 'we don't bury the dead at night, not in Coatbridge.'

'A word up front,' the stern paramedic nodded to her colleague, 'radio the police,' I overheard her say.

'Really? He seems like a harmless *hombre*.'

'Police, *now*.'

'Okay, but I don't think he'll be happy. He seems keen to get back on his horse.'

'Idiot. Honestly. Shut up. Anyway, he's going nowhere,' she shouted at him. 'I've taken his boots and socks off.'

I looked down at my bare feet and thought of Hands. Feet are fucking amazing too, I wanted to tell him as I jumped out of the back of the ambulance and ran across the road. Think of all the places they've taken you.

I walked into the first pub I came across, The Hindenburg, and ordered a pint. The barman looked at my suit and bare chest. Thankfully, he couldn't see my feet. Still, he looked concerned.

'I've had a long day. I'm fine now,' I assured him.

'If you say so.'

Since I hadn't made it to Johnny's funeral, I decided the least I could do was call him. I took out my mobile and dialled his number and when the answering machine kicked in I began to leave a message.

'Hi Johnny. I'm sorry I didn't make it to your funeral. I tried. I got close. I'm in a pub, the Hindenburg. At least we're going out with a bang,' I joked.

'The Heidelberg,' the barman, who'd been listening to me, interjected.

'What?'

'The pub, it's the Heidelberg, not the Hindenburg.'

'*The Heidelberg?*'

'Aye, The Heidelberg.'

'I'm sorry Johnny. I've fucked up again. It's not with a bang after all, but with a whimper.'

The night was closing in around the pale light of the bar like earth around amber. In this misnamed place the day was ending and dragging the dying world behind it. It felt like the last night on earth. It was for Johnny. He was in the ground and never coming back.

I remembered staying at Johnny's flat once and being woken in the middle of the night by him shouting his dead mother's name over and over. In the morning he couldn't get out of his dreams. At breakfast he kept talking to her as if she were there with us. He put extra eggs on for her, made extra toast. When I sat at the table he asked me if I'd mind swapping chairs, so that his mother didn't have the sun in her eyes. He poured coffee from the pot into a cup that wasn't there and didn't stop until he noticed it spilling across the table onto the floor. It wasn't till later in the afternoon — after I'd been to the corner shop to buy beers to wash our breakfast down and we'd gone to the pub for more drinks — that he finally forgot about her. Or maybe he didn't forget about her, but was okay now with her being dead. Or else with her being undead and hanging around as a ghost or whatever it was he saw. Either way, after enough drink he was back in his head and feeling fine about what he could or couldn't see, about who was or wasn't by his side.

I didn't know if it was possible to drink my way back into my head, or if I even wanted to. Then just as the fruit machine paid out a rain of coins to a punter, I caught my reflection in the mirror and it hit me. I'd never see Johnny again. I tried fighting back the tears, but in that solemn light, somewhere between the high-rise and Johnny's grave, I couldn't help myself, I broke down crying. I would have given anything to have him sitting there by my side again.

'Are you sure you're okay, mate?' the barman asked.

'Yeah, yeah, I'm okay. Honestly. One more drink and I'll be fine,' I told him.

8

The day Pete left, I was up on the twenty-first floor. The design of the top floor was slightly different to those below it. With no stairwells, it was a larger, open space, and in the corners where the stairs would have been there were intersecting walls of glass bricks from floor to ceiling. The abundance of light falling in disparate angles through each corner gave the landing a shifting, rarefied air, as if you were on a platform floating above the high-rise and not attached to it at all. I'd hammered a narrow section of glass bricks out of one corner and positioned a sofa where I could sit and watch the jets flash across a vertical shaft of sky, like images in some huge Zoetrope. In addition to the sofa, I'd added a standard lamp, a coffee table, a sideboard, and an old boom box. This is where I was sitting, listening to a *Best of Frank Sinatra* CD, folding sheets of white A4 into paper planes and throwing them out the window, when I saw Pete again.

'Hey, son,' he said, suddenly appearing beside me.

'*Pete!*' I exclaimed, startled.

'Sorry to scare you,' he said, holding up the palms of his hands as if to settle me.

'I didn't even know you were still in the building.'

'You wouldn't, not since they cut the power to the lifts.'

'I suppose not.'

'I like what you've done with the landing,' he said, smiling and looking around.

'It's a bit sparse,' I replied.

'According to the TV it's all the rage. Spartan chic, they call it.'

'Spartan chic, my trademark style at the moment. How are you, anyway?' I asked, seeing he was out of breath following his climb up the stairs.

'I'm fine, son, absolutely fine.' He said, adjusting the jacket of the blue three-piece suit he was wearing, with a white shirt, a green tie, and a red plastic rose in the buttonhole of his lapel.

'What on earth are you doing way up here? You look like you're on your way to a wedding.'

'Close. It's a vow renewal.'

'Where about?'

'Not too far from here. Do you mind if I join you?'

'Of course not.'

Pete sat down next to me on the sofa and put an unopened bottle of White Horse and a glass on the table. There was a pile of paper planes on the arm of the settee and a strong gust of wind blew in through the window, pushing several of them onto the floor and lifting one of them up over Pete's head.

'Whisky?' he asked, looking over his shoulder, then pouring himself a drink once he'd got his breath back.

'Sure, thanks.'

He pulled a glass from his coat pocket and poured me a large measure.

'Has no one said anything to you about what you're doing, breaking into the flats, leaving furniture everywhere?' he asked as he sat back and looked out the window.

'Not so far. I don't think they care. They've pretty much given up on us.'

'Aye, right enough. Are you watching the planes?' he asked, gesturing towards the sky and smiling.

'Yeah.'

'Martha was forever doing that. She'd stand at the window all day, watching them take off and land. Imagining we were on one of them. Flying off to someplace or coming back from someplace. She'd read up on places she dreamed of visiting and talk about them like we'd been there. Sometimes I think she believed we had.'

'Did you ever go?'

'Where?'

'Anywhere she dreamed of visiting.'

'We made plans to. We even saved up enough money once. But before we got the chance she became too ill to get out the front door, let alone on a plane.'

'And you never managed?'

'No.'

'That's a shame.'

'Aye. Eventually, she stopped looking outside altogether. Drew the curtains in every room and refused to open them again.'

'Why?'

'It was too upsetting for her. Watching them fly off, knowing she'd no chance of getting on one.'

'You never thought of leaving after she died?'

'Never. She was my world.'

'Not even a trip somewhere in her honour?'

'Without her? That would have been like leaving her behind. I couldn't have done that. No, there's nothing left for me down there.'

'No family?'

'Nope.'

'You must miss her so much.'

'Even more than I miss my childhood. Anyway, why are you still here? Nobody chooses to live here, not these days.'

'I split up with my girlfriend and she threw me out of the place we shared. After running out of couches to sleep on I applied for a housing association flat. This was the first place I was offered.'

'So, it's love's fault we're here, then.'

'How's that?'

'In my case I had too much of it. In yours, you didn't have nearly fucking enough.'

'I suppose so. Yin and Yang.'

'You're young, you should take the money, get out. I'm almost eighty. I had no reason to leave. You've no reason to stay.'

'I like it here. It suits me.'

'It'll drive you mad, living up here on your own.'

'I'd miss the views.'

'It's the views that'll drive you crazy. You become so hooked on the horizon, you lose sight of what's in front of you.'

'I'll be fine. Honestly though, Pete, I know it must be hard, but you really shouldn't be here on your own now.'

'I know. I agree. That's what I wanted to talk to you about.'

'Okay.'

'Can I try that?' Pete asked, pointing to the reams of paper at my feet.

'Of course.'

He picked up a pristine piece of white paper, carefully folded it into an aeroplane, then floated it clean out the window into the sky.

'I've heard you with that sledgehammer.'

'Really?'

'A fucking deaf man could hear you.'

'Oh, right. You want my sledgehammer?'

'I want *you* and your sledgehammer. I need your help to get up on the roof.'

Most of the flats were easy enough to break into. A screwdriver positioned in the centre of the lock, then a solid hit with a mallet and you were in. Those with heavier duty locks needed a little more force. Big Bertha — a 20 lb sledgehammer I named after a woman who used to tend bar at the Satellite — usually did the trick.

'You want to go up on the roof?' I asked him.

'Yeah, we could finish the whisky up there, and throw more of these,' he said, gliding an aeroplane out the window.

'Sure, why not?'

'And bring your stereo with you. We'll need music,' he smiled.

—

The first swing of Big Bertha missed the lock and battered the door frame. The force of the impact reverberated back up the shaft of the sledgehammer into my bones and I thought I might pass out with the pain. Shaking off its resistance, I managed to raise the hammer back over my right shoulder, steadied myself, and prepared to go again. The second swing hit the lock dead on with a satisfying report, and the wood splintered around the lock casing and up the edge of the door with a sound like ice cracking across the surface of a lake. When I stepped back to get ready to hit it again, Pete laid his hand across mine and took the sledgehammer from me. After gently swinging it back and forth several times, like a woodcutter limbering up to split a log, he swung it anticlockwise up over his shoulder towards the top-left corner in one fluid movement. The third punch from Big Bertha took the top hinge clean off and the entire door swung out and backwards like a heavyweight spinning on their heel as they're knocked out in a boxing match. Pete composed himself, then stepped over his adversary and walked out onto the roof, smiling like a pugilist who'd come out of retirement to claim victory in one last fight.

This was the first time I'd been on the roof and gazing out over the four other high-rises that descended incrementally down the sloping landscape, I was struck by how sad and forlorn they looked in the gloaming, as if loneliness had lent them its clothes. Above their dark silhouettes the evening sky was cool and keen. I breathed deep draughts of blue air and was filled with the sadness of past summers. Overwhelmed by the sheer immensity of it, I teetered on the edge of something beautiful and ominous and distant that I never wanted to see fulfilled.

Pete kept the whisky coming and I kept the music playing. We danced together, sang 'Come Fly with Me' together, laughed at how we'd come to be on this roof together, and all the time kept throwing paper aeroplanes up into the air together. We must have folded hundreds of them, because at one point I looked up and they were everywhere. Floating above us. Swaying and swooning all around us. Diving and gliding over the edge of the building. Pete couldn't stop smiling as we launched more of them up into the sky. He was still smiling as he refilled our glasses then sat the White Horse on top of a ventilation duct and took a good look around. I was trying to smile along with him, but I knew what he was going to do next, and I knew I couldn't stop him. Instead, I started crying.

'For fuck's sake, son. Stop crying and get a grip of yourself,' Pete said. 'You're just drunk.' He clinked his glass against mine, then swept the air with a gesture that indicated the high-rise. 'Soon there'll be no evidence of any of this. And you know, it's not like knocking down the odd house here and there. When it's gone there won't be a street to walk along and reminisce. What would I do, stand and look up at some random point in the sky and think, "That's where I brought her a cup of tea in bed in the morning? There's the room where we'd play cards most nights. That's where I kissed her for the last time." No. It'll all be gone. There'll be nothing. Actually nothing. I don't intend to be here when that happens.'

'You might find something somewhere else.'

'Have you ever woken from a dream you didn't want to leave and found your life so empty you felt like throwing up?'

'Yeah, a few times.'

'Well, I wake up like that every morning. I'm tired of it. Everything I love is out there.'

'Where?'

'There,' he said, indicating the sky. 'Do me one last favour?' he asked.

'Of course.'

'Play a song and keep throwing those planes.'

Pete may have been getting on in years, but he was strong and squat, with a low centre of gravity, and agile for his age. Still clutching his glass, he managed to pull himself up onto the parapet that bordered the roof. A gust of wind caught him as he got to his feet and he swayed back and forth, teetering in the loose air, before managing to steady himself. Looking up, he sidestepped along the ledge and fixed his vision on something high above him. I'd stopped crying, but my chest was still heaving. I folded and threw some more paper aeroplanes, then I stopped. I thought there was something I should do, but I was too terrified to move. I was frightened that doing so might push him over the edge. I thought if I concentrated hard enough, I could somehow hold everything where it was. And for a moment I thought I had. Everything seemed to pause. Pete with his glass raised above his head. The paper aeroplanes around him. The music. A lone jet, burnished by the evening light. And then he broke the spell with an audacious piece of magic that set everything in motion. I'd seen him do this countless times before, but to see him do it now, I was transfixed. He started doing that old soft-shoe shuffle, and after dancing and singing his way along the ledge, he finished his drink and stepped off into the air.

I never looked over the parapet. I lay on my back staring up at the sky and didn't move. After I've no idea how long, I heard emergency vehicles approaching through the streets with their sirens wailing. When they reached the foot of the high-rise their sirens stopped, but their lights continued rotating. Even from the rooftop I could see them. Their electric blue sweep pulsing the darkness like signals to another world. I had no idea what was happening. I couldn't hear much, only the occasional word or phrase breaking loose and drifting up from the conversations between those gathered around Pete's body down below ... *bloody* ... *sad* ... *no one else* ... *fallen* ... *inevitable* ... *lonely man* ...

I always found it remarkable how ribbons of words would travel up through the air and reach you no matter where you were in the high-rise. Sometimes, depending on the weather and other environmental conditions, an entire conversation might drift by me as I sat by an open window in my flat. I may have been fourteen floors above whoever was talking, but their words were so clear I could have just as easily been standing on the ground right beside them.

I waited for the police to appear on the roof, but they never did. After a while I heard the doors of several vehicles slam shut. A moment later their engines turned over and purred warmly, idling, as final orders were issued and leaves were taken. Their emergency lights were switched off, and I watched the photons of their collective blue pulse scatter and dissolve, like tiny fireflies into the void. Then they drove off, at first collectively and loudly, then fading quickly as they chose different routes for alternative destinations.

In their wake, a vast multifoliate silence burgeoned from the car park and bloomed all the way to the heavens. I didn't move. I lay in the darkness, watching the lights of jet planes blink overhead. Drifting in and out of sleep, I dreamt that Pete and Martha had flown away together. I dreamt we had all flown away together. I dreamt we were all dreaming.

Little fuss was made over Pete's death. The police found a suicide note in his flat and assumed he'd killed himself. They never suspected or just didn't care that someone else may have been involved in some way. I wasn't even spoken to. His blood stained the concrete slabs where he'd landed a deep rose red like a late, shocking bloom. A week passed, and it darkened. After a few weeks, it was indistinguishable from all the other stains on the pavement in front of the building.

Though he chose not to share what remained of his life with the world, I like to believe that the world nevertheless shared in Pete's death. That someone walking through the surrounding streets may have looked up for a split second and seen a shocking yet beautiful sight. Perhaps they, too, thought they were dreaming. An old man dancing off the high-rise and falling through the air, while paper aeroplanes swooped around him, the first stars of evening glittered on the horizon, and the 'Summer Wind' drifted across the rooftops.

9

I met Mia at a party in a nearby high-rise after almost coming to blows with a gay, amputee junkie. I'd gone along with a couple of friends. An amputee acquaintance of my own, as it happened, Jimmy Two-fingers, and Dave. Jimmy got his name after frostbite liberated three digits from his right hand while he was on a climbing holiday in the Pyrenees, leaving him with only his index and middle finger. Dave was just plain Dave. Really we should never have been there at all.

It was a month or so after my block had emptied and they'd come to see how I was doing, or at least Dave had. Jimmy just liked the idea of hanging out somewhere he considered fashionably dystopian. On the way to mine, they'd noticed there was a party in the high-rise further down the hill. Given the madness and stupidity on display, they couldn't have missed it. It wasn't at all uncommon to see some poor bastard being held by his ankles and dangled out of a window, while he wriggled and screamed for his life at one of these lofty soirees. It didn't matter what floor they were on — in this instance, the ninth. We watched from my kitchen window as he was hauled back in and immediately replaced by a teenager who sat with his legs dangling over the ledge, yelling at passers-by while music blared behind him. Cans and bottles were being hurled from the other windows and every so often a piece of furniture would fly out into the air, then explode at the foot of the building seconds later. I wasn't convinced a party in a local high-rise was what I needed,

but Jimmy managed to persuade us to crash it on the warped pretext that it
would do me good to get out.

We'd not been there long when Jimmy managed to ingratiate himself with
the amputee I mentioned. A junkie called Bobby, who'd undergone surgery to
remove his entire right arm, after mistakenly injecting an artery and developing
gangrene. No sooner had Jimmy bonded with his limbless brethren than I was
abandoned in the kitchen with him, while Jimmy and Dave went off to find
a dealer Bobby had told Jimmy about. They'd been gone so long I thought
they'd scored, got high, and had forgotten all about me. Which, as it turned
out, was pretty much what had happened.

Bobby was a skinny, hyper character in his late twenties, who talked a lot
about his life. His parents, who were Jehovah's Witnesses, had forced him to
undergo conversion therapy after he told them he was gay. He was seventeen
and the pastor running the course employed what Bobby referred to as reverse
psychology conversion methods. This involved regular sessions of oral and
anal sex with the pastor himself. When Bobby confided in his parents about
what was happening, they asked him to leave their house. When he refused to
do so, they told the elders, who arranged for muscled servants to pay Bobby
a visit and essentially throw him out. He wound up on the streets, turning
tricks to survive. Then he started taking heroin, so that he didn't have to think
about being on the streets turning tricks to survive. It was variously, in Bobby's
own words, a bad run of cards, a downward spiral, a vicious cycle, as well as a
right fucking bummer. While telling me all this, he stared at me with a dreamy
intensity that never wavered. He kept saying how beautiful my eyes were, and
after talking me through the procedures involved in his operation, he asked
if I'd ever fucked an amputee. When I told him I hadn't — not knowingly,
anyway — he took it personally and became quite animated. He demanded to
know what I had against one-armed men? I tried to reassure him that I didn't
have anything against them, that I just didn't want to fuck him. No matter how
many or how few limbs he had. He grew angry then and threatened to hit me
with a fish slice covered in what looked like dried fried egg. At this point a

couple of guys who'd been watching and listening to all this decided to get involved. They started winding him up with cheap insults. Telling him to put the fish slice down, that he was armless. That his right hand didn't know what his left was doing. That if he kicked off it'd be fucking Armageddon. It was all very shameful. Any other time — if I'd been a bystander witnessing this — I would have intervened on Bobby's behalf. Given the circumstances — that the three of them were clearly equal in the no-limits-fucked-up stakes — I promptly washed my hands of the whole affair and slipped away. I was on my way out, when I spotted Dave and Jimmy dipping their heads towards a coffee table in one of the bedrooms, before coming back up, smiling like idiots. They were sitting on a sofa, in between them was Mia.

'There you are,' Jimmy said when he saw me walk into the room, 'we were wondering where you'd got to.'

'*Where I'd got to?*'

'This is Mia,' Dave said, introducing us with a wink. 'You know, who we've been looking for,' he affirmed, sniffing repeatedly and wiping powder from his nostrils with the back of his hand.

'Looking for all our lives — or at least every day since I smoked my first joint in high school,' Jimmy laughed.

Mia was the dealer.

'Hi,' I said.

'I've seen you before,' Mia replied.

'Really? I don't think I've seen you before.'

'Yeah, right, you'd remember if you had,' Jimmy grinned, in a nauseating manner.

Given it was Jimmy saying this, I didn't like to admit it, but he was right. I would have remembered her if I'd seen her before. In her late-twenties, with popcorn-blonde hair falling in loose curls around her shoulders, she had a beauty that was flagrant and faraway, like a ballerina in a tattered music box come to life. Her lips were painted red, her eyelids glittered gold and her pupils, encircled by light blue explosions, were two black stars that burnt right through me. She looked damaged and exuded damage. A beautiful face with a shipwrecked heart, she made me think of the calm just before a storm. Only she was the calm *and* the storm.

'I saw you in the Satellite a couple of weeks ago,' she said.

'Did you?'

'Yeah. You're Jack McCann,' she smiled.

'Okay.'

'You kept playing "I'm So Lonesome I Could Cry" on the jukebox. You'd put it on, and by the time you got back to your seat it would have finished, so you'd turn around and walk back and put it on again. You were maybe a little bit drunk.'

'I don't remember that.'

'A little?' Jimmy remarked, disdainfully.

'You started arguing with some guy,' Mia continued, ignoring Jimmy. 'You were yelling about some ornaments and plants that were on the table in front of you. I thought you were going to hit him. Then you stood up and told him he could have it all and stormed off.'

'Still don't remember,' I said.

'He never remembers anything. It's the drink,' Jimmy interjected again.

'Before you walked out, you stood at the entrance shouting over and over that you'd never earned a nickel on another man's sweat. That *Jack-fucking-McCann has never earned a nickel on another man's sweat,*' Mia mimicked.

'You remember all that?' I asked.

'How could I forget?' She laughed.

'Who the fuck is Jack McCann?' Dave wondered.

'Gene Hackman,' I said.

'What?' Jimmy asked

'So, who was who?' Dave wondered again.

'Never mind,' I told them both.

I had a vague memory of the evening she was talking about. I'd taken a collection of random household furnishings and personal items from the high-rise into the Satellite with the intention of trying to sell them. I don't know how it happened, but I wound up so drunk I forgot why I'd taken the stuff and ended up arguing with a guy I thought was insulting my dignity by asking how much I wanted for a collection of small glass animals and a bulrush and pampas grass arrangement.

'Yeah, I remember now. Sorry about that.'

'You don't have to apologise. It was hilarious. Did you ever get your stuff back?'

'No.'

'That's a shame.'

'It didn't belong to me anyway.'

'You didn't need to return it?'

'The people it belonged to didn't need it back.'

'They're probably dead. He steals shit from dead people,' Jimmy chipped in once more.

'Excuse my friend's manners, he thinks he's funny,' I said.

Dave looked at Jimmy and shook his head. 'But he's not.'

'I've people I need to see. It was nice to meet you both,' Mia said to Jimmy and Dave as she stood up, 'and you too, Jack McCann,' she said, turning to face me, 'maybe speak to you again sometime.'

'Yeah, maybe,' I said.

Five minutes later Jimmy told us it was time to go, *pronto*. As we were leaving a mass fight broke out — due, it transpired, to something Jimmy had written in lipstick on the bathroom mirror. A spurious denouncement, claiming a girl at the party had given a blow job to the boyfriend of another girl at the party. He didn't know any of the individuals mentioned and none of this had actually taken place. Having eavesdropped on other people's conversations and picked up on underlying tensions, he'd thought it would be a hoot to use what he'd heard to fuel a little trouble. The girl found her supposed rival standing in the kitchen and smashed a bottle over her head and pandemonium ensued.

By this point, numbers at the party had swelled considerably. People were spilling out onto the landing, and pockets of fighting were breaking out all over the place like blazes in a spreading forest fire. Someone must have called the police, because suddenly the night was layered with the sirens of police cars. I headed down the stairs with Jimmy and Dave and a dozen other revellers. Jimmy was laughing as we leapt down flight after flight. He didn't care that one girl was lying with her head split open or that another was going to wind up in jail. Not to mention the attendant general fucking carnage he'd unleashed. He thought the whole thing was a big joke. Everything was always a big fucking joke to Jimmy.

I remember once when he was stoned he started cracking jokes about people with cancer. The sister of a guy in our company had recently died of leukaemia and I was standing behind the guy, trying to make it clear to Jimmy that he should stop. That he wasn't funny. But the more I gestured for him to stop and the more uncomfortable the situation became, the funnier Jimmy seemed to find it. That's the kind of guy Jimmy was. You might have understood a little if Jimmy had started being like this after he'd lost his fingers. If the pain and disfigurement had embittered him. But the truth was, I'd known Jimmy since we were teenagers, when we'd worked in a restaurant together. And even then, when he had all ten fingers, Jimmy was a dick. Especially around those he felt superior to — and he felt superior around pretty much everyone. If anything, he wore the two working fingers on his right hand like a badge of honour. A physical display of his dick-head-ness that he loved to hold up in front of your face.

'Stupid fuck!' I was yelling at Jimmy. 'Stupid, ignorant fuck! Seriously, what am I doing with you? This isn't friendship, it's fucking Stockholm Syndrome!'

'He's right,' Dave joined in, 'one day you're going to pay for all the shit you've caused. Seriously, all this shit is going to come back to fucking haunt you one day!'

Someone further down shouted that the police were on their way up the stairs and we ran through a door onto a landing. People were hitting the buttons for the lifts and piling into them, heading up and down to give the police the run around. I joined a group heading down the stairwell on the opposite side of the building. When we spilled onto the street I couldn't see Jimmy or Dave. As it turned out I was never to see either of them again.

Weeks later, I did talk to Dave on the phone. After we'd been separated he'd run into one of the lifts with a group of people he didn't know, and one of them slashed him. The guy wielding the blade was only fifteen, a boy. He hadn't even been at the party. He'd just got involved in the aftermath with his mates. At his preliminary hearing, he said he didn't know why he did it. That Dave was standing in front of him and it just happened. When I spoke to Dave he was living in Brighton and said he'd had enough of Glasgow. He'd found a flat and a job as a trainee chef in a seafood restaurant and had no plans to ever come back. I told him I was sorry for not visiting him in hospital, but he said it didn't matter. He was more disappointed to hear I hadn't moved out of the high-rise. When I phoned him again a few days later, his mobile number was no longer in use.

As for Jimmy, Dave's prediction came true. Jimmy inadvertently snorted a dose of liquid LSD at a party one night, thinking it was poppers, and wound up spending a year in a secure unit in Leverndale psychiatric hospital. According to a guy I knew, who was present the night it happened, the woman whose party it was looked out of her kitchen window and saw Jimmy rolling around, half-naked, in the back garden, kissing and fondling a furry white hat. She called some people over to have a look, and they were all laughing until someone asked if that was a rabbit hutch in her backyard? She said it was and continued to laugh. But when the guy pointed out that its door was wide open, she stopped laughing and started screaming. They ran outside and found Jimmy rolling around on the grass with his pants around his ankles, an erection, and a dead rabbit clamped between his thighs. Apparently he'd crushed her daughter's pet rabbit in an amorous embrace.

Later, on the way to the hospital, Jimmy imagined the ambulance had driven head-on into an eighteen-wheeler and they were all killed. The acid had fried his brain so badly that even once he was treated and discharged, he was convinced he'd died that night and that everyone was lying to him about the fact he was alive. The last I heard of Jimmy, he spent most of his time wandering around cemeteries all over Glasgow, looking for his grave. Determined to prove to everyone that he really was dead.

The scene outside the high-rise was chaotic. Drunken teenagers were running back and forth, taunting and dodging the police, while lone junkies staggered around like trauma victims at the site of a bomb blast. A car was going round in circles with mad banging techno blaring from its speakers. Ambulances had joined the police vans and cars, and multiple lights strobed the night sky, lending the scene the atmosphere of a travelling fairground. A guy with long pink hair streaked across the car park in a skin-tight green nylon jumpsuit. Clutching green glowsticks and waving his arms like a demented aircraft marshaller while whooping and hollering, he climbed into the cab of one of the ambulances. He must have centrally locked the doors, as neither the paramedics nor the police were able to get him out once he was in the driver's seat. The vehicle's lights flashed on and off a few times, and the siren let out several abbreviated whoops, then the engine roared wildly as he lowered the windows and let out a sustained '*Gerrronnnimooo!*' before reversing the ambulance at high speed into a lamp post. The door opened and he jumped out and shot off again, this time running across a grass embankment and straight down the middle of the road. It was like an episode of the *Keystone Cops* directed by Quentin Tarantino. I had no intention of hanging around and getting caught up in the chaos, but neither did I want the police or any of these bampots following me into my high-rise, so I cut down a path towards the main road leading into the city centre. When I slowed down and stopped to make sure I wasn't being followed, Mia was right behind me. She asked if she could walk with me, I told her she could. Then she offered me a pill, and when I accepted, she placed it on the tip of her tongue and half-kissed it into my mouth.

On the way into town, we stopped at a bar called the Laurieston for a drink. We carried our drinks into the lounge, where we were the only customers, and sat down in the corner at a little circular table and drank amaretto and played songs on the free jukebox. There was a street light directly outside the window behind us, and its grainy orange vapour drifted through the wire mesh and frosted glass like atomised heartache. After a couple of drinks, Mia leant across the table and very gently kissed my cheek, then we stood up and danced with our arms around each other to Lana Del Ray's 'Video Games'.

After we'd danced we went outside, so that Mia could smoke. She brought out a tin of tobacco and a packet of Rizlas and began to roll a cigarette, and every gesture dispatched in its rolling pulled me in. The careful, deliberate movement of her fingers. The tip of her tongue running along the edge of the paper. The way she held the flame of the lighter in the air before lighting the cigarette, like she could've set the universe on fire with the faintest flick of her wrist. By the time Mia had taken her first drag, then exhaled and glanced at me through the smoke, I wanted to sacrifice myself to her. I wanted to cut a tiny perfect wound in each of us, through which we'd experience life. I wanted nothing less than a bevy of falling stars constellating in our fucked-up, tortured hearts.

'Who are you?' I asked her.

'You know who I am.'

'I know your name.'

'Isn't that enough?'

'Yeah. It's just, you seem a strange fit?'

'A strange fit for what?'

'Dealing drugs, especially in the high-rises.'

'As long as they're paying, I don't care who's buying or where they're buying. It makes no difference to me. I've never been good at fitting in. What about you?'

'What about me?'

'How did you end up where you are?'

'I came here with you,' I smiled.

'Well, that's too bad.'

'Who for?'

'Let's find out,' she said, and ran her hand slowly up the inside of my thigh, then down inside the front of my trousers.

The rest of the evening passed in this manner. In furtive touches and kisses. Dancing with and around each other. Dropping in and out of conversations. Flashes of dialogue. Crystallised visual impressions. Alternating between states of consciousness like in a continually interrupted dream. In fact, the rest of our relationship passed as if in a constantly interrupted dream. With the line between dreaming and waking blurred and shimmering like a mirage, so that I was never fully aware which was which.

For the brief time I was with Mia I was never entirely sure what was going on. Everything she told me may have been true, or none of it. It was impossible to tell with Mia. She was one of those people who make something true by the conviction with which they say it. Not that I cared. Who was I to judge? A drunk who occasionally went by the name Jack McCann and yelled at people about random items of stolen furniture.

As for Mia, she said she'd grown up in Glasgow's leafy West End, the only child of a wealthy couple. Her father was a successful lawyer, who beat the shit out of her mother. Mia had begged her mother to leave him, but her mother insisted it was a price she was willing to pay for all that he gave them. Convinced she'd be ruined if she tried to divorce a lawyer, she made it clear to Mia that she hadn't suffered countless humiliations and years of beatings to wind up with nothing.

When her father slapped her because he didn't approve of what she wore to her high school graduation party, and then her mother persuaded her not to go to the police, Mia left home and moved to London. Once there, she started dating a gangster and then dealing drugs. Now she was twenty-six and back in Glasgow, saving to study photography at art school. She said dealing was the only way she knew how to make a living. It also happened to be the quickest and most lucrative, which suited her fine, as she didn't plan on doing it for long.

'It's only temporary. As soon as I've enough to buy the equipment I need and to pay my fees, that'll be it,' she claimed.

When the bar closed we wandered around the city, and when the sun came up and we were too tired to walk any further, we went back to the room Mia had at the George Hotel.

From the outside the George looked like it had been laid siege to. A century and a half of Scottish weather had left its façade looking like a hotel on the edge of a city ravaged by war. Weeds and bushes sprouted from every crack and crevice, and its once golden sandstone was layered in varying degrees of grey, pock-marked, chipped, and covered in bird shit. Its statues, inset in crumbling alcoves, had faces without features and outstretched hands that could no longer hold the rain. They'd begun as dust and were on their way home to end as dust. Above the entrance a large metal canopy supported by two marble pillars extended out above the pavement. The canopy was in ruins, a rusted skeleton of its former self, and the signage on its front was missing the second letter, renaming the place the G ORGE.

There were no windows in the foyer of the George. The only natural light that made it in from outside fell through the glass panes of the heavy oak revolving door. You had to push hard and lean in against it to make it turn, and when it moved it sounded like someone was hushing you to sleep. Whenever anyone entered, long beams of light would cut across the foyer in rhythmic snapping bursts. Sunlight during the day, street light at night, throwing the shadows of those who entered across the walls and into the hotel like captives thrown into the brig of a ship.

The only internal light came from the television that was permanently on beneath the reception desk with the sound turned down. There were light fittings, ornate brass wall lights with dainty shades throughout the hotel, and two massive chandeliers hanging from the ceiling in the foyer, but over time all the bulbs had blown and had never been replaced.

In the long hallways of its five floors you had to use the glow of the exit signs at each end to guide you to your door. Matches or lighters would suddenly flare up, revealing a face or a hand, before a cloud of smoke curled into the air and the image disappeared into the darkness again. The entire place reeked of vomit, piss, and booze, and you could hear wailing and moaning coming from most of the rooms. Often you'd hear footsteps in the hallway and swear they'd stopped outside your door, but when you opened it, there'd be no one there. As for staff, I only ever saw two who seemed to be official employees. The wizened, shrunken concierge, in his oversized grey suit. He looked like he was going to keep on shrinking until he'd disappeared, leaving only his suit behind the reception desk. And the Polish barman, whose grasp of English seemed to start and end with the word *drink*, posed either as a question when you were ordering, or as a command when he wanted to stop serving and close up.

A once grand institution, the George hadn't functioned as a genuine hotel with staff and regular paying guests for more than two decades. The only people who stayed there now were derelicts and addicts. The forgotten, or those who wanted to be forgotten. Mia said she loved the fact that the place was in a state of terminal decline. That once you were inside, you could do whatever you wanted, and no one bothered you. That it was haunted by its former glory and condemned by its current disrepute.

I stayed at the George with Mia for almost three weeks. We'd sleep from morning till late afternoon, drink and get high in the evening, then fuck until we could no longer see each other's faces and our spirits disappeared into the darkness of the room. Afterwards, we'd get up and walk through the city just like we had the first night. Between 5 a.m. and 6 a.m. was our favourite time. The hour that sits between the last of the revellers leaving the city to go home and people coming into the city to start work. The deserted hour. The liminal hour.

At the outset, the sky would no longer be black, but dark blue. Looking into the immensity of it from the top of a fire escape on the side of some building, it felt like we were leaning out into the heart of the universe, reaching towards a destination it was impossible to arrive at. With the day still only a suspicion, we'd watch the sky soak up sunlight like blotting paper and flower gradually through folds of midnight, cobalt, turquoise, crimson, and gold. Just at the point when the night had almost pulled away from us, we'd come down from the fire escape and follow it. Compelled to chase it through the streets like a magnet drawing two solitary iron filings after it.

Of course, we never caught it, no matter how quickly we ran. We'd end up in some alley, listening while all the declarations of love and hate from the night before, the collective sigh of countless regrets, settled in the streets around us. Minutes later, as dawn broke over the edges of the city and slipped gracefully down the sides of buildings like a golden visual hymn — the words to which were common noises — we'd walk out among the swelling crowds.

Moving from the old night into the new day, was like crossing over from an invisible world. And having crossed over, it seemed we remained invisible. After several days we began to notice that having become invisible, we were able to see things that had previously been invisible to us. Each morning we'd pick out details of the city that we'd overlooked the day before, and Mia would photograph them with her instant camera. When we got back to the hotel, we'd lie in bed together, studying the images, finding worlds within worlds. Sometimes Mia would photograph the same section of a building over a period of days, and we'd watch as it came into focus and revealed itself like someone removing a series of veils from their face.

Walking back to the crumbling grandeur of the George to add another image to those already spread across the room like some map of captured time, I realised how mutable the city was. How vulnerable it was, and ultimately, how mortal. I could have stayed there with Mia forever. Fucking and drinking. Bearing witness to the merciless glory of time's creativity and destruction. But nothing lasts forever. We were as open to time's vagaries as any statue, or street corner, or door that Mia photographed. As any of the forgotten faces we passed each morning.

There was a bar in the George called the Anchor — a nod to Glasgow's once thriving shipyards. I'd drink in there in the afternoons, if Mia was out, and most nights we'd have a few drinks in there together. It was decked out like a fo'c'sle, with old barrels for tables and canvas hammocks strung along the walls. Booths ran all the way around the room, and above each one there was a brass porthole with the same yellowed image behind the glass of an ocean sunset viewed from a golden beach. The punters would sit for hours gazing into them or out through them, as if they were real views, seeing ships or shipwrecks, depending on how low in their lives they'd sunk.

The strange thing was, I'd stood on that exact beach, gazing at that exact sunset countless times before. On the pavement outside the travel agent next door to the Western Bar on Great Western Road. Only in the window display the image was enlarged just enough beyond life-sized to make it seem like you could walk right on into it. It hung there for over a decade, like a huge screen on a projector tripod — the image itself seeming to recede with every passing year, as it bleached and faded a little more. I'd stand gazing at it, before ducking into The Western at 4 a.m., beneath the shutter they'd leave partially open for those of us who couldn't stop drinking until our pockets or bodies called closing time. At some point the Western had an arty revamp and reopened as the Belle. Its illicit hours vanished and along with them its old clientele. Not so long after that the travel agent closed down. I think they sell musical instruments there now.

But it was the same image, and when I saw it again in the Anchor for the first time I wondered if perhaps only I could see it. That I'd carried it with me. Until I asked someone one afternoon if they could see it too, and they confirmed they could. After that I began to wonder if it moved itself from location to location like some Fata Morgana, luring drunks further and further from their lives. That without realising it, all of us had seen it before, and were following it to our deaths.

One evening, after taking an assortment of pills, the bar began to list heavily to one side and I found it difficult to stand up. Mia sat me down in a booth, then lay me in the recovery position with my head towards the wall and my feet dangling over the edge of the seat. After a while I started to feel a little better, but when I tried to sit up the whole room went sideways again. I was fine if I stayed lying down, but the room would start spinning and I'd keel over every time I tried to sit up.

From the position I was lying in along the booth, with the underside of the table obscuring my view, I could see the full sweep of the bar and everyone in it from the waist down. All I could see were legs, trouser legs, and a couple of skirts to be precise. After a while, the bar began to fill with more of them. They looked like they were walking around on their own, unattached to bodies and multiplying. It was easy enough to keep track of Mia though, as she was still one of the few women in the bar, and the only one wearing black stockings.

The busier the bar became, the more Mia's legs seemed to be moving around the room. I figured either she knew a lot of people who were in the Anchor, or she was dealing. Then I saw her stockings walk with a pair of jeans into the men's toilets, and then her stockings walked back out on their own, minutes after. She came over to check on me and I asked her what was going on. She told me not to worry, to stay down where I was, that she was just doing a bit of business and that she'd come back for me soon. A little later, I saw her walk towards the men's toilet again, only this time there were a pair of grey tracksuit bottoms on one side of her and a pair of fawn chinos on the other. I couldn't see enough of what was happening to make sense of it, but I knew something was wrong, and I managed to force myself up off the seat and sat slumped across the table, looking towards the toilet. This time the tracksuit bottoms and chinos emerged first, and now they were attached to large bodies with misshapen heads and grotesque faces. Then Mia emerged from the bathroom carrying her stockings, her eyeshadow blurred in rings around her eyes and her red lipstick smudged across her mouth. I looked at her and she mouthed, 'Don't get involved. I don't need a saviour.'

But it was too late. I was already careering across the barroom towards the two men like a sailor floundering across the deck of a pitching ship. Neither of them moved an inch, while the bigger of the two started laughing as his smaller companion swung out what looked like a remarkably large fist the closer it came to my face.

I woke up lying face down on the bed in the hotel room. Someone was knocking on the door. When I opened it I couldn't see anyone. I flicked the light switch and a woman in her sixties, wearing a red leather mini skirt and yellow high heels, came tottering like a marionette out of the darkness of the hallway into the light. She adjusted her left breast, which was sagging clean out of her boob tube like a balloon that had seen all yesterday's parties, then asked if she could come in. Before I got the chance to respond, she pushed passed me with an agitated gait, and when she wheeled round to face me, I saw that it wasn't only her breasts that were heading south. Her entire body had been ravaged by the gravitational pull of her past. One shoulder drooped lower than the other, while her face looked like a subsiding tenement. To cover over the cracks, she'd applied her make-up so heavily she looked embalmed. Her eyes had disappeared behind folds of wrinkled flesh that she'd made up in dramatic purple and high gold, and her lips had all but vanished. She'd made a valiant stab at painting where they'd once been with green lipstick, but what was there didn't add up to a mouth, and when she spoke her words seemed out of sync with the movement of her lips.

'Sorry honey,' she said. 'Mia asked me to tell you she's not coming back.'

'Tonight?'

'Any night.'

'Did she say anything else?'

'She said you were fun for a while.'

'Nothing else?'

'That you should move on.'

'That's it?'

'Aye.'

'Who are you, anyway?'

'I'm Irene.'

'Are you her friend?'

'No, not exactly.'

'What does that mean?'

'I take care of things for her when she stays here.'

'What do you mean?'

'She didn't tell you?'

'Tell me what?'

'Honey, Mia's on the game.'

I was confused and couldn't quite take in what she was telling me. The information was taking a little time to filter through the haze of the chemicals and the throbbing pain on the side of my head.

'I know she's a dealer,' I said.

'Yeah, and an addict, and prostitute. Come down to the bar and have a drink with me, sweetie. I'll help you forget about her.'

I wasn't ready to go home, and so I did go down to the bar with Irene that night. And the next night, and the next. I stayed on at the George for over a week, staring out through the portholes in the Anchor at either moon shots or shipwrecks, depending on what I'd taken. When Irene came up to my room each night and slipped into my bed, then climbed on top of me, I'd reach over and switch the lamp on. Seeing the faces of all the women I'd ever known, I'd lose myself in her painted face and watch the shadow of her crooked back rise up and down the wall like Max Schreck's Count Orlok climbing the stairs in *Nosferatu*. Finally, despairing at the mess I was in, I'd pull Irene close to me and implore her to keep fucking me.

When I woke in the morning, Irene would always be gone. Still drunk and high from the night before, I'd roll out of bed onto the floor and look up through sparkling clouds of dust motes, imagining the room was a snow globe someone had shaken, and that I was a little plastic figure floating around in it.

After I went back to the high-rise I'd occasionally get up just before the dawn and walk into the city. I'd walk around for hours, trying to find my way back to that other land. But I never did find my way back there. When I looked up at the buildings all around me I wouldn't notice anything different from the morning before, I'd just see the same details, day after day, and give up and walk home.

Pretty soon I forgot all about Mia, though I did see her one more time. Months later, in a dream. I saw many people I'd forgotten in that dream. Living on the upper floors of a high-rise it was easy to forget about people, about everything. To lose track of time. It was like being on a spectacular journey, but never actually going anywhere. Everything moved on all around you, while you stood still. You could lose days, weeks, months, entire seasons, looking out the window at the sky. Watching the dramatic shifts of light and shadow move across the landscape. One day it would be summer and all the windows in the high-rise would be open. There'd be people calling out to passers-by in the surrounding streets. All the swarming sounds of the city. The sweet warm smell of it in the fetid air. At such times, it would feel like great events were unfolding all around you and you'd be convinced you were somehow part of them. Then you'd look out the window and the entire landscape would be covered in snow as far as you could see. There'd be a thin sheet of ice on the inside of the glass as well as the outside, and you'd realise the light of the world was faraway and that everything you felt you were a part of was out of reach and had been for a long time.

10

I woke up lying on my living-room floor, surrounded by an array of household items I'd dragged in there while working my way through a bottle of whisky. At around 1 a.m., revelations delivered from the burning cosmos had started entering my soul, and determined to decipher them, I'd arranged the objects around me like some monumental stone circle. Revelations, the burning cosmos, standing stones — that's not hyperbole. Caught in the maelstrom of the whisky, that's *exactly* what I saw and believed. Add all that to the vast loneliness of the high-rise and I was tumbling beyond my visible surroundings to infinity. But the line between wonder and dank oblivion is a thin one, and just when I thought I was about to cross over into the realm of white horses, intoxication flung a heavy, wet blanket over my awakening.

In the hours since, the cold had set about my bones, the cosmos had been extinguished, and whatever secrets I had knowledge of had been leached from my marrow. Now everything looked like nothing besides exactly what it was. There was an old wooden hat- and coat-stand. A tall grey metal filing cabinet with its drawers open to differing positions, and knives balanced around the edges of the drawers. A huge toy giraffe. Stacks of newspapers. A tin mop bucket with a mop and two brushes sticking out with their heads up. And lengths of red thread tying it all together like some insane evidence board. As well as my miniature Stonehenge, I'd attempted to mark out a pentagram on the floor with white emulsion, and had drawn little signs and arrows all over the walls, which pointed nowhere and meant nothing to me now. The ceiling light was on and the bare bulb on the end of the wire lit the grimy magnolia-painted walls in a harsh caustic light that exposed everything, yet illuminated nothing. Having attempted to commune with gods, I'd wound up in my own private Guernica.

Intermittent squalls were being whipped against the windows by a wind that was howling around the high-rise and wailing up and down the lift shafts like a banshee foretelling the death of humanity. I felt like I'd been hit with a metal bar and the slightest movement caused my brain to jar and rattle agonisingly in my skull. Attempting to hide from the pain, I held on to the base of the coat-stand and got up off the floor, as gently and discreetly as possible, and looked in a mirror. There was a bruise and swelling on my right temple, and the word *ARSE* written in pink lipstick on my forehead. I touched the swelling, then smeared the lipstick down across my face and began to recall fragments of the previous evening. The girl I was on a date with smiling sweetly when we met beneath the clock in Glasgow Central Station. Sitting at a table in a bar, laughing and drinking wine with her. Holding hands across the table. Furtively ordering shots of whisky whenever she went to the toilet. A party. Standing alone in the dark in a bedroom, drinking from a bottle of something I'd swiped from the kitchen. Someone walking in and switching on the light. The girl I was with yelling at me. Being pushed out a door into the street and staggering into the middle of the road, still clutching the bottle. Someone shouting, 'For the last time, stay away. Do you understand?' Stumbling back towards the voice. Trying to say I was sorry. That I didn't know what I was doing. Wretched tears streaming down my face. Looking up and yelling something about the stars. Or maybe I was yelling at the stars. My foot catching the edge of the kerb. Glimpsing a beautiful crescent moon flying off through the night sky as I plunged towards the ground.

When I turned away from the mirror my reflection slid across the surface like a smashed-up car skidding off the road. I felt physically and emotionally wrecked and walked into the kitchen to brew a pot of coffee. The wind was blowing so strongly that the high-rise had begun to sway from side to side. By the time I'd made it to the kitchen sink I'd added seasickness to my afflictions. Peering through the rainy blur of the window, I tried to concentrate on the horizon, to fix the contours of the city to the earth. But it was still dark out and the skyline kept shifting and disappearing in the gloom.

I checked the time on an old microwave I'd taken from one of the voids. It was no good for cooking anything, this microwave. The inside was covered in rust and the turntable didn't turn. I only used it for the clock, and even that was fucked. I had to move sideways to read the ghost segments of the tiny green numbers on the LCD properly and was always misreading it. I'd thought it was closer to morning than it was. It was only 3 a.m. When I saw the actual time, the rotting apple of gravity dropped through me and I felt terrifyingly aware of being fourteen floors above the earth and surrounded by space. This happened from time to time. Without warning, it would suddenly hit you where you were, and all the concrete surrounding you might as well not have been there at all. You never got completely used to living up there. Certainly not if you lived above the ninth floor. Most residents experienced it at some point. The ninth-floor nightmare. Its knockout blow was similar to that moment when you realise that one day you're going to die. A fact that most of us take for granted, like it's nothing. And yet when it *truly* hits you — it's terrifying.

I drank a cup of black coffee, then closed my eyes and clutched the edge of the kitchen worktop. I felt like an actor who needed a drink to conquer stage fright. Intoxication sheltered me from reality, but after sobering up mid-performance and seeing the audience for the first time, I'd realised where I was and panicked.

I drank another cup of coffee and continued to hold on. I stood there until the first faint light of morning began to seep into the day, then undressed where I was standing and dropped to my knees. Clutching the floor like I was trying to hold on to the ceiling, I crawled out of the kitchen, then across the living room and along the hallway towards my bedroom and into bed. From where I lay, I could see the elements scar and bruise the pale sky. It looked like nature was readying for war. It was my thirtieth birthday.

—

When I awoke again, I decided to stay in bed listening to my radio. I loved my radio and considered it the most beautiful thing in my life. A Chairman Supersonic Chassay, a truly charismatic object. I'd found it in a charity shop when I was fourteen years old, and it had been at my bedside ever since. Photographs, clocks, lamps, countless books, bottles of booze, had all come and gone, but not my radio. Over the years I'd stopped believing in most things, but I'd never stopped believing in my radio. As a teenager I fell in love with the sound of it. Its tone, its voice, the way it talked to *me*. I'd sit in front of it all day, moving from station to station. Listening to music, news, cultural discussions, sport, sermons, anything at all I could find. A babel of voices sent out from every corner of the world. While at night I'd lie in bed and tune in to the space between the stations, searching for obscure transmissions and signals. Recurrent loops of high-pitched sound, long sequences of bleeps and blips. Listening to what I believed were nocturnal communications. Nebulous dispatches. Numbers stations operated by revenants. Ciphers scribbled on the underside of radio waves by palmists attempting to interpret the dreams of the living and the dead. Sacred vectors charting the direction of the human heart.

Whenever I turned my on my radio, no matter how terrible I felt, it always managed to pull a song out of the ether to soothe or help me in some way, but not that morning. When I reached over the edge of my bed and turned the dial, I couldn't find a voice or song that I wanted to hear. And when I tuned in to the cracks between the stations, there were no secret dispatches, only empty static. I lay staring at the ceiling, cast adrift upon a sea of white noise. Pushed and pulled by electromagnetic waves travelling around the world. Abandoned along with all the other fuck-ups who'd been thrown overboard by life, then scattered like flotsam and jetsam across the goddamned universe.

—

It was after midday when I finally got out of bed. Unsure what to do with myself, I considered walking to the nearest supermarket, buying a birthday cake and candles, wine, then throwing myself a party while listening to Tom Waits all day. But the thought of blowing out the candles of my birthday cake alone in a derelict high-rise, while listening to 'Christmas Card from a Hooker in Minneapolis' was too maudlin to contemplate. Fucking hell — even for me.

I opened the living-room window and leaned out to check the weather and to try to clear my head. Around here the squalls had eased off, but in the distance the forecast continued to look bad. Great columns of rain were slanting in every direction across the landscape like legions going into battle, while galleons of black cloud remained moored above the city centre. War was definitely on the horizon. It was inescapable. All hell was going to break loose, and there was nothing any of us could do about it. With death and destruction an inevitability, I decided to take my chance and get out while I still could.

Outside there was an uneasy calm in the streets. It felt like the day had been condemned and was waiting anxiously to hear its punishment. I walked all the way from the south of the city to the west, but still couldn't shake the feeling that something terrible was on its way. When I passed the Kelvingrove Art Gallery I hurried up the front steps and pushed in through the doors like a cursed man seeking refuge in a church. Once inside, I felt safe and calmed by the vast, antique interior.

For a while I wandered around the museum, weaving in and out of the galleries, looking at the exhibits. I sat in the central hall and listened to the organist perform a rendition of 'Eleanor Rigby'. Afterwards, I stood looking up at Sophie Cave's *Floating Heads* and attempted to say hello to them all. I left that hall and stopped at the cross-section of an ancient oak and counted its growth rings until I lost my way near the middle of its life. Finally, I sat down in front of Dalí's *Christ of Saint John of the Cross*. Every time I visited the gallery I would end up here, yet it wasn't a painting I particularly liked. To be honest, I found it kitsch and couldn't stand it. Floating him face down on a crucifix in darkness above some port seemed excessive, even for a Nuclear Mystic. I always imagined that Christ would suddenly look up and start shouting, 'In the name of fucking God! Have I not been through enough already? What daft bastard stuck me back on a cross *and hung me up here?*' Maybe that's why I always stopped in front of it, hoping I'd be there when he spoke. I sat there for over an hour, waiting for him to raise his head — it was my birthday after all — but he never did look up.

I was sitting at the bar in a pub in the city centre a few hours later, when I was approached by a guy who asked if I'd studied at Glasgow University. When I told him I had, he started smiling and shaking his head from side to side in amazement.

'I knew it. *I knew it*,' he said.

'Did you?' I asked.

'Yeah, straight away,' he assured me.

'How did you know?' I asked him, with no idea what it was he knew.

'Because it's me — *it's me*,' he said emphatically, then stepped back with his arms held out and up at shoulder height, as if displaying himself fully would somehow bring his identity into focus for me. He was around my age, but dressed like a twenty-year-old, or at least parts of him were. With his black winkle-pickers, skinny, cropped black jeans, blue denim shirt, heavy arran cardigan and yellow, lightweight duck-down walking jacket, I wasn't sure quite what to make of him. I don't think he was sure what to make of himself. Unable to decide on a single look, he'd settled on several opposing styles.

'Is it *really* you?' I asked.

'Yeah, yeah, it's me, Henry.'

'*Henry?*'

'Yeah, Henry. You remember,' he beamed.

I had absolutely no idea who this guy was, with his Leninesque goatee beard and hair tied back in a ponytail. But I got the impression he was down on his luck, and since I was down there too, I decided to go along with him.

'Of course, of course. Do you want to join me?' I asked.

'If you don't mind?'

'No. Great. You can help me celebrate.'

'What's the happy occasion?'

'It's my birthday.'

'Fantastic,' he said with a distinctly hollow enthusiasm, 'absolutely fantastic.' And then neither of us spoke for what seemed a long time. With all the excitement of reacquainting ourselves taken care of, and given we were actually complete strangers, we didn't have a lot to say to each other. It was mostly long silences, with Henry buying another round of drinks every so often, then wishing me happy birthday and slapping my back.

'Can I be honest with you?' he asked, breaking in on an unbearable period of dead air between us.

'Of course, weren't you always?'

'Yeah, I was. *I was*. The truth is — and I thought you might remember this — I hate birthdays.'

'Really? No, I don't remember that.'

'Never liked them. Fucking depressing events.'

'Even when you were a child?'

'They were the worst, especially the teenage ones. That's what did it for me. None of the kids I knew even liked me. It was my mum they liked. That's the only reason they came to my parties in the first place. To watch her bend over the dining table with her cleavage hanging out her blouse when she poured their fucking orange squash.'

'Yeah, I see how that would put you off. I'm sorry to hear that.'

'Don't be. I'm over it now. Totally. It's you I feel sorry for.'

'Yeah?'

'*It's your fucking birthday.*'

Henry had been glancing at a group of young people who were seated around a couple of tables on the opposite side of the room. He was particularly taken by a girl who must have been ten years younger than him and was way out of his league. He'd been trying unsuccessfully to catch her attention for the best part of an hour. In response, she'd spent most of the time deliberately ignoring him in the hope, I imagine, that he'd either give up or go away. But there was no way Henry was going to give up. Similarly, there was no way anything good was going to come of this.

Oblivious to the reality of the situation, Henry kept buying rounds of tequila, knocking his back, then trying all over again. Using the demented and inappropriate telegraphy of the drunk, his spasmodic efforts were becoming increasingly desperate with each attempt. When it was no longer possible for the girl to ignore him, she finally looked over. When she did, Henry lost it completely, raising his hand above his head and waving like he was greeting another long-lost friend. Unfortunately, in his exuberance he forgot his glass was full and threw his drink across his face. The girl started laughing, then her friends started laughing. It was the moment to appraise the situation and take a step back. They were laughing at him — not with him. However, Henry didn't read it like that at all.

'Shit. Napkin. Napkin. *Give me a fucking napkin*,' he hissed loudly under his breath, while smiling like a third-rate ventriloquist.

'Are you all right?' I asked, handing him a bundle of cocktail napkins.

'My eyes are fucking burning,' he winced, trying to look cool. 'I'm in there now, though,' he continued, wiping tequila from his face and ordering another round.

'Are you sure?'

'Certain.'

'I'm not quite as sure,' I cautioned.

'Didn't you see the way she smiled at me?'

'I did.'

'Well, then.'

'Do you think she might have been laughing?'

'Same thing.'

'Is it?'

'More or less.'

'Listen, Henry, maybe you should back off a little. Take it easy. Just see what happens,' I suggested in an effort to steer him from embarrassment or possible imprisonment.

'No chance.'

In a way his excitement was touching, but mostly it was troubling. One thing was certain, poor Henry was heading for disaster. When the girl stood up a little later and made her way across the room to the stairs leading down to the toilets, Henry declared that his time had come.

'This is it,' he said, a spasm of joy spreading through his entire being and fixing a nausea-inducing grin on his face. 'Cometh the hour, cometh the man.'

'Henry.'

'Yes?'

'Please don't.'

'Once more unto the breach,' he proclaimed, before striding off after her.

'Good luck,' I told him as he headed for the stairs, knowing all the luck in the world wouldn't help Henry now. Henry might have deserved whatever was coming to him. For all I knew, he may have been capable of committing unspeakable acts. Though I would have found that hard to believe. For all his general creepiness, the underlying impression I had of Henry was of someone who didn't have a bad bone in his body. He was a Tin Man who'd been taken apart and put back together incorrectly. When he tried to move his right arm, his left leg moved instead. When he tried to smile, he pulled the lining of his pockets out his trousers. When he tried to shake your hand, he yelled fuck off. And when he tried to say what was in his heart, he was silent, because his heart had been misplaced. No matter how hard Henry tried, you got the impression that nothing he did ever achieved the outcome he'd intended.

Still feeling lousy from the night before, I'd been deliberately holding back and not matching Henry drink for drink. But now I looked down at the collection of shots I'd accumulated in front of me on the bar and finished three of them in quick succession. I had the feeling I'd need them. When Henry walked back up the stairs only minutes later, I realised the situation must have deteriorated far more rapidly than I'd expected. My hunch was confirmed when I saw the look of utter dejection on his face and what looked like the red blush of a slap on his left cheek. When I asked what happened, he didn't respond and instead ordered more shots and started muttering to himself.

'Are you okay?' I asked him.

'Fuck. Shit. Fuck. Shit.'

'It didn't go well?'

'I told you I hate birthdays.'

'At least it's not yours,' I tried to joke.

'Fuck. Fuck. Fuck.'

'Did you talk to her?'

'I tried.'

'And?'

'She didn't want to talk to me.'

'Then what happened?'

'I waited for her to come out of the toilets.'

'You waited for her, after she'd blanked you?'

'Yeah.'

'Why?'

'To kiss her.'

'*What?* You can't just go around trying to kiss people you don't know, or even people you do know for that matter.'

'Why not?'

'You just can't. Or shouldn't.'

'Jesus did.'

'Jesus, what's Jesus got to do with it?'

'He kissed people all the time.'

'So? Anyway, I'm not even sure he did. I think that was only in books and movies.'

'The Bible says we should greet each other with a holy kiss.'

'I don't think they meant literally.'

'How do you know?'

'I don't know. Jesus, you don't think you're Jesus do you?'

'Of course not. That would just be daft.'

'Okay. Good. I've had enough of Jesus for one day. Forget about Jesus.'

'I'm only saying. I just wanted a kiss.'

Right then the girl appeared at the top of the stairs and hurried over to her table. A moment later two of her girlfriends turned in their seats and sat glaring at us. Then one of her male friends stood up and strode across the room to talk to the barman. I didn't like the way her friend kept pointing at the both of us, as if we were somehow in this together. I decided to approach them to try and straighten things out.

'Is there a problem?' I asked the barman.

'Yeah, get your mate out of here before I call the police.'

'You should call the police anyway,' the friend stated.

'He's not my mate, I only met him tonight,' I told them.

'Just get him out of here,' the barman reiterated.

'Why, what's he done?'

'He assaulted my friend, that's what.'

'Assaulted her?'

'Yeah.'

'How?'

'He tried to kiss her.'

'Assault with a kiss. Is that a crime?'

'If the person tells you to fuck off beforehand it is,' the friend said.

'Fair enough. Definitely. I agree. I honestly don't think he meant to upset her though.'

'Well, he did, so why don't both of you fuck off?'

'He claims it was a holy kiss.'

'A what?' the barman asked.

'A holy kiss,' I repeated.

'Are you all there?' the friend asked me.

'He's only a Tin Man.'

'What the fuck?' the barman exclaimed.

'If you don't call the police on these weirdos, I will,' the friend said to the barman.

'You both need to leave *now*,' the barman declared.

'Okay, okay, take it easy. I'll get him out,' I told them. 'He didn't actually kiss her, though, he only tried too,' I said, before walking away.

'So?' the friend asked.

'Well, that wouldn't be assault. That would be attempted assault.'

'Are you taking the piss?'

'I think that was your friend,' I said with a final flourish, believing I'd carried the day for the weirdos.

Victorious, I turned to walk away and fell flat on my face over a small stool I hadn't anticipated. Henry looked over at me lying on the floor and shook his head. He looked so disappointed and tired of his lot in life. Even his made-up friends were failures. Recognising that look on his face, I realised we really were in this together, and I pulled myself up off the floor and put my arm around him and got him out onto the street.

'I'm sorry I got you thrown out,' he said after vomiting all over the pavement.

'Forget it. It doesn't matter.'

'Thank you. Really. Thank you,' he repeated, then burst into tears.

'I told you, it doesn't matter. I wanted to leave anyway.'

'Not for that,' he sobbed.

'For what then?'

'For letting me join you. I didn't go to Glasgow Uni and I've never met you before.'

'I know.'

'You do?'

'Yeah, of course. Don't worry about it,' I reassured him.

'It's all my fault. Everything is my fault,' he heaved and sighed through his tears.

'Henry …'

'That's not my real name.'

'It's not?'

'No.'

'I did wonder.'

'My name's Staxx.'

'*What?*'

'I'm called Staxx.'

'Staxx. *That's your name?*'

'Yeah.'

'Are you making that up as well?'

'No.'

'*Fuck.* That's the greatest name ever.'

'It was the name of a disco in North Yorkshire where my mother met my father.'

'All the more reason to use it, instead of Henry.'

'She worked there. He was a soldier. She met him. I never did.'

'Hey, that's all right. Still a great name. You should definitely use it from now on.'

'You think so?'

'What, are you serious? It's a gift. A name like that could change the rest of your life.'

'I feel terrible about that girl.'

'That's a good sign.'

'What an awful thing to do.'

'It was.'

'I'm so sorry. What was I thinking?'

'You were thinking like Henry, *Henry*. From now on you think like Staxx. Okay Staxx?'

'I'll try.'

'Promise?'

'I promise.'

'Good. I'll be back in a minute.'

I left Staxx leaning against a lamp post, then went back into the bar and approached the girl and her friends.

'I just want you all to know there's a man in tears out there. A man called Staxx' I said to them. 'He said he's sorry,' I added, looking at the girl he'd followed to the toilet, 'and I believe him.'

For several seconds no one moved or said a word. They were waiting to see what I'd do next. When I didn't do anything, the guy who'd spoken to the barman said, 'So what? He shouldn't have perved on our friend.'

'He's leaning against a lamp post.'

'And?'

'It's going to rain.'

'What are you going on about?'

'It's going to rain hard.'

'Great.'

'I just wanted you to know.'

'Thanks for the weather report. Now fuck off.'

'I hoped you'd consider things for a moment.'

'What things?'

'Everything.' In the middle of one of the tables there was a little vase with pink carnations in it. I picked up the flowers, bit off their heads, and ate them.

'What the fuck *is* wrong with you?'

'There's nothing wrong with me,' I responded.

'No, then why did you eat those flowers? You're a fucking looney tune.'

'Total fruitycake,' a boy with an Italian accent added.

'It's fruitcake,' I corrected him, then continued. 'I ate the flowers because I wanted you all to know how it feels.'

'How what feels?' asked a girl with her hair dyed blue and wearing a Kurt Cobain T-shirt.

'To eat flowers and not to be afraid.'

'How would we know how it feels? You're the one who ate the flowers,' she retorted.

'Exactly,' I said, then turned and walked away.

When I got out onto the street, Staxx had gone. A strange flash lit up the sky an electric green, then a few heavy drops of rain exploded on the pavement around my feet. Seconds later a wave of thunder rolled across the city. I hailed a black cab and told the driver my address, then sat back and allowed myself to be pushed and pulled like a rag doll across the seat as the driver swung the taxi around and sped through the streets.

Back in my flat, I lay down on top of my bed and switched on my radio and searched for a song. As I fumbled with the tuner my mobile beeped and vibrated to indicate I'd received a text. It was a message from the girl I'd gone out with the night before and read — *HAPPY BIRTHDAY YOU SAD DRUNK!* Next to the message there was a row of laughing emojis with tears streaming from their eyes. Just then, the promised storm broke directly above the high-rise like an orchestra falling from the sky, and a moment later a song I'd never heard before, 'Lover's Spit', crashed out of my radio and washed right through me.

11

I'd been hiding in my flat for over a week, ever since I'd messed things up with a dealer. I'd done something foolish and no amount of grovelling or money — not an amount I could afford anyway — was going to make it okay. I knew this, because I'd tried both and had just received a phone call from an acquaintance telling me neither approach had worked.

The Afghan was always looking for a way into your life. For such a huge man he could slip in through the tiniest crack as swiftly and easily as the shadow of a bird. If that was the required approach. Otherwise, he'd simply kick your door down and walk right into your life. I'd seen what happened to people who'd pissed him off, or who had tried to stop doing what was asked of them, or that he'd simply tired of. As a result, I kept transactions with him as brief as possible, I never accepted free drugs, and I always avoided telling him anything personal about myself. But this last time, when I'd turned up unannounced — also something I never did — I'd done all three.

The evening before going to the Afghan's I'd washed down some Adderall capsules with a half-bottle of gin, then wandered around the high-rise, staring at a photocopy of a photograph that had fallen out of my copy of Rilke's *Duino Elegies*. I had no memory of putting it there and couldn't recall how I'd come by it in the first place, but there I was with my parents at a fairground on a sunny day. I must have been around five years old and was standing between my mother and father in front of a merry-go-round, the brightly coloured horses slightly blurred behind us as they flew by on the carousel. In the far right there was a whiteish vertical strip about two centimetres in length. A defect or some covering, like Sellotape, used to hide something in the photograph or perhaps erase a fourth figure from it before it was photocopied.

All through the night I drifted from floor to floor, shifting between the photograph and panoramic views of the city, until they overlapped and merged in a haunting procession of double negatives in my head. Just before dawn, I stood at the bedroom window of a flat on the ninth floor and watched the night fade slowly into the brightening sky, as great yellow swathes of street lights blinked off across the city like fields of scythed corn. I was expecting some sort of epiphany, but then the morning came in an unremarkable way. The sun rose like a glaucomic eye through layers of primordial mist, and I watched the light seep into the day in lonely shades of grey and amber through the cages of the massive gasometers ranged across an area of land in the distance.

Empty and exhausted, I walked down to the Trinity and wandered around the empty avenues and platforms like the lone inhabitant of some brutalist, post-apocalyptic world. When the Satellite opened, I went inside and ordered a beer. The only customer, I sat at the end of the bar feeling out of kilter, like a kid sitting alone on a seesaw. I dozed off nodding at the stranger in the mirror behind the gantry and when I woke up, I was still nodding at him. The black dogs were circling and the relief I felt at seeing my beer untouched on the bar, was overwhelming. I lifted it and drank it down, and the world balanced out like someone had sat down on the opposite end of the seesaw. Convinced there was only one place in the city that I could possibly go, I stood up and headed for the Afghan's in the thoroughly mistaken belief that I knew exactly what I was doing.

———

It was early afternoon when I turned up, unannounced, at his apartment. I should never have been there, the last thing I needed was more drugs. But there I was standing in the doorway of a huge open-plan lounge and kitchen-diner in a luxury apartment, waiting on one of his thugs to return with my pills. I'd been told to go in to the Afghan, but I couldn't see a fucking thing. My mind was still wandering through the previous night, and my eyes couldn't adjust to the harsh light flooding in through the floor-to-ceiling windows. I knew the Afghan was there — I could hear him breathe and feel his presence — but I had no idea if he was watching me. All I could see was a white ghost hovering in the centre of the room. When my eyes finally adjusted, I saw he was sitting on what looked like a throne, wearing a bright white perahan tunban. With his bronze skin and shaved head, he looked like Marlon Brando in *Apocalypse Now*, only younger, and he was staring straight at me.

'What are you reading?' he asked, indicating the book sticking out of my jacket pocket.

I'd picked it up on the way out my flat and had forgotten it was even there. 'It's a book of poems,' I answered.

'Whose poems?'

'Rilke.'

'I don't like him. I like Shelley. His poem "Ozymandias",' he smiled. 'I like this poem very much. I studied history at Kabul University. Did you study?' He asked, in a deep voice that wreathed you in opium and sex.

'Yes.'

'Good. Very good. You are here for Mandy?'

'Who?'

'Mandy, crystals, MDMA?'

'Sorry, yeah, I am.'

'My guy will be half an hour. Take a seat,' he said, indicating a small sofa. On a table on one side of his throne there was a revolver and an old sweetshop jar filled with pills. On a table on the other side, a box of wine. He pulled out a bottle of red, opened it, and called over his shoulder. A minute later, a door off the lounge opened and two girls, strung out on drugs and booze, drifted in dressed in their underwear. One of them looked in her late teens, the other in her mid-twenties. I caught a glimpse of several naked bodies entwined on a double bed in the room behind them, then someone kicked the door closed.

'Get some glasses,' he told the older girl. She returned with four wine glasses and sat on the floor with her friend between me and the Afghan.

'I'd introduce you all, but I don't actually know your name,' he said, looking at me, 'and I don't know theirs either, not today anyway.'

'Sorry?' I asked.

'They choose a new name every day, don't you girls?' he said, turning to them.

The younger girl stretched her hands above her head. 'Yeah, it makes us feel free,' she yawned.

'Pleased to meet you. I'm Loretta and she's Lynn,' the older one smiled.

'You should choose a name, too,' the Afghan said to me.

'I'm okay, thanks.'

'Maybe later. Everyone needs a name. If you don't have a name no one will ever know who you are.'

'The man with no name. Like Clint Eastwood. Only we could call you Cunt Eastwood. You could be our cuntboy,' Loretta laughed.

Lynn ran her index fingers around the elastic of her underpants and repositioned them. 'He doesn't look like much of a man to me,' she said.

'Girls, please, show our guest some respect and hospitality,' the Afghan said. He opened another bottle of wine, then passed Loretta a small wooden box filled with cocaine, which she passed directly to me.

'I'm sure I've seen you around, at the Sub Club or the art school? Aren't you a journalist?' Loretta asked.

'I was,' I said, then snorted a line.

'And what are you now?' she asked.

'Nothing,' I answered.

'You don't do anything?'

'I drink.'

'Is that an occupation?' Loretta continued.

'It's more like a vocation.'

'Yeah, a vocation from reality. I'll drink to that,' Lynn laughed and raised her glass.

'Vocation, not vacation,' Loretta rebuked her.

'What's the difference?' Lynn asked.

'Where did you go to school again?' Loretta responded, sarcastically.

'You know exactly which school I attended. The High School of Glasgow, thank you very much,' Lynn snapped, before draining her glass of wine.

'Well, your parents pissed that money right up the wall, didn't they?' Loretta laughed.

'Girls, girls, please. Everyone's welcome here,' the Afghan declared.

'Even ex-journalists?' Loretta asked.

'Ex-journalists, cowboys, rich girls, poor girls, everyone,' the Afghan continued. I passed the coke back to Loretta and she did a line, then handed it to Lynn. After she'd had a line, too, they started kissing each other and I wasn't sure where to look or what to do.

'They get on well,' I said, as the girls slipped their tongues into each other's mouths.

'Very well,' the Afghan answered.

After the box had been passed around a few more times, the girls removed their bras and started touching each other's breasts.

'You don't need to do that on my account,' I said, but they ignored me and continued anyway.

'They're not doing it on your account. Does it make you feel uncomfortable?' the Afghan asked, as he brought a bag of coke out from under his robe and refilled the box.

'Not if they're happy to do it.'

'Do you think they're happy to do it?'

'I wouldn't know.'

The girls had stopped what they were doing and were listening to our conversation now.

'I'm happy,' Lynn said.

'Me too,' Loretta said, then started kissing Lynn's breasts.

'And you, are you happy?' the Afghan asked me.

'I'm trying to be,' I answered.

'You look miserable. You should try fucking harder,' Loretta smiled.

Just then, a tall skinny guy came out of a room off the lounge and walked over to the kitchen and filled a glass with water at the sink. His eyes were wild and he walked with his body facing in one direction and his head held up facing the other direction, like someone was leading him while holding the tip of a knife to his throat. When he walked back to the room he'd come out of he'd taken on a theatrical limp that I hadn't noticed previously. Nothing here was quite as it first seemed, as if the sheer volume of drugs that had been consumed within the apartment had melted everything and everyone over the edge of reality. It was still early in the day, but the light had been blocked from the sky by a huge black cloud that was sitting in front of the sun like the moon during an eclipse. The darkness felt like it was pressed tight against the floor-to-ceiling windows and was trying to come in on top of us. I looked at Loretta and Lynn and imagined them months before. Not as innocents or perfect, but as attractive, ordinary girls, going out on a Saturday night. Now, lost in doomed love affairs, their veins filled with black tar, they moved around the room like animated Francis Bacon portraits. The Afghan always had two girls with him when he was out, but it was never the same two for long. They probably had no more than a month before the Afghan fucked the life out of them and tossed their butchered reflections to his henchmen. I was lost in some reverie that involved me saving them, when a gust of wind battered the windows, then died away. I finished my wine, then without asking, reached for the bottle on the table beside the Afghan and refilled my glass.

'I'm sure Loretta and Lynn would make you happy, wouldn't you, girls?' the Afghan said, while watching me closely.

'Definitely,' they replied in unison.

'I'd certainly like to see them try,' he smiled.

In the room the girls had come out of earlier I could hear a bed creaking, and loud moaning and sighing. In another room an orgy of violence — I couldn't tell whether real or staged — was unfolding on a television or computer screen. It felt like the day was shaping up to come to some sort of bloody conclusion, and that I was running out of options to do anything other than surrender to the coming carnage. I had to get out of there before I ended up handcuffed to a bed, screaming for Tonto while being pistol-whipped by Loretta-fucking-Lynn for the Afghan's pleasure. But I'd come for MDMA and I wasn't about to let them ruin what was left of my afternoon with their crazy fucking shit for nothing. Fortified by the wine and animated by the cocaine, I was determined to get out of there and to leave with something to compensate for the time and dignity I'd lost. I'd sunk pretty low, but not as low as these people, I assured myself. Not yet, anyway.

'Can I use the bathroom?' I asked the Afghan.

'Of course,' he replied.

As I stood up I emptied all the cocaine into my pocket, then placed the box down on the sofa. I had the feeling the Afghan saw exactly what I'd done and was just letting things play out for the fun of it. I didn't care. I was going to get to the front door and make a break for freedom.

'Loretta will show you where the bathroom is,' the Afghan said when I stood up.

'That's okay,' I said.

'No, *really*, I insist,' he said.

At the door to the toilet, I told Loretta to wait outside.

'Don't worry, I've seen a man piss before.'

'I'm sure you have.'

'I could drink it if you want?'

'It's not a piss that I need.'

'I don't mind that either.'

'*I do*,' I told her.

'Suit yourself. I'll be waiting right here for you, though.'

I couldn't get near the front door, and going back into the lounge wasn't an option, so I opened the window, and sitting down, turned and swung my legs out over the ledge. It was only three floors up and didn't look so bad. Besides, I was invincible now. As I reached out and held on to the drainpipe I could hear Lynn knocking on the door, asking what the fuck I was up to. It was difficult to get a good grip of the drainpipe, but I managed to shimmy down to just below the first floor, before it came loose and snapped, and I jumped on top of the bin shed. Someone had joined Lynn at the window and was yelling death threats at me. Without turning around, I ran hooting and hollering along the back alley and out into the street. I was on such a high that I forgot all about the coke in my pocket and didn't think about the rain when it came on. By the time I got home and remembered, it had all dissolved. My first thought was to suck the lining of my jacket. But that seemed like a seriously stupid fucking idea. Instead, I squeezed the lining out and managed to wring about two centimetres of inky blue liquid into a glass. I did consider not drinking it, but only for a moment.

The next day, when I realised just how much shit I was in, I was so scared I couldn't stop throwing up. I'd no idea what to do in a situation like this, so I did the only thing I knew how — I got drunk and came up with a plan, an actual plan this time. At 6 a.m. the following morning, I pressed the service button and snuck into the Afghan's apartment block and posted an envelope through the letterbox of his flat. Inside the envelope I put one hundred pounds and a letter in which, while continually pleading for mercy, I described in rambling detail how much of a fuck-up I was, and how magnificent and all-powerful he was. Convinced the door was suddenly going to swing open and the Afghan was going to be standing there, naked, holding a huge ceremonial sword, my legs almost gave way as I dropped the envelope through the letter box and started running back along the hallway towards the lift. Afterwards, I stopped at a mini-market and stocked up on bread and jam and peanut butter, before heading home, locking the door, and sitting with all the lights and the television and radio switched off for the rest of the day and night.

I'd been sitting in silence, praying for forgiveness ever since. But when my mobile rang and I saw Richie's name on the screen, I knew I was fucked. I'd met Richie through a girl I was dating. He was her best friend, was in love with her, and as a result despised me from the day I met him. I was never entirely sure why we'd bothered staying friends after I split up with her. I think I believed I owed him after she completely cut ties with both of us when I broke up with her. While on his part he was happy to remain friends, because he took great delight in watching me screw up my life and even greater joy in constantly telling me I was doing so. I could hear the satisfaction in his voice when he phoned me that afternoon and told me that, according to a girl he'd met in a bar the night before, the Afghan regarded the one hundred pounds as an insult, and my letter the ramblings of an idiot and coward.

'He has a car full of thugs permanently cruising the streets looking for you,' Richie said.

'I'm going stir-crazy as it is — I can't hide in here much longer.'

'I don't think that matters so much now,' Richie said, in a consoling tone.

'What doesn't matter?'

'Hiding.'

'Why?'

'I think they might know your address.'

'How did they get my address?'

'How should I know? Maybe they asked the postman.'

'Asked the postman? Are you the fucking postman, Richie?'

There was a brief silence, and then he said, 'Not exactly. The girl already

had an idea where you lived anyway. I think you might have fucked her once.
She didn't seem to like you very much.'

'And you just filled in the details.'

'Sort of. More or less.'

'*I knew it.*'

'Listen, what's done is done. Really, you've no one to blame but yourself.
I mean, you did steal his drugs. What matters now is the only way you're going
to pay for your utter-fucking-out-of-this-world-mind-blowing-stupidity is
with blood. Unless you have enough money?'

'How much do you think it would take to pay him off?'

'Not for him. For you, *to run*. You could head south. Start again. Your
life's a pile of shite anyway.'

'Your support's as fucking heart-warming as ever,' I told him.

'It's honest. You know the Afghan. It's all about respect and reputation.
He's got to fuck you up, even if he doesn't want to. But he definitely does want
to. I heard he once made another dealer kill his own dog, then cook it and eat it.
That guy hadn't even done anything. Of all the drug dealers to rip off, you really
are a class A idiot.'

I didn't want to give Richie the satisfaction of being the person who
dispatched me to a rooming house in some seaside town in England, but he was
right. The Afghan would never let this go. Anyway, I was almost out of peanut
butter and jam.

'I've still got some savings I could use.'

'Good. Get the fuck out of here. Don't come back for a long fucking time.
In fact, you've fucked up so much this time, don't *ever* come back.'

I was on my way to withdraw money from my bank and still only two streets
away from the high-rise, when I turned a corner and saw an old, beat-up, silver
Vauxhall Astra coming along the road. I didn't think anything of it at first,
but when it slowed and cruised past me, then stopped and idled in the road a

hundred yards or so behind me, I knew it was them. They reversed at speed and in an instant were up beside me. My only escape route was over a tall wooden fence bordering a back garden. I ran towards it, but as I tried to get over it, my legs turned to jelly and I flapped to the ground. When I looked up, the Afghan's thugs were standing over me.

There were three of them, a Glaswegian and two Pakistanis. The Glaswegian was clearly in charge. He sat in the front passenger seat, while one of the Pakistanis drove and the other one sat in the back with me.

'Right, Ahmed, let's go,' the Glaswegian told the driver.

'No names, remember?' the driver said.

'Names don't matter, not this time.'

'You fucked up, big shit,' the guy next to me smiled, revealing a mouthful of rotten teeth.

The Glaswegian turned around, leaned over his seat, and slapped me across the face with the back of his hand. 'I'm Mohammed. He's right, by the way, you're one fucked-up piece of shit.'

'I'm sorry, I'm really sorry. What I did was really fucking stupid,' I said, shaking uncontrollably.

'Yeah, it was. But don't worry about that just now. First we're going to go for a spin around the city and you're going to have a wee drink.'

'Can we talk about this?'

'We can talk about it as much as you want, but it's not going to make a blind bit of difference. I bet your balls don't feel so big now,' he said to me, then turning to the other guy, 'Do they, Akbar?'

Akbar was the guy sitting next to me. He'd drifted away from proceedings and was gazing out the window, smiling absent-mindedly at the alien world outside. '*Akbar!* For fuck's sake, pay attention,' Mohammed snapped.

'Yes?' he asked.

'His balls, are his balls big now?'

'Don't know.'

'Well *feel* them, for fuck's sake.'

'His testicles?'

'Aye, *his fucking baws.*'

Akbar cupped his hands around my groin and squeezed. I had to summon every ounce of will I had not to start crying or piss myself. Even so, a few tears welled in my eyes and a dribble of piss blossomed on my trousers at my crotch.

'No, Mo, fucking tiny,' he confirmed, then started crying with laughter.

'Here, dickhead, drink this,' Mo said, and passed me a bottle of Buckfast with the cap already unscrewed. 'Come on. You're the Afghan's guest, remember? Might as well drink up,' he said, after I'd taken a quick sip. 'You're going to drink every fucking drop of that shite one way or another anyway.'

I took a longer drink and immediately felt as if my brain had been removed from my head and tossed out the window. Which was a positive development really, because I forgot all about crying and pissing myself. A second later, Mo turned on the radio. The Kylie Minogue song, 'Can't Get You Out of My Head', was playing, and Mo started tapping the dashboard to the beat and moving his head from side to side with the music. Next to me Akbar was laughing so much he was having difficulty breathing.

'For fuck's sake, Akbar, it wasn't that funny. I love this song and you're fucking ruining it,' Mo chided him, before turning up the volume on the radio. When the chorus kicked in Mo started pumping his hands in the air and dancing in his seat. A minute later we swung onto the motorway and headed towards the city with visions of Kylie naked and wild conquering my mind.

I don't know how long we drove around for, but it seemed like a long time, like the sun had gone down and come back up again. I'd drunk more than half the Buckfast by now and had forgotten all about why I was in the car, when for reasons unknown to everyone besides Ahmed, we slowed to a halt at the top of a steep hill in the west of the city and didn't go any further.

'What the fuck?' Mo yelled, grooving in his seat to 'No Diggity'. He turned the music down and all three of us looked at Ahmed, waiting for a response.

'No gas,' Ahmed said, nodding towards the dashboard.

'No, no diggity,' Mo joked, singing along.

'No, no gas,' Ahmed repeated, nodding towards the dashboard, emphatically.

'What?' Mo asked.

'No gas in the tank,' Ahmed explained.

'We call it petrol here, not gas. This isn't fucking America. What the fuck do you mean we've no petrol?'

'None. No more.'

'Get to a petrol station, then.'

'Can't.'

'Why?'

'No gas,' Ahmed shrugged.

'I don't think it promising idea, taking this shit to a station for gas,' Akbar joined in, indicating me with both of his thumbs.

'Sorry to interrupt, but would you mind turning that song back up, Mo?' I asked, lost in my own silent disco.

Without thinking, Mo turned the volume back up, and then started yelling, '*What the fuck? What the fuck? What the fuck?*', over and over, seemingly unable to process what was happening. 'And it's petrol, fucking petrol, not gas,' he said, turning back to Akbar. 'Fucking hell. I don't believe this. Fucking morons. I told you to always keep the tank full.'

'*Enough already! Do not call my cousin a moron! You're a fucking moron!*' Ahmed yelled back.

'*Enough already?* Stop all this American shite. And I'm not calling just him a moron, I'm calling you both fucking morons. There's a petrol station near the bottom of this hill, just get us there. I'll knock this fuck-wit out before then.'

Ahmed turned the ignition, but nothing happened.

'Try it again. There must be something left,' Mo told him.

'I told you, no gas. *Fucking moron.*'

I was so out of my mind on the cocktail of drugs they'd laced the Buckfast with that I didn't care about anything that was going on around me, least of all that I may have been living through my last few hours on earth. In fact, as far as I was concerned these guys were my friends now and they were in trouble.

'Guys, guys, come on. Let's not fight among ourselves. We're all in this together,' I counselled, shouting above the music. 'Maybe we could syphon petrol out of one of these parked cars, or we could call a taxi, or we could—'

'*Shut the fuck up!*' Mo screamed at me. 'Freewheel it — freewheel it down the hill. Do you know what that is?' he asked Ahmed.

'Yes, float it.'

We were causing a tailback, and the guy in the car directly behind us had started beeping his horn.

'That's right. Float the fucking thing down,' Mo encouraged Ahmed, while trying to stay calm. 'Get out and push us over the top of the hill. We'll meet you at the bottom,' Mo said over his shoulder.

'No problem,' I said and moved to open the door.

'*Not fucking him!*' Mo yelled, grabbing me by the hair and pushing me down into the seat. '*You, Akbar. You get out and push the fucking car.*'

I sat back up and turned around and tried to indicate through the rear window to the driver in the car behind us that I needed help. But I couldn't stop grinning, and he just glared at me, then started making the unofficial hand gesture for a crazy person, jabbing his forefinger into his temple and twirling it round. I continued to smile benignly, as Cher singing 'Believe' blared from the radio, and the guy in the car behind switched to the official hand gesture for wanker.

Akbar got out and pushed the car over the crest of the hill, and Mo started yelling at Ahmed, 'Freewheel it, *freewheel it.*'

'What?' Ahmed asked.

'Float it, *fucking float it.*'

'*Okay, okay,*' Ahmed responded.

We were rolling now, and I glanced back and saw Akbar running down the hill after us. He was running faster and faster and rapidly losing control. It was clear that his legs were increasingly unable to keep up with his body and when I looked away for a moment, then looked back, it was just in time to see him hit a lamp post. At the same moment the music stopped mid-song and I realised Ahmed must have turned the ignition off. Even completely out of my head I knew this was a bad idea. I'd been in a similar situation before. A near-fatal situation, when the driver of a vehicle I was in, decided in their stoned wisdom, to switch the ignition off as we drifted down a hill towards a bus stop that we subsequently ploughed right into.

'I wouldn't do, do, do, do,' I stammered, managing to slide my seat belt into place.

'What the fuck are you stuttering about?' Mo barked.

'Turn the ignition ... off ... steering ...' I managed to get out, before my speech slurred off towards incoherence.

Passing in and out of consciousness as we drifted towards oblivion, the crash unfolded not in a series of frantic rapid flashes, as I would have expected, but as if I were watching an event unfold in slow motion. Mo was leaning across the gearstick, trying to grab the steering wheel, while Ahmed screamed, '*No steer! No brake! No steer! No brake!*' Bemused faces of onlookers turned and gazed into the car from the pavement as we floated past. A couple did a double take and laughed a little manically, as if unsure of what they were laughing at. A woman in a red headscarf cupped a hand to her mouth in shock. A child smiled and waved at us as if we were riding a magical, wild horse. The car strayed towards the centre of the road and the evening sun poured in through the windows, filling the interior with a warm, honey-yellow glow. I was somewhere else now, floating in the golden light of childhood, of tranquillity, of liberation.

Our descent may have unfolded in slow motion, but impact with a tenement wall brought the crash up to speed in a flash. Glass rained through the vehicle, and the interior filled with smoke and the smell of burning rubber. Unfastening my seat belt, I crawled along the back seat and fell out of the car onto the pavement. I tried to stand, but found that for the second time that day, I had lost the use of my legs. Too terrified to look down, I was screaming, 'I can't feel my legs! I can't feel my legs!' as I dragged my body twenty feet or so along the street. Then some guy was walking beside me and stooping down to talk to me as I crawled along.

'Call an ambulance,' I pleaded with him. 'Please call an ambulance. My legs, *my legs*.'

'Pal, you're all right. There's not a mark on you. It's probably just the shock,' he said.

I looked down and discovered he was correct.

'Can you help me up?' I asked.

'Of course.'

He pulled me to my feet and I leant against a wall.

'I need to go,' I told him.

'You should probably still wait for an ambulance, mate, just so they can check you over,' he cautioned.

'No, you're right, I'm fine,' I said, and staggered off.

'What about your friends?' he asked.

'They're just out of gas,' I called back, as I headed around the next corner.

When I came back to the world I was utterly stupefied and had no idea how I'd ended up where I was — sitting with my legs dangling over the edge of the railing on a bridge spanning the M8 at Charing Cross.

I was rocking back and forth in a psychotic state, while one hundred feet below, two long lines of traffic hissed like mechanical snakes crawling through the heart of the city. Everything was super-real — the outlines of buildings, vehicles, the birds in the sky, their shadows slipping across the earth. Certain objects that were far away appeared shockingly close, as if I were looking through the lens of a telescope. Colours had a terrible vividness, were so intensely *real*, I worried my eyes might start bleeding. Cars, like beasts slick and wet with sex, rose shimmering out of a heatwave spilling across the motorway in the distance. I was standing at the gates of Bethlehem looking at a planet destroying itself. Its end heralded by a colossal red sun sinking slowly into a pool of blood spilling over the rim of the world — while four blazing clouds rode across the sky like the Four Horsemen of the Apocalypse.

I'd no idea how long I'd been there, but evidently no one had stopped to ask if I was okay or to talk me down. When I tumbled back off the railing onto the pavement and a man allowed his dog to its full business right beside me, then calmly walked on, I wondered for a moment if I'd died, and no one had noticed.

I walked down under the massive concrete hex of the M8 junction at Charing Cross to where the city centre breaks down into a patchwork of vacant lots and derelict buildings. At the top corner of one such lot I ducked beneath a mangled section of chain-link fence, then headed to the corner diagonally opposite where the fence ran parallel to Clyde Street. The concrete footprints of the buildings that had once stood here were still visible beneath the grasses and ragged bouquets of ragwort sprouting between the cracks in the foundations. The land here was dusty and broken and strewn with bricks and twisted masonry. Dotted across it were several small, burnt-out buildings. The entire site felt preternaturally opened to the sky and charged with an occult energy, like an abandoned airfield or ancient staging post. The sky above Glasgow was a rippling molten sea, while the surface of the lot vibrated as if it were about to separate from the earth and fly off, or else in some elemental synergy with the alien sky, burst into flames. I was in the heart of Glasgow, yet I felt like I was light years from earth.

In the corner next to the fence there was a single mattress, some soiled clothes, odd shoes, several used condoms, and at least a dozen empty two-litre bottles of Frosty Jack's cider. The cider had been sucked from the plastic bottles until they'd collapsed in on themselves like the buildings that had once stood here, and the lives of those who'd drunk them. I considered lying down on the mattress and ending the day in this scratched and sacred corner of wasteland. Then the clouds moved off across the sky towards the coast like a burning armada making for the open sea and the light shifted and I left the lot and crossed the road, then the George V Bridge over to the south of the Clyde.

I turned onto a street with no traffic and followed the white lines in the middle of the road towards a stretch of railway arches over which early evening trains, going in and out of the city, beat an effortless refrain of *hope and regret, hope and regret,* on the tracks. I watched partially erased faces float by like ghostyheads in the fallow light of the carriages. People dreaming in the crimson evening, completely oblivious to the world going on in the units and lock-ups below. Shady business transactions, random beatings, real games of poker on packing boxes, and virtual games of *Mortal Kombat* on Xboxes. Groups of men, dripping with gold and filling the air with smoke and heavy wafts of expensive cologne, standing at the entrances to the businesses housed in the arches. Scots, Africans, Eastern Europeans. Individuals from the three groups, calling back and forth to each other, exchanging banter, sizing each other up. All of them pretending to ignore me, but watching my every move.

I passed a row of flat-roofed, one-storey buildings. At one end there was a Celtic bar, flying the Irish tricolour, its flaked and peeling façade painted green, white, and gold. At the opposite end, a Rangers bar painted royal blue, with a torn and tattered Union Jack hanging on a flagpole above its entrance. Separating them was a halal butchers, a fancy-dress shop — its windows covered in grime and dust — a locksmith, a pawn shop, and an Army & Navy surplus outlet. On the other side of the street there was a huge warehouse. Its advertisement, painted in large, white letters directly across its red-brick front, stated: *PURVEYORS OF FANCY FOOD! WE HAVE IT ALL! FROM HOTDOGS TO HAMBURGERS!* The whole area felt lawless. A stretch of no-man's-land, an old love song sung by a crooner whose throat was being slowly strangled. Already plastered with FOR SALE signs, in a few years it would be bulldozed, rebuilt, rebranded, and surgically *un*-imagined in stainless steel.

I walked along Nelson Street, beneath the Central Station railway bridge, then crossed back over the river and started walking up through an area where lucrative land deals had already been made. Where the architecture of the new waterfront rose like the outer walls of a fortress city. Towering, cold, blank blocks of steel and mirrored glass. Row after row of telescopic bollards, huge concrete plant pots, sleek marble and maple seating areas. The first lines of defence against terrorists driving transit vans packed with fertiliser and ball bearings. Not religious terrorists. Economic terrorists, eco-terrorists, spiritual terrorists. Those disaffected and abandoned by future resets. Barbarians, bampots, and *bodhisattvas* going mad on benzos, Buckfast, and Bakunin. Banded together, waiting for the sign. Riding shotgun with the fucking Valkyries. Militarised architecture, developed and tested in Baghdad, Basra, Mosul, but always intended for the home front. Latter-day Czech hedgehogs and Dragon's teeth, rendered aesthetically pleasing for the cities of the West. The potential for war so seamlessly embedded in our everyday lives, we don't even notice it. Weaponised motorways and rooftops. Dark architecture commissioned by Academi Blackwater. Multinationals with private military wings as city planners, guardians of commerce, custodians of the free world.

The temperature plummeted in the shadow of these buildings. I saw no pedestrians, no litter, nothing. Only the contradictory sensation of space and claustrophobia. Immediately beyond this zone there was an area of red neon. A bleeding. A manufactured haemorrhage, tempting people to dance and fuck and drink each other's blood. Carnage as necessity. Sanctioned. Encouraged.

I passed a bar and caught a glimpse inside as the doors swung open. In the dimly lit interior, to a nightmarish electronic thump going at more than 800 bpm, a voice that sounded like Dolly Parton jacked-up on helium and shot full of amphetamines sang about getting fucked up the ass all night long. Out of sync with the music, a crowd of girls and boys — devoid of emotion, absent — moved like mannequins on a malfunctioning conveyor belt. Their eyes blank and flat, their mouths fixed like facial prosthetics designed for oral sex.

The pavements here were lubricated with blood and booze, the overspill of condoms, the grease of fast-food joints. Cankerous, humping shadows lurked down alleyways. The stench of dumb animals, reared and slaughtered simply to satiate the pleasure of dumber animals, drifted from the air vents of restaurants.

Each step I took traced the air, leaving a luminous photocopy of my body in its wake. I was shedding chakras. Washing myself in the blood of the Lamb. I'd gone out of the world fucked up in the back seat of a silver Vauxhall, with Cher singing 'Believe' pumping through my veins and re-entered on the evening of Revelation.

Too fucked and terrified to go home, I wandered back down through the town to the river and headed west. Not far from the Transport Museum, I squeezed through a narrow gap in a long stretch of hoardings advertising a new retail and residential development, and a derelict building, and walked down through a huge area of wasteland. A murmuration of starlings swung through the air above the Clyde like a black fist, while great swathes of red and indigo tinged with yellow blushed across the bruised sky. High above it all, in a vault of midnight blue, a crescent moon with its ancient razor-edged blade sharpened and burnished by the light of dying stars and burning solar winds, hung above the world like a giant swinging pendulum, ready to lacerate the poisoned world down the middle of her swollen womb.

I walked on and stopped near the water at a clearing, where an old oil-drum brazier stood rusting and flaking away at the edges into dust on the cool evening breeze. Across the river a wire fence encircled an abandoned dry dock. Around its perimeter I could see the flukes and crowns of several huge anchors jutting out above the tall grasses and weeds like the broken, scavenged ribcage of a great whale. A forbidden place that, a sacred place. I'd been here before and knew that if you listened hard enough, especially at night, you could still hear the men down there in those concrete basins. Their shouts and hammering a resounding requiem that never quiets.

I gazed further along to where the few red-brick buildings still standing around the Graving Docks glowed with a quiet sadness in the dying light. The evening air was cold and filled with hopelessness. I turned my collar up and rubbed my hands together, then warmed them at the brazier by a crackling, spitting fire that wasn't there. And then a whispering, and then voices, and I wasn't sure if I was being sung to or singing ...

... This is where I carve my heart. In these endless folds of rosy dusk. In memories of sheet-metal harder than meteorites. More brilliant than stars. This is where I inscribe what remains of my love. Upon this river. In that holy broken place, I swim forever ...

I never saw the Afghan again. No one did. I assumed he'd gone into hiding after the police arrested Mo and Ahmed at the scene of the crash. Then word got around that he'd returned home to attend to his father, who was terminally ill. His father was a warlord in Kandahar. Richie called me one evening to tell me that he never wanted me to leave town, not really. He said he'd miss me if I was gone and that I might as well stick around. Especially given there was no way the Afghan would be coming back, not since he'd been killed by a US drone strike while attending his father's funeral. But then, you couldn't believe a thing Richie said, not about friendship, the Afghan, or anything else.

Not too long after he told me all this, Richie himself was almost killed by a woman he'd met on the internet. She'd flown over from America to meet him, and on their second night together, while he was cooking her dinner and they were drinking, they got into an argument about French New Wave cinema, and she stabbed him in the ass. The knife hit a nerve and he was temporarily paralysed from the waist down. He got the use of his legs back, but now and for the rest of his life he'd have to shit using a stoma bag. I never managed to save the two girls who were at the Afghan's flat. I don't know what happened to them. I like to think they made it back to their everyday lives and put all that behind them, but I very much doubt they did.

The only person I saw again was Akbar. It was months later and he was working in a continental fruit and veg shop I wandered into one day to buy a mango. He recognised me straight away and greeted me with a huge smile, a new set of teeth, and open arms. I put my arms out and smiled too. Then the strangest thing, we hugged and cried in each other's arms, like long lost brothers who'd made it through a war.

And what was it all for? A photocopied image that broke my heart for the child I once was. A breaking so sweet and so terrible, I wanted my heart to keep breaking over and over. To remember every ray of sunshine, every breath of wind, every smell and sensation from the day the photograph was taken. To feel each element, with its own aching quality and infinite architecture, all over again. To remember it all at once in one overwhelming memory that would carry me over from the regrets and disappointments of this life into the blissful arms of the one I never got the chance to live.

That's what it was for. That's what *all of it* was always for. An impossibility. And how do you explain something like that? The way in which moments that occurred long ago move through space and time like obscure radio signals. You can't explain it. More than twenty years down the line, after having bounced off countless other moments, a message I didn't even know was on its way, finally reached me.

What does that tell you about life? What does that tell you about time?

12

It was early November when I finally went to visit my father. By now he'd been hospitalised, and after an initial assessment, followed by the introduction of a palliative care regime, they'd done what they could and had transferred him to a hospice. When I'd phoned to ask about visiting, his doctor had warned me that my father's condition had deteriorated so quickly and severely that I might find the experience challenging. Especially as such a long time had passed since I'd last seen him. *Deconditioning syndrome*, he called it. I hadn't heard of this before and wondered how this syndrome would affect me. Then he explained that's not what I would feel, that's what my father was suffering from. A physical, psychological, and functional decline that occurs through decreased physical and mental activity. In my father's case, a combination of ageing, prescribed bed rest, and historical neglect.

According to the doctor, prolonged hospitalisation and spaceflight were its abettors. The scourge of geriatrics and astronauts, he explained cheerily, drawing what I felt was a touching parallel. I appreciated his attempt to relate difficult news with a healthy dose of good humour and bonhomie, but all the same felt anxious after his pep talk, and had prepared myself to experience a vertiginous drop when I saw my father again.

As it turned out, the shock wasn't as great as I'd anticipated. In fact, I wasn't particularly shocked at all. Not because he hadn't changed much, but the opposite. He'd changed so immeasurably I found it difficult to connect the man lying in front of me — what little remained of him — with the man who'd left me at my mother's house that afternoon all those years before.

We hold on to all sorts of foolish delusions in life. I once knew a man who believed he had a special connection with William Blake. He believed a bond existed between his own life in the here and now and that of Blake's in the afterlife. I've since met many men who believe they have a special relationship with William Blake. It's always men who have these quasi-literary-spiritual delusions, and more often than not it involves William Blake. Anyway, this guy was a big-bearded barber not a writer, but he kept a ream of blank paper on his bedside cabinet, utterly convinced that one morning he'd wake to find the completed manuscript of a new work written by Blake's ghost and bequeathed to him. A prophesy to pass on to the world as his own.

Then there was a friend of a friend, whose sister fell pregnant when she was seventeen. The biological father was a drunken one-night stand that she never saw again. Finding herself short of a partner, she raised her child as the daughter of her childhood heart-throb, Justin Timberlake. When she moved into her own place, she printed pictures of JT that she framed and placed around the house. She spoke about him to her daughter as if her *dad* were away on a long tour, promising her that one day he'd return. At six years old the little girl was still yelling 'Daddy! Daddy!' whenever she saw Justin Timberlake on TV. The saddest element of that delusion wasn't the central one — that this was pure fantasy. It was the mother's unwavering conviction that one day she'd meet JT, that they'd marry, and that everything she believed would come true.

For a while I myself believed I was destined to find a lost, winning lottery ticket. For almost a year I went around picking up discarded tickets from the street, certain each time I did that *this one* held the numbers of the jackpot. A clinical psychologist would probably say that those mentioned above, myself included, had developed some form of psychosis. But then none of these delusions seem particularly outlandish when you consider the wishful thinking that millions of so-called sane people believe it perfectly reasonable to indulge in. There are people who believe revolutions will make the world a better place. All sorts of people are convinced — against all evidence to the contrary — that all sorts of utopias will come to pass. Others believe God created heaven and earth in six days and rested on the seventh. Many of them even believe that the best among them will go to heaven when they die and the worst to hell. Some people believe in the power of money. Others hold fast to the healing power of crystals and urine therapy. There's a multitude of sad and troubling delusions out there. But among the saddest and most fatal belief of all, is the belief that those we love or hate will be there when we finally decide the time is right for us to face them and tell them exactly how we feel.

My father was awake and staring at the ceiling when I approached his bedside. When I went closer and stood over him, he looked right through me like I wasn't there. It was such a distant look it was impossible to tell if he was oblivious to his situation and had no idea what was going on, or if he knew exactly what was happening and was already gazing into the abyss. The only parts of him visible were his head and his hands, each so frail and vulnerable. He looked as if he'd inhaled and held his breath until his gossamer skin had been sucked in around his straw skull. Another deep breath and I worried his head might crumble like a crisp autumn leaf. Before the singing, he'd been a steel fixer, tying it by hand with pliers and steel-fixing nippers. Now his hands lay across the white fold of the bedsheet like exoskeletons shed by spiders, his bloated blue veins standing out on the back of them like petrified rivers. I remembered being held aloft by those hands and being thrown into the air above his head with his muscled arms. A small boy tottering on the brink of happiness, dizzy with laughter and the fear of not being caught. Now his hands didn't have the strength to peal even the ripest fig and his arms were only good for drowning.

I'm not sure what I'd expected to happen the moment I saw him again, but I'd expected something. Not necessarily some great revelation or reckoning, but at least some sort of meaningful acknowledgement. For my part, despite the years blurring and even erasing some of the resentment I felt towards him, I'd nevertheless kept my shoulder pressed against the door to the past, waiting for an opportunity to push back in there and run amok — or so I'd thought. When I finally saw him lying there, tucked into those crisp white sheets like an old letter slipped into an unaddressed envelope, the anger didn't vanish, but it was profoundly altered. Like a word being translated consecutively through many languages and losing a little more of its original meaning each time, my anger had undergone so many mutations, that in its final translation, through the language of the heart, it had fallen into some lexical gap. It was still there, but devoid of form. I couldn't take hold of it. But then the dying have that ability, don't they? To disarm us with their un-blooming. Even those who have hurt us. Indeed, perhaps those who have hurt us the most, most of all.

It was a clay-cold November day, and an anaemic band of yellow strung between the range of hills in the distance and the underside of a dark ridge of sodden cloud had been gradually erased by a great boreal drift slanting across the land. There must have been snow in the offing, because the sky was dotted with patches of that curious ultraviolet light, and through the partially open window you could feel the haunting chill of it in the fragile air.

My father's bed was next to a window in the far corner of a ward on the sixth floor. I'd been watching him for some time, when his body began to tremble ever so slightly. The tremble turned into an ongoing tremor and a moment later the alarm on one of the monitors started sounding. A nurse approached the bed and began adjusting the tubes fastened to his mouth and nose and the backs of his hands. After this, she checked and pushed some buttons on a monitor, where a lonely blip travelled along a green line of light. It rose every few seconds with an elusive beep, beep, beep, then moved on and receded like the ebb and flow of an electronic wave that was carrying him further and further away.

'He's fine now. Probably a bad dream,' the nurse smiled. She smoothed out his bedding and tucked it tighter beneath the mattress, then pulled the curtain round the bed and left us alone.

Standing there, watching him, it struck me how people are often impossible to find, even when they're right in front of you. We're only vessels for our blood and wills, and now that my father didn't have much of either, what remained? He'd left most of what he was somewhere in his past, what chance did I have of ever knowing him? I wondered why he'd bothered to stick around as long as he had and not gone already. Other than the waning influence of the moon, there was nothing keeping him here and only one direction he was going. His body a fragile boat borne by the tide to the place where the river meets the sea.

His hands twitched and his eyes darkened into life as a whisper issued from his mouth like a burst of white noise from a radio.

'I'm thirsty,' he repeated more loudly the second time.

I poured water from a jug on the table by his bed into a white plastic cup and lifted it to his mouth. 'It's water. Drink a little water,' I told him. I tipped the cup gently towards his lips, but he shut them tight and the water ran down his chin on to his neck.

'Why did you wake me?' he asked

'I'm sorry, I didn't mean to,' I said.

'I was dreaming.'

'What were you dreaming about?'

'Where's the boy I usually talk to?' he asked, ignoring my question.

'What boy?'

'The boy who talks to me.'

'Dad, it's me. I'm talking to you,' I said.

'Who are you?'

'Your son.'

His head began to shudder like a cog jammed in a damaged mechanism, as if one part of him was trying to turn and look at me and another part of him was preventing it from doing so. Confronted by my presence and unable to escape, his eyes began to tremble violently in their sockets. Then his body started shuddering and then the tears started flowing. I could see him trying to fight them back, but it was no use. The cords of life were being severed one by one, and his body no longer responded to his commands in the way it used to. Mostly it did whatever it wanted. All he could do was lie there, helplessly, like a puppet abandoned by its puppeteer.

'It's okay, it's okay,' I tried to reassure him. 'Don't worry. You're all right.'

'Am I?' he asked as the tears poured down his cheeks.

'Yes.'

'Really?'

'Yes.'

'No, I'm not. You're a bloody liar. I'm not okay,' he said, his mood changing abruptly and aggressively.

The door to the past had opened wide. He was in there and couldn't get out. All I had to do was walk in and tell him the truth.

'No, you're right, I am lying. You're not okay. You're dying and there's nothing you can do about it.'

'I know that. Say whatever you want, but don't lie to me.'

'And can I ask whatever I want?'

'Yes.'

'Why did you never come back for me?'

He took three, four, quick thin breaths, through barely opened lips, as if he was afraid and trying to compose himself, and then he settled.

'I was dreaming about your mother leaving.'

'Answer my question.'

'I am.'

'You know about her leaving?'

'Of course.'

'Do you know where she is?'

'No.'

'But you knew she'd gone?'

'Yes.'

'How did you know?'

'I saw her. I watched her go.'

'You were with her?'

'Of course. You were too. We were all together.'

'What do you mean?'

'When your mother left.'

'What are you talking about?'

'Christmas Eve.'

'What Christmas Eve?'

'When she disappeared for a week.'

'I don't know anything about that.'

'You were only a toddler.'

'What happened?'

'I looked out the window and saw her walking away.'

'Where to?'

'I didn't know. It was snowing. I ran out. I followed her footsteps.'

'And?'

'The snow was falling so heavily. It was lying. I got confused, so confused.
I lost her. Eventually, I walked home. That's when he first confronted me.'

'Who?'

'When I got back to the house he was waiting for me at the front door.'

'Who was waiting for you?'

'The Devil.'

'What are you talking about?'

'The Devil, he was waiting for me.'

'What? Why would you say something like that?'

'Because it's true. I tried to tell you.'

'When?'

'I called, but you never answered.'

'You mean at the phone box?'

'Yes.'

'I got there. I could hear it ringing.'

'But you didn't answer.'

'I tried. It stopped when I got to the door. You could've called back.'

'I couldn't.'

'This is bullshit. All of it. Total bullshit.'

'It's not. It's true.'

'Really, what did he want then, the Devil?'

'Don't ask me that.'

'I'm asking. What did he want? Why was he waiting for you?'

'I can't.'

'Tell me, you fucking coward.'

'I can't, not now.'

'You can. Or is this just more bullshit? Even now. Even as you're fucking dying.'

'You. He wanted *you*.'

'This is mad. You're mad. Sick.'

'When I got inside, I stayed in bed until Boxing Day morning. I forgot all about it being Christmas. I wanted to forget about everything. Including you. Then I came downstairs and saw you. You were in the living room, sitting beside the Christmas tree. You'd torn open a selection box. Your face and hands were covered in chocolate. I had no idea how long you'd been sitting there on your own. I didn't know what to say. I didn't have the words. I didn't have the words. You were such a gentle boy. You looked up and smiled at me. You asked me if you could open your presents now. And that was that.'

'*And that was that*?'

'Yes.'

'You said that's when he first confronted you — when was the other time?'

'When I took you back. I saw him then. He said I could never escape him. That I had to face the truth.'

'And that's why you left me?'

'I had to get away from him.'

'You're telling me you left because you were running from the Devil?'

'Yes. I had to.'

'Why did you have to?'

'I had no choice.'

'This is bullshit.'

'It's not.'

'Why me? Why did he want me?'

'Christ, why did you have to come here?' He sighed, like someone completely and utterly exhausted with life.

'To see you.'

'Why?'

'Because I'm your son.'

'Are you?'

'What do you mean by that?'

'Oh, where's the boy?'

'*What boy?*'

'The boy I want to talk to. My boy.'

He started to sing, but he was mumbling and kept losing his way and the tune and the words. It was impossible to make out what he was singing. Then he stopped.

'I can't, I can't,' he said.

'*No.* Not this time. Not this fucking time. Tell me what you're talking about.'

'The words.'

'Just wait, they'll come back to you,' I said desperately.

'I can't. I never had them,' he said, then that distant light returned to his eyes and he was gone again.

Some of us spend our entire life trying to escape or find ourselves. We know there's little chance we'll succeed, but we keep trying anyway. The problem lies in the fact that one undertaking is dependent on the other. To find ourselves we must escape ourselves, and to escape ourselves we must first find ourselves. In this manner we become trapped in a hapless struggle with all of life's impossibilities raging within us and no hope of resolution. My father, having failed to escape himself by running, or find himself through singing, was in the process of finally conceding defeat. Yet even death wouldn't provide the escape he longed for. That possibility was being mercilessly wrested from him by illness. Wrapped in the blanket of his own curse, his would be a cheerless farewell. A man alone at the end of his life, forgetting who he was, before he was able to escape who he was. His mind a confusion of memories like reflections in a broken kaleidoscope. His heart a tired organ forgetting all the old tunes. And now I could feel something of what he felt, hear something of what he heard. A grief of song lodged in the heart, and that longing to give up the ghost.

Illuminated by the sallow glow from the nightlight above his bed, we looked like actors on a stage set at the end of the final act. I leaned over and switched off the lamp and our curtained corner of the ward went dark. The light flickered on and off a few times, and I wondered if we were about to blink out together, into the darkness. Then a nurse drew the curtain open and told me visiting hours had ended and it was time to go.

I moved to the window and stood face to face with the night. The sky immediately around the hospice glowed with that deep purple light, like the town was on fire. But there were no fires, and no snow, not yet anyway. Only a rising wind that swirled around the building, rattling the old metal window frames, and tearing the fabric of the night, like a raging, wordless prayer.

13

I met Linda the first evening I visited The Satellite. I'd just ordered a drink at the bar when she walked up and stood in front of me.

'What the fuck?' she asked, obliquely, her eyes rolling towards the ceiling as her right hand reached for the bar rail, and her left tried to remember the glass of wine it kept forgetting was there.

'What the fuck what?' I asked back.

'Is someone … like you … doing … in … the Satellite?' she asked, getting behind each word like she was beating it down. The glass fell from her hand and looked lost for good, before she manged to catch it and lift it to her mouth in an astonishing flourish. Whereupon she drained it in one of those theatrical acts of defiance against everything and nothing. It was clear Linda was already bevvied.

'I'm mapping the stars,' I told her, having had a few myself.

'What sort of shite is that?'

'Okay. I'm hoping to encounter extraterrestrial life.'

'Fuck off.'

'I might. After I've finished my drink.'

'Take it from me, you don't belong here.'

'I don't?'

'No, you don't.'

'Why not?'

'Look at you.'

'Yeah?'

'You're a fake.'

'A fake?'

'Yeah. A fucking fake.'

'What am I faking?'

'Yourself. Being in here. Everything. You look like you're faking fucking everything.'

It was a harsh judgement, but honest. Though one which didn't deter me from remaining in the Satellite that evening, or of course from subsequently frequenting the place. In fact, it made me feel right at home, because everyone in the Satellite was faking something or other. Faking their life, their death, their hate, their love. Or their indifference to life, death, hate, and love. Just like Pessoa's poets — they faked their lives so completely, they even faked they were suffering the pain *they were really feeling*. And many of them were poets, too — or traded in something similar. A peculiar glossolalia located somewhere between incoherence and lucidity that they'd impart in unsolicited pronouncements. Whispering it to you enigmatically as they brushed past you, or suddenly exclaiming it in vatic utterances from the other side of the bar like mad Glaswegian Rasputins.

Yeah, the Satellite was full of fakers just like me. All of us secretly hoping that someday, God, the Devil, or some alien destroyer of worlds, might come along and tear the roof off the Satellite and expose our cowering lonesome souls and put an end to the whole shooting match.

As for Linda, it turned out she was willing to put all my faking to one side, since she also thought I was, in her words, a fucking handsome bastard. At least compared to the competition in the bar that evening. After her uncompromising introduction, she asked if I was interested in a line of coke and a blow job. I thought she was joking, but a minute later I was following her into the women's toilets. As soon as I closed the cubicle door, she told me to get my fucking trousers off, then she handed me a wrap and got down on her knees. Linda had

a filthy mouth, but a velvet tongue. I'd only just managed to unfold the wrap
and dab my finger into the coke when it was all over. Without missing a beat,
she shoved me out of the cubicle and told me to go buy her a drink, while she
took a piss.

Linda lived nearby in the house she'd grown up in, though she hadn't
always lived there. At some point she'd moved to one of Scotland's remote
islands after winning a competition aimed at boosting the island's population.
From the little she said about the few years she lived on the island, it seemed
she was happy there. Then one day her father reversed out the drive at speed
and didn't notice his wife on her knees, pruning a rose bush. He drove his car
right over her and killed her. Linda had come home for the funeral, stayed
on a while to look after her grieving, guilt-ridden father, then he died, too,
only months later. One afternoon he taped up the garage doors and windows,
attached a hose to the exhaust pipe of his car, then fed it through a gap in the
driver's window and got inside and started the engine. Linda never went back
to the island after that. But we did go back to hers that first night and on her
insistence fucked in her parents' bed.

Ever since, Linda would call me when she felt the need, or I'd call her when
I felt the need. What we had was an arrangement. A very basic arrangement
that had nothing at all to do with romance or friendship. We comforted each
other in dark and sometimes terrible ways, lanced the boil of time, drew the
puss out of our days. On this particular occasion it was me who'd called Linda.
Though for once I wanted a little more than comfort — or a lot less, as Linda
would see it. I wanted company. Any company other than my own. When I
walked into the Satellite she was sitting at one of the booths waiting for me.

Almost an hour had passed and we'd hardly talked. We'd been concentrating
instead on drinking half pints of Buckfast — with me trying to swerve
the inevitable and Linda drinking straight towards it — when a guy selling
designer knock-offs approached our table. After some flirting disguised as

haggling, Linda bought a fake Louis Vuitton purse for twenty quid, and for a fiver I bought a sheet of kitchen roll that he swore had been dipped in acid.

'Are you still working at that newspaper?' she asked once the guy had moved on to a different table and we sat tearing and chewing our half-sheet of kitchen roll.

'I'm on leave.'

'What sort of leave?'

'Extended leave.'

'You've been sacked.'

'Not officially.'

'How about your writing?'

'I'm working through ideas.'

'You said that the last time we met.'

'Did I?'

'You need to get out of that fucking high-rise.'

'I'm out now.'

'I mean *really out*. What do you do up there on your own all the time anyway?'

'I watch.'

'Watch what?'

'The view. The weather. People. Aeroplanes. I like watching the aeroplanes.'

'*You like watching the aeroplanes*. Listen to yourself, you sound like there's something fucking wrong with you. It's not healthy.'

'It's therapeutic.'

'It's abnormal.'

'And your life is normal?'

'I make it in to work each day. I earn a living.'

'You work from home on a chatline.'

'So? Believe me, compared to you I'm the fucking definition of normal. What floor are you on again?'

'The fourteenth floor.'

'I thought so. Like the Stations of the Cross.'

'I suppose.'

'How very fucking biblical.'

'Is it?'

'Honestly, you fucking Catholics and your Stations of the fucking Crosses.'

'It's just the one *fucking* Cross. And I didn't get to choose the *fucking* floor.'

'Whatever. Stuck up there like that fucker swallowed by the big fish.'

'Jonah?'

'That's the fucker.'

'The big fish was a whale.'

'Exactly. All alone in your big fucking concrete whale, suffering for your writing. Only it sounds like it's all suffering and no writing to me. You should stay there till the end, let them tear the fucking thing down with you in it.'

'Do you really have to say "fuck" and "fucking" so often?'

'I like fuck and fucking.'

'I know.'

'You could fucking write about it. It could be your final fucking story. Something of yours some fucker might actually want to fucking read. That place, it's your very own Hotel fucking California.'

'I thought it was a whale.'

'Whale, hotel, who gives a fuck? You can check out anytime you like, but never fucking leave,' Linda laughed.

'Fuck you.'

'Please fucking do. That's why we're here isn't it?'

'I was hoping for once we could just have a drink and a chat.'

'We are drinking and chatting.'

'I mean properly.'

'If you wanted a drink and a chat you should have opened a bottle at home and called the Samaritans. Did you know Samaritan call-handlers can't trace or record your number or involve any other services unless you ask them to?'

'I don't think that's correct.'

'Fucking is. You can phone and tell them you're going to kill yourself and they can't do anything about it except talk to you. Just sit there and listen. Can you fucking believe that?'

'No, not really.'

'Talk about a fucking captive audience. More like do-no-fucking-good-Samaritans.'

'If it's true, which I doubt, I imagine the idea is to foster trust, so you can talk openly.'

'What type would you want to talk to?'

'Type of what?'

'You'd probably be a caller, not a handler, but if in another life you were a call-handler, what sort of suicide would you want to talk to?'

'The kind that decided not to do it.'

'I'd definitely want someone who was going to OD with pills. I definitely wouldn't want a fucking cutter.'

'You've thought about this?'

'Yeah, I couldn't stand any wailing. I think a pill-popper would be less noisy. Or maybe a jumper. A jumper would definitely be quicker.'

'Jesus.'

'Jesus would make a good fucking call-handler.'

'Do you want another drink?'

'Are you feeling anything from that acid?'

'What acid?'

'If it was fucking acid.'

'What acid?'

'I think I saw something there.'

'Where?'

'You don't remember taking acid? *If it was fucking acid.*'

'No. I don't.' I had no recollection of taking anything.

'Shit. Shit. Shit. It was definitely fucking something.'

'Do you want another drink?'

'Why not? One for the road,' Linda said, then lit a cigarette.

'You can't smoke that in here.'

'I know, I'll be going soon,' she smiled, benignly.

On the way to the bar I went via the jukebox. On the dancefloor a middle-aged man sporting a drooping, Wyatt Earp moustache, and wearing a fringed and tasselled brown suede jacket, stood clutching his pint at arm's length, like he was strangling someone. He saw me flipping the song cards and started yelling, 'A Horse with No Name! A Horse with No Name!', over and over. I gave him his song, followed it with Roy Orbison's 'Crying', then Sonny Boy Williamson's, 'Help Me'. As I passed him, he yelled, 'Fucking tune, man!' Then he put his pint on the floor and started march-dancing around it, while shooting imaginary holes in the ceiling with hands shaped into pistols. When I made it to the bar, the barman was standing waiting for me.

'Tell her to go outside and smoke that,' he said, nodding over at Linda.

'I did. I told her. I'll tell her again,' I promised him.

When I returned with our drinks, Linda was flopped across the table with her face pressed into the burnt and scratched surface of the Formica tabletop, and her arms stretched out like she'd been nailed there. The cigarette stuck between the index and middle finger of her right hand had burned down to the stub, leaving a delicate rainbow of grey ash hanging in the air. I sat our drinks on the table, then slipped the butt out from her fingers and slid into the opposite side of the booth and sat facing her.

'Where has all the tenderness gone?' I wondered out loud, thinking she was asleep.

'We drank and fucked it all away,' she answered, drowsily, her head still on the table.

'And that's it?'

'That's it. Sayonara fucking tenderness.'

'What a mess.'

'Aye.'

'We could run away.'

'Who?'

'Me and you.'

'Don't be fucking stupid. Anyway, you're the one in a mess, not me,' Linda slurred, before drifting off again.

Linda was correct about one thing. The kitchen roll may not have been dipped in acid, but it had certainly been dipped in *something*. I stood up, and clutching my glass, staggered into the bathroom in a drug-and-drink-induced stupor. By the time I'd made it from the urinal to the sink I was no longer capable of coordinated movement. I stood with my eyelids slowly opening then closing, drifting in and out of consciousness, swaying in an ever-decreasing circular movement like a punchbag that's been hit hard and is gradually coming to rest. I opened my eyes as wide as I could and lifted my face to the mirror. I looked wretched, diabolical, like a freak produced by an act of necromancy, abandoned just before completion. I knew there was no way back, though, not now. And like an idiot fooling around with a loaded gun, I lifted the half pint of Buckfast to my lips and drank the entire glass. The wine exploded in my stomach like a tiny atom bomb that sent a million burning stars exiting through the pores of my skin. I stopped swaying and felt a hand reach up inside me and pull out what was left of my heart. Afterwards, I felt like I had absolutely nothing left to give and completely at peace.

I've no idea how long I was in the toilet, but when I came out there was no sign of Linda. Her drink lay untouched on the table, so I assumed she'd also gone to the toilet and slid into the booth and waited for her to return. But this time, true to her word, it seemed she really had gone.

Before I had time to wonder what may have become of her, a guy dressed in a tight-fitting grey suit, cream shirt, and brown tie, slid into the booth and sat exactly where Linda had sat.

'Hey, man, mind if I join you?' he asked in a sunny, freewheeling American accent.

'Sure,' I told him, 'why not?'

'Cool. Cool. Is that drink free?' he asked, staring at Linda's half pint of Buckfast.

'It wasn't when I bought it, but it is now.'

'Do you mind if I try a little?'

'No, go ahead.'

'Thanks. I only flew into Glasgow today, but people sure are friendly,' he said, smiling and looking around the Satellite, while nodding at everyone and no one in particular. He said he was here visiting relatives and was a professional poker player who went by the gambling name Flamenco Riviera. He said he was happy to meet me, and I was certainly happy to meet him.

'You couldn't buy me another?' he asked, staring at the already empty glass like a father staring at the photograph of his missing child. 'I've got money. I promise I've got plenty of money,' he said. 'Hit the jackpot in Las Vegas the night before I flew over the pond. I just haven't had the chance to get to the bank. I'll tell you what, will you be in here tomorrow?' he asked with what can only be described as a winning smile.

'There's every chance,' I told him.

'Well, as God is my witness, I'll be right by your side, and for every drink you buy me tonight, I'll buy you *two* tomorrow. Cross my heart and hope to die.'

The kitchen roll was seriously messing with my mind, so that Flamenco's words hung around me like perfectly weighted apples in a tree on a warm summer day. I wanted to pick each one out of the air and bite into it and savour it. I could see the colour of everyone's aura, soul, or whatever, that was in the bar. Most of them looked dark and toxic, but Flamenco's glowed with a pure, golden Californian light. This guy had walked straight out of a goddamn Ready Brek commercial. I felt honoured that he'd chosen me among all these lowlifes to buy him a drink, and the honour began to swell into an uplifting pride that rose magnificently in me like the darkness being swept from the face of a mountain by the rising sun.

'Flame — you don't mind if I call you Flame?' I asked him.

'Hell no. I like it. In fact, *I love it.*'

'Well, Flame, you put that roll back in your slacks. You are my guest and tonight is on me.'

'Now you're talking my language.'

'Yes, by God! We'll drink, go further north, strike for the pole!' I exclaimed, then bowed with a theatrical flourish after giving the best impersonation I could muster of Albert Finney in *Under the Volcano*.

'Whoa, big fella, you take it easy there now,' Flame laughed.

All I could respond with was, '*Slacks, slacks, slacks.*'

Slacks. I'd no idea how that word had got into my head, but I loved the feel and sound of it. It felt like a woman had slowly put her warm tongue in my mouth and was moving it gently around. I loved the feel of it and kept saying it over and over as I floated towards the bar.

'You, ma man, are one mother-fucking, star-spangled banner,' Flame, who was *actually* on fire now, called after me.

It turned out the guy who'd sold us the acid had returned to our booth when I'd gone to the toilet. For a free matching fake handbag to go with the purse, Linda had agreed to take him home for a fuck. I only learned this weeks later, when the guy stopped me in the street one day to apologise for stealing my date, and to thank me for introducing him to his fiancée.

As for me, I stayed and kept buying drinks for the Flame, until I looked up and the Flame had either gone to find a casino or been extinguished. I stayed until all the lights went on and they opened the doors and let the cold air blow in to drive the last of us out — then I floated out of there on a river of brotherly love. I drifted past the shell of a burnt-out ice-cream van, past the playground where a toddler's back had been ripped open by a nail someone had driven through the slide, past the tatty shrine with the plastic flowers that marked the Birdman's murder back at the end of June, and on past all the closing times, until there was nothing else to do but keep walking.

I walked beneath a sky lit cobalt-green by a brilliant display of the northern lights too far south and freakishly visible above the city's light pollution. I didn't want to go back to my flat on my own and ended up at the Trinity. For a while I wandered around the upper parades and walkways, marvelling at the increasingly spectacular aurora borealis flowing across the night sky in broad ribbons of supernatural light — certain I could hear and feel static bursts emanate from the heart of it out across the universe. Each burst echoed through the shopping centre like a psychic pulse, crackling across the broken slabs of the central concourse and fizzing around the splintered doorways and shop fronts of the derelict stores, as if searching for some trace of an ancient broadcast analogous to itself, or some other sign of life to correspond with. Following the echoes, I circled further and further down into the Trinity, passing one boarded-up shop after another, until at the lowest level I found myself surrounded by darkness. A haunting darkness like in the negative of an old photograph. I was hearing voices, shadows were passing through the walls, and tenebrous chasms were opening all around me. The spirits of the vanished went about their business as if life went on as it always had, but it didn't. All commerce had ceased there years before. They kept disappearing, then reappearing, as if they were trapped down there in a blind pocket of the universe where forgetting was impossible. I followed them around through the thick, pixelated darkness, until my atman collapsed in a doorway, unable to go any further. She was shivering and whispering something about gathering up the lost and sold, and I lay down beside her and put my arms around her to keep her warm, and we fell asleep in each other's arms.

I once happened to watch an episode of a documentary series on TV one afternoon. It was 1997 and I was twelve years old. I remember because it was the year Tony Blair became Prime Minister in a landslide result and the year when I was terrified to fall sleep. Ill again with something or other, I was wrapped in a duvet on the couch instead of being at school. Which wasn't unusual — I don't recall attending school much back then, regardless of whether I was ill or not. I do remember I had a fever that day and that before going out, my mother had given me a dose of Benylin and a Valium. And I remember how the day looked and felt. Diffused by the net curtains, the sun filled the room with a thin, absent light, and as I drifted from malady to a hazy almost erotic euphoria, the afternoon began to feel less and less inhabited, as if everyone had moved on and I'd been left behind somewhere. I'd been sneaking the odd swig of booze for a year or so, but it was around this time that I started drinking more regularly. It went from a necked shot of something and a beer every now and then, to an emptied Barr's bottle, refilled with diluted juice and a good measure of whatever booze was in the drinks cabinet. On this particular afternoon I was sipping orange juice laced with Malibu, when I switched on the television and found what looked like a home movie shot in Super 8. It opened with a Seventies white Oldsmobile flickering in and out of consciousness and time, in bursts of blinding sunshine on a long stretch of empty American highway. Then we were inside the car, drifting past a group of forlorn children sporting the tragedy of life. Foundlings standing on a dusty verge and turning their heads to follow the car. Looking directly into the camera, gazing right at me through the TV screen from a bygone world, a ghost world. Even from so many years away I could tell they were broken-hearted, unwanted, without love.

'I passed through Sawtooth at 11.15 a.m., a town so small it didn't even have a stop light,' the voiceover said.

Then a crude cut, like a page torn from a book, and from a high snowy bluff there was Reno beneath a blood-red winter sky, all lit up like a neon royal flush. And then girls with flowers in their hair, smiling, swimming through mountain pools, their skin and the surface of the water, sun-kissed. Summer bathers mouthing silent epigraphs of love that resonated down through the years like barely legible epitaphs.

Then multiple dawns and dusks, and fields of golden corn stretching towards the horizon. Freight trains riding parallel to the car as the sun rose up over the Rockies. Twilit Badlands, otherworldly beneath a red ochre sky *the colour of love and Spanish mysteries*. Voiceovers like old, scratched records. Kerouac reading from *On the Road* mixed with hallowed commentaries of baseball games. Preachers prophesying the end of the world. Flickering images filled with a deep, aching longing. And that music naively following its own hope, over and over without end. Perpetuum mobile, perpetuum mobile, perpetuum mobile, perpetuum mobile.

I didn't know then it was Kerouac. Had never heard of the Penguin Café Orchestra. Didn't know what Super 8 was or a baseball game or speaking in tongues. Didn't know an Oldsmobile from a stop light and was only vaguely aware of what America was. Maybe it was the Valium and Malibu-laced Kia-Ora. And yet there was something about that footage and that music that had me gasping for breath. It was ridiculous how much I cried that afternoon. Bawled my eyes out with absolutely no idea for the love of God why. Christ, even now when I hear that music I'm right back in that day, and that room, with those feelings.

We've no idea of half the worlds contained with ourselves. Far less of those contained within the person standing next to us at the supermarket or at the bus stop or even lying next to us in bed. We can tell ourselves otherwise all we want to, but that moment of darkness right after we reach out and turn the bedside light off, that's the truth of everything right there, and it's the same for all of us.

14

The day before my father was buried, I visited the funeral home where his body had been embalmed and dressed. My Aunt Mags told me he'd be laid out in an open coffin for the Prayer Vigil, and I wanted to take one last look at him before they put him in the ground.

When I arrived, there was no one at the reception desk and no visitors in the waiting room. I took a seat and looked around while waiting for a member of staff to appear. In the centre of the room there was a large rectangular G-Plan-style coffee table, with several similar styled wood and black vinyl chairs arranged around it. The walls were covered with brown wallpaper embossed with vegetation and fruit sprouting from the mouths of Green Men, and there was a bookcase tightly packed with *New Jerusalem* bibles, that on closer inspection turned out to be fake resin moulds. On top of the bookcase there was a temple-design mantel clock in green onyx. Someone must have been a collector or bought the clock as part of a lot at auction, as there were several themed pieces carefully placed on surfaces around the room. A rotary telephone, an ashtray, a cigarette case, a set of scales, and a caravan of camels, all in green onyx. Brown floor vases filled with pink plastic lilies stood in each corner of the room, and hanging on one of the walls was a collection of mirrored pictures with inspirational Christian quotes like: *Unless you are born again, you cannot see the Kingdom of God*, and *God will take you places you have never dreamed of.*

On top of the reception counter there was a white plastic push button that when pressed triggered a loud *ding-dong*, as if you were at the front door of someone's house. I pressed it repeatedly, but no one answered. After I'd waited a while, I walked from the waiting room through an archway elaborately decorated with red velvet curtains and layers of swag, fringes, and tassels, into a hallway. The transition from the public area into the private was disorientating. In contrast to the lobby, the inner sanctum was furnished in cheap rococo with an abundance of velveteen in varying shades of red. Even the walls were covered in red velvet flock. The multiple layers of scarlet, ruby, vermilion, cardinal, claret, and other red textiles lent the place an air of tranquillity that bordered on sedation. It was as if time – unable to fully penetrate the layered fabrics within the building — didn't function properly here. The separation between body and spirit was enhanced by the heavy piled red carpet, and endless cycle of classic love songs performed on pan pipes flowing from speakers hidden behind faux air vents. The whole place had the vibe and decor of *Tales of the Unexpected* circa 1979.

Finding the room my father was laid out in wasn't difficult — in fact, it would have been more difficult to miss it. On an easel just outside the door someone had placed an enlarged promotional photo of him from his cabaret days. With his perfect, cut-out smile, sun-kissed complexion, and white silk shirt unbuttoned to his chest, he was every bit the handsome crooner. Set beside the velveteen drapes and tasselled tie-backs that adorned the entrance, it felt more like I was entering an entertainment lounge in a hotel than a visitation room at a funeral home.

I'd missed the Prayer Vigil, or else it was still to take place. Either way, there was no one there and I was relieved, as I didn't want to talk to any of my relatives. Large bouquets of white lilies were arranged around the coffin, and a group of nine gilt chairs were aligned in three rows of three in front of it. I sat down in a chair in the front row, said a short prayer, then stepped forward and looked down at my father.

He'd been dressed in a white suit with a black silk stage shirt and white patent-leather boots. A large ornate silver crucifix had been laid on his chest, and a set of black rosary beads had been wrapped around his clasped hands and between his fingers which were decorated with an array of rings set with colourful stones. His face looked just as it had when I saw him in hospital, only more shrunken and skeletal. His eyelids were closed and dark, as if they'd been smudged with mascara or ash, and they'd rouged his cheeks and touched his lips with a hint of scarlet. I'd come with the hope of experiencing some sort of epiphany. Of achieving a connection with him in death that I hadn't been able to achieve with him when he was alive. But it didn't happen.

There was a momentary jolt after the initial shock of seeing his lifeless body, one I hadn't experienced when I'd previously seen him. A leaden sense of inertia that plunged through me and for a second seemed determined to pull me down through the earth with it. Then that was it. A momentary jolt, and he was gone. I was desperate to weep, but how can you weep for an absence. In the end, he remained as removed and unreachable in death as he had done in life. When the music shifted from the pan pipes to Bette Midler singing 'Wind Beneath My Wings', I turned and walked out through a realm as plush and chintzy as a Mayfair brothel and as otherworldly as the surface of Mars.

After leaving the funeral parlour I bought a bottle of rum from the first off-licence I passed, then wandered around town, stopping at locations that held some meaning for me from my youth.

The house where my first proper girlfriend lived.

The lake where my friend's girlfriend fell into the water after losing her balance on the bow of the rowing boat we'd stolen.

The lamp post around which I watched a local virtuoso jazz musician who suffered from schizophrenia walk for over an hour, playing 'My Favourite Things' non-stop on his alto sax.

An area of woodland in the local park where a boy approached me one afternoon and asked if I could see dead children hanging in the trees.

The stretch of road my mum was driving along when she screamed that she wished I'd never been born.

The spot where the phone box stood that my father called me at.

After I'd drunk more than half the rum, I walked into the town centre and entered a pub down a lane off the high street. There were no chairs between the entrance and the bar, and though the open space was probably no more than two metres, to me it seemed vast. Undermined by the unexpected distance, I approached slowly and cautiously in an exaggerated manner, stepping over objects only I could see. When the girl behind the bar moved forward to serve me, the barman, who'd been watching my measured approach the whole time, stepped in front of her, puffed his chest out, and smiled at me.

'Yes, mate?'

'Rum, please,' I asked.

'Don't think so, mate,' the barman replied.

'A glass of wine then.'

'Nope,' he smiled.

'A small beer?'

'I think you've already had enough.'

'I've not had enough.'

'I think you have,' he said, and nodded towards the bottle sticking out my jacket pocket.

'Okay, maybe a little, but I'm perfectly sordor.'

'You're what?' he laughed.

'*Sober.*'

'Okay, on your way.'

'No.'

'Just leave, mate.'

'I'm not your mate.'

'Don't make a dick of yourself.'

'I'm not making a dick of myself — you are.'

'I'm making a dick out of you?'

'You are, with no good reason.'

'Listen, pal, just call it a day.'

'Mate? Pal? I ask you, is this any way to treat your friends?'

The barmaid giggled, which seemed to irritate the barman further. 'Fuck off,' he said.

'There's no need to swear.'

'Seriously, get to fuck.'

'Me?'

'Aye, *still fucking you*.'

'Fine, I'm going.'

'*I know you're fucking going*,' he snapped.

I stepped outside and walked back onto the high street. The day was overcast, yet unreasonably bright. Trapped between the earth and the pale grey sky, the light was intense and glaring like a migraine. It seemed to have no fixed source and its omnipresence had a disorientating effect that made everything it illuminated ungraspable. In a daze, I walked past shopfronts, watching my refection undulate across the glass. I stopped outside a mobile phone shop and looked in through the window. Inside, the customers and staff floated around in a pearly haze like ghosts. I felt like I was drowning, sinking slowly past all the old landmarks I'd visited earlier that day. And now I was reliving the events that had written each location into my memory.

I was standing in front of Daisy Lane's parents' house, the first girl I'd kissed with all my mouth, and an erection. It was early evening and the long brown-brick American style bungalow glowed with soft electric lamplight beneath a deep raspberry-ripple sky. It was a few days after our first kiss, and I was peering in through her living-room window, watching her. She'd told me her parents would be out and that she'd be waiting for me. I hadn't set out to spy on her. But when I peeked in over the ledge of the living-room window to make sure she was alone and saw her dressed in nothing but her bra and underpants, I couldn't help myself. I followed her from room to room. Watched her drink a glass of water at the kitchen sink. Saw her run her hands down inside her bra and around her large firm breasts as she stood in the centre of the living room. Watched her cross to a mirror to check her hair and make-up. When she sat down on the settee and leaned back and put her feet up on the coffee table and opened her legs, then switched the television on, it was the most beautiful thing I'd ever seen.

I'd heard of peeping Toms and was sure I wasn't one. Then again, the sensation of watching Daisy Lane that evening was so electrifying, I realised how easy it would be to become one. I watched her for so long I forgot all about going in and didn't hear her dad pull into the driveway. Didn't hear him come up behind me. Didn't hear him ask what I was doing. I wasn't doing anything, besides watching her, but when he saw what I saw he grabbed me by the neck and hauled me around the side of the house. He didn't call the police, which was something, but he did beat the shit out of me. Daisy was at a different high school from me, and after that evening I never saw or heard from her again.

We never saw my friend Jason's girlfriend again either. Not alive anyway. Vivienne drowned that afternoon. Police divers lifted her body out of the lake later that day and laid her on the grass beneath a police-incident tent they'd erected on the main lawn, in front of the park's grand country house. I remember her mother standing just beyond the harsh glow of the floodlights at the crime scene later that evening, screaming her daughter's name, then prostrating herself on the ground. Jason was in shock and still stoned from the jellies we'd taken and all the weed we'd smoked earlier. When he walked over and lay down next to her and put his arms around her, she went berserk and started punching and clawing and kicking him. The police had to pull her off him and drag her away across the lawn. Jason never came back from wherever he went after Vivienne died. A year later he was a heroin addict. A year after that he was dead too. He broke into Vivienne's house one night and overdosed in her bed. In the paper it said he was burgling the home of the girl whose death he was responsible for. I know he wasn't responsible for her death, and I don't believe he was burgling her parents' house. I don't even believe he intended to overdose. You might imagine that he just wanted to be close to her. But I don't believe that either. I think he was attempting to bring her back from the other side.

After he'd finished playing 'My Favourite Things', Micky Miller began to batter his head off the lamp post until it cracked and bled. An ambulance arrived, and when the paramedics were done with him, he was transported straight to the main psychiatric care facility in the area. Set in the grounds of a crumbling Victorian asylum, the services at Bellsdyke Hospital were cut back soon after, and Micky was moved from institution to institution. I knew the brother of someone who'd been in a band with Micky, and when I bumped into them years later and asked after him, they said that after the institutions, he moved through several supported housing accommodations, each one further away from his family home, until no one was sure of his whereabouts. It seemed somewhere along the line people stopped caring and Micky vanished, just like the notes he'd played on his sax that afternoon.

I only spoke to the boy who'd seen the dead children in the trees once or twice after that — just passing hellos in the street. But years later, while I was living in Glasgow, the CID turned up at a flat I was renting. I didn't know what I'd done, but I assumed it must've been something serious since they'd sent a detective. Recognising the panic in my face, he assured me that I needn't worry, that I wasn't in trouble. He said he was here in a semi-official capacity. A case was being wound down and he wanted to check something before it was closed. He asked if I knew someone called Rupert Simmons. I told him I didn't know anyone called Rupert Simmons. I imagine he wanted to see how I'd react, because next he told me that Rupert Simmons had recently hanged himself in an area of woodland in a park in my hometown. He waited for me to respond. When I didn't, he asked 'That doesn't mean anything to you then?'

'It means something in that it's awful. But no, not personally. Why, should it?'

'I'd hoped so. In a diary he'd left behind he mentioned meeting you in that park beside those trees.'

I had no idea who he was talking about. Then he told me a little more about Rupert Simmons. He'd become obsessed with exposing a paedophile ring, members of which he claimed had abused him and other children in the town. As soon as the detective said this, *I knew exactly who it was*. I remembered the boy in the park and talking to him. I was only thirteen years old. He couldn't have been much older. It was such a brief conversation, but unforgettable, given how strange it was.

He appeared from nowhere and handed me a plastic toy soldier.

'You can keep that,' he said, with a nod that indicated the little green figure throwing a grenade in the palm of my hand. And then he looked up into the woods and asked, 'Can you see them?'

'Who?' I asked.

'The children hanging in the trees?'

'What?'

'I think they're all dead now.'

'*They're what?*' I responded, totally freaked out.

'Dead. See them, right there?' he asked again, pointing calmly up at a tree.

'*No. No I can't.*'

'Yes you can.'

'*I can't.*'

'You can. You just don't want to say so.'

'Who are you?'

'Your friend.'

'I don't see them. And we're not friends. I've never seen you before.'

'But I've seen you. And one day you'll see them,' he smiled, looking up at the trees. 'Then you'll understand,' he said, then walked off.

I remember I was going to call after him, 'No, I fucking won't see them, and we'll never be friends!' But I couldn't get the words out. I was too scared and confused. I just stood there, watching him fade into the shadows of the tree-lined path he followed up into the woods. I saw him in passing a few times after that. We'd smile and say hi with a half, awkward wave, but we never stopped to talk.

'I do remember a boy approaching me in the park one day years ago. I'd have been about thirteen. It was the strangest thing. He asked if I saw dead children in the trees.'

'What?'

'Yeah, it was weird.'

'You think that was Rupert?'

'Obviously. It must have been.'

'And did you?'

'Did I what?'

'See them?'

'*Dead children?*'

'Yes.'

'No, of course not.'

'How about Rupert? Did you see him after that?'

'I said hello to him a couple of times.'

'And that was it?'

'Yeah.'

'You don't have any other information?'

'About what?'

'A paedophile ring?'

'What? No.'

He looked out the window, then down at his feet, before finding the right look to fix me with as he asked the next question, 'How about Satanists?'

'Satanists, are you serious?'

'Yes. Not necessarily connected. But possibly connected.'

'*A Satanic paedophile ring?* No, I don't.'

According to the officer, Rupert had started knocking on the doors of the great and the good of the town — MPs, businessmen, councillors — and throwing accusations around. In the end, people stopped listening to him and he was written off as a fantasist. And yet the truth was, the CID believed what Rupert was saying. In fact, they said they knew there was a paedophile ring. As for Satanists, apparently they'd found evidence of Satanic rituals having been performed in secluded spots all across the district and had good reason to believe they were connected. The problem was, Rupert had accused so many different people — some guilty, others innocent — that he'd compromised their entire investigation. Rupert had written my name in his diary, and beside it the word *trust* in bold capitals. The detective had hoped I could help them corroborate Rupert's allegations. He seemed genuinely crestfallen when I couldn't.

'So, you were never actually friends?' he asked.

'No.'

'How was he back then?'

'When, that day?'

'Yeah.'

'It was a long time ago now.'

'I know, but is there anything you can think of?'

'What he was saying was so bizarre, I wasn't really focusing on how he seemed.'

'Nothing?'

'Well, he wasn't angry or worked up. If anything, he was sweet. You know, warm, nice. And sad, I suppose. Though I don't know if I'm just filling all that in now, because of what you've told me.'

'Did your parents know each other?'

'Hopefully. They got married and had me.'

'I mean your parents and Rupert's parents.'

'Not that I know.'

'And there's nothing else you can think of? Nothing more you can tell us?'

'There isn't,' I assured him. And at the time there wasn't — I couldn't think of anything. But there was something I could have told him. I didn't hold it back intentionally. I just didn't put it together that afternoon. Even now I'm not sure it was connected.

—

As far as I'm aware, my mother didn't know what the man she'd allowed into our house on and off for years had been doing. With that in mind, it wasn't so much the damage she'd done, at least not directly. It was the damage done by the damage she'd failed to prevent.

That afternoon in the car, for the first and last time, I tried to tell her about what happened. How it started. He'd climb up on to the banister at the top of the stairs in our house and watch me in the shower, or bath, or on the toilet, through the window above the bathroom door. I'd look up and he'd be looking down at me, smiling benignly. A kind of end-of-the-world smile. Like he had a revolver in his mouth and was in the process of pulling the trigger and blowing his head off. I stopped bathing and toileting at home after that.

I told her about how I woke one night and opened my eyes to find him sitting by the side of my bed, staring at me through the scrunched-up darkness. Sometimes weeks would pass and I wouldn't see him. His face and presence would gradually fade from my memory like a bruise from my skin. Then without warning, he'd appear suddenly in the middle of the night, like an afterimage or an X-ray. I'd awaken and he'd be leaning over me, his lips millimetres above mine. I could never focus on the disorganised static of his face in the darkness, but its visual burn was branded on my soul.

One night I awoke to find he'd snuck into my bed and slipped his hands down the front of my pants. That's when I stopped sleeping. Soon after, I started hearing the grim, measured clip, of what I was certain were the Devil's hooves approaching our house and stopping directly below my window every night. Convinced he would enter and claim my soul while fucking me if I went to the window and looked at him, I'd clutch my mattress and hold on as tightly as I could in an effort to stay in bed. After several months, and doubting my resolve not to look down, I resorted to tying one of my wrists to my headboard. I'd wait out the night wracked by cold sweats, my heart pounding, constantly on the verge of throwing up. When dawn broke and I was utterly exhausted, I'd finally fall asleep.

He never said a word to me, not when we were alone, not while it was happening. At other times, in front of people, he'd talk away to me and act as if everything was normal. But there was always a sly smile and a wink when no one else was looking. A gesture so light, yet so leaden. Compromising, threatening, duplicitous. As if I were his willing accomplice, and he'd reveal my true nature to everyone if I did anything to upset him.

I already knew the world outside could be merciless. But to know it in your own home.

It terrified me how multiple realities could co-exist, not only beside one another but overlapping and within one another. How you could be in several at once, like alternate universes, and no one could see you or reach you. They say that ghosts are the restless, tortured souls of the dead, but I wonder if they're actually those of the living.

That afternoon in the car I could tell by the way my mother kept tightening, then loosening her grip on the steering wheel and refusing to look at me while I spoke to her, that she knew I was telling the truth. But the last thing in the world she wanted was the truth. The last thing in the world my mother had ever wanted was the truth. Her entire life was built on an illusion so complete it was impenetrable. And yet at the same time it was as fragile as a starling's egg and she did whatever was necessary to protect it. She wanted to be as far from the truth as was humanly possible. As far as starlight from the dead star that released it.

We'd just pulled out onto the main road when she accelerated and screamed, 'I wish you'd never been born.' That's when I opened the passenger door and stepped out onto the road, hitting it at a run, and lurching towards the oncoming traffic. I kept running, following the white lines along the middle of the road, and didn't stop until I managed to cross the opposite lane and collapse on a grass verge. I lay in the long green grass, looking up at an Arctic-blue sky, imagining I was lying in my mother's arms. Everything was spinning and

disordering. Spilling beyond the fast-moving clouds and the sun and the moon
and the stars. And further, beyond everything I'd imagined we were.

I stayed at a friend's house for the next few weeks. Then my Aunt Mags
called me one evening to say, among other things, that my mother had taken off
somewhere, and that I might want to go home and check everything was okay
with the house.

The house was cold when I got there, and there was no sign of my mum.
She'd left me a note that I suppose was intended as some sort of apology. In it
she told me that when she found out she was pregnant with me she'd made an
appointment to have me terminated. In the waiting room before the procedure,
she said she'd picked up an issue of *Cosmopolitan* and opened it at an article
about abortion. She said she couldn't remember if the article was for or against
abortion, but after she read it she walked out. She said walking out of there was
one of the few things she'd done in her life that she didn't regret. I suppose
we're talking about love here. But a love hidden in the backrooms of days.
A love filled with remorse. A love pregnant with regrets. It was never a love
that would hold you. A love that would wrap its arms around you. That knew
you like a mother's love should. Even if it *was* the one thing she didn't regret,
because of everything she failed to do subsequently, I could never bring myself
to believe she really meant what she'd written. And I never got the chance to
find out whether she meant it or not, as she never returned.

Waiting at that phone box for my father to call became a regular part of my
life. I'd go there most evenings at the time I'd missed the call. Standing in its
damp, rusting iron carcass, with its cracked red paint and odour of piss, the
darkness threatening and swelling outside, I'd will the phone to ring. I'd wait
for hours in the pale white prayer of its light, but you never called. When I
started drinking more heavily, I stopped hoping you'd call me. Instead, I started
playing a version of Russian roulette. In my version the gun was the handset
and the bullet a man's voice. I'd call random numbers and if a woman answered

I'd apologise and put the phone down. If a man answered, I'd ask, 'Dad, is that you dad?' You would usually say something like, 'Who is this?' And I'd say, 'It's me. I miss you.' Then I'd stay on the line, listening to your voice, until you hung up on me.

When I reached the bottom of the high street I decided now would be a suitable time to go to the church where the Mass for my father's funeral was taking place. I wanted to talk to the priest about what he was going to say at the service. When I arrived at the church, just like at the funeral home, there was no one there. It seemed neither God nor his attendants were present in my home town that day. Alone in the vast, echoey interior, I genuflected in the central aisle, then sat in one of the pews, pulled down the kneeler, and bowed towards the life-size Jesus crucified above the altar. I was trying to pray, but I was too distracted. Every movement I made, no matter how slight, produced a noise. And every noise resounded and bounced against the walls like a reproach. Even my breathing echoed loudly in the air.

With my disturbed prayers and the sweet smoke curling up from the petering wicks of votive candles, I walked up to the sanctuary and stood by the altar. I called out to the priest, but he didn't answer. I called several times, but there was no response. The air up there seemed more concentrated than down in the nave, where it felt thinner. It felt as if the weight of my words increased the closer I got to the centre of things. I called again, but still didn't get a response. I liked it up there and didn't want to go back down. At the side of the sanctuary there was an ornate wooden door, I pushed it open and walked along a short, dark passageway to the sacristy. I knocked on the door, and when no one responded I went in and had a look around. There was a bottle of wine and a chalice on a table. Next to the table there was a clothes rail with an assortment of vestments on coat hangers. I unscrewed the cap of the wine, filled the chalice with it, and drank it. After I'd drunk most of the wine, I started looking through the vestments. I chose a white chasuble with ornate golden embroidery across the shoulders and down the front, and a long purple stole with embroidered gold crosses to complement it. As soon as I dressed in the vestments, I felt the spirit in me. I walked out robed-up and headed back into town. I was in a state, but a fine state, of exalted intoxication.

When I walked back into the same pub I'd been asked to leave only a couple of hours earlier, an uneasy hush descended. I approached the bar unhindered this time and stood looking up and down the length of it, like I had the measure of the world all figured out. The same barman from before approached me. He looked confused, like someone who's just watched a card trick they can't figure out.

'Can I help you?' he asked, falteringly.

'A rum, please.'

'Uh …'

'Anything wrong?'

'Eh. No. Nothing. Dark or light?'

'Dark. Make it a double.'

'Mixer?'

'Just ice.'

He put the drink down on the bar, reluctantly, as if someone were holding a gun to his head and he was being forced to do and say things against his will.

'Would you like to pay now, or do you think you'll …?'

'Have another drink?'

'Yes.'

'Do you remember me from earlier?'

'Aye.'

'You said then I'd had enough.'

'I know.'

'But you'll serve me now?'

'Aye, you seem, well, better.'

'*Better?*'

'You seem fine now. I didn't know you were a …'

'A priest? A padre? *A man of God?*'

'Aye.'

'No, you didn't, did you?'

'No.'

'For that alone, I'll have another rum.'

'But you haven't drunk that one yet.'

'I know. Put it in with those two there.'

'That's a treble.'

'It is and I need it badly. I've been doing God's work.'

'Right.'

'*Ministering.*'

'Okay,' he said, pouring another measure with a shaking hand.

'Do you know how much it takes out of you?'

'I can imagine.'

'Can you? *Can you really?* This morning I buried a child. An orphan. An orphan who'd recently been placed with a family and was being driven to meet her new parents. The car she was in crashed. She died. You can imagine that, can you? Did you imagine that when I came in here earlier looking for a drink? Seeking refuge? Did any of you imagine that?' I yelled, knocking back the rum and turning to face the room.

The rum scorched my insides and my vision shuddered. When I focused again, all the customers were trembling in a freakish manner. Outside the front of the bar a small crowd had gathered and were looking in through the floor-to-ceiling window. They were trembling too. One woman was particularly animated. She was pointing at me and shaking wildly, while conferring with a policeman who was also shaking wildly. It was like a mass outbreak of St Vitus' Dance.

'I know all of you in this godforsaken town. I know what you've done, and I'll have the fucking lot of you. Hell will be your kingdom,' I drawled.

I raised the glass above my head, ready to hurl it against the window, and then gave up. I was tired of fighting for the sake of fighting. Tired of manufacturing conflicts I knew I could never win. Surely there were nobler ways to foster a sense of resistance in a numbed soul than getting the shit kicked out of oneself.

For the most part, life is a struggle, but it doesn't have to be a war, not always. I lowered the glass and turned back to the barman.

'I'm not a shadow. I am flesh and blood,' I told him. And then just to be nice, I blessed him. 'In the name of the Father, and of the Son, and of the Holy Spirit. Amen.'

'What a total arsehole,' I heard him say, as the police led me away.

'I think he's quite cute,' the barmaid replied.

I was still blessing people and muttering benedictions at lamp posts as they escorted me along the lane, where they put me in a cage in the back of a van, then drove me to the local police station.

I spent the night in a cell and never made it to my father's funeral service. I tried to get to the burial, but by the time I made it to the cemetery the mourners had dispersed, and the grave had been filled in. The woman gesticulating outside the bar was the church caretaker. She'd seen me leave the sacristy and called the police. When they realised who I was, the priest chose not to press charges and I was let off with a caution. They told me later that they'd delayed the service as long as possible, but since my father wasn't the only dead person in town that day, they couldn't hold it back for long. It's normal for the dying to queue — that's a never-ending line — but they like to get the dead in the ground as soon as possible.

And what remained of the day? A few feet behind my father's grave, a gentle slope led down to a burn where someone had dumped a shopping trolley and some wooden pallets. The pallets lay in the long grass and weeds on the near side of the ditch, the trolley was on its side, rusting in the shallow stream. On the ledge of the opposite bank there was a burnt-out car, beyond which a series of football pitches stretched out towards a disused signal box, where several decommissioned carriages had been shunted down sidings. An air-raid like siren slowly gathered volume and expanded through the air signalling the end of the shift at a local factory. A few gulls, trapped beneath the flat grey roof of the clouds, circled and swooped angrily in the diminished sky. Standing off to one side of the grave, four groundsmen leant on their spades, smoking and staring absent-mindedly at a funeral procession winding its way slowly through the graveyard as if it were moving on a conveyor belt. They must have had some idea of why I looked at a loss, because they regarded me with a collective look of tenderness. I felt the interaction deserved a response, so I walked over and thanked them for their work.

'No problem,' the oldest of them smiled. 'I take it you're a relative?'

'I'm his son.'

'Sorry for your loss.'

'I arrived late. I missed the burial. But you know that.'

'Aye. We do. That's a shame.'

'Yeah. I suppose there's not much happens now,' I asked.

'There's nothing at all happens now, son. That's the finale right there,' he replied.

I turned and looked at what he was indicating with his spade. My father's grave. A mound of cold black earth. The full stop at the end of a man's life.

15

I'd developed a habit of losing my house keys when I was drunk, then having to contact the housing association to have them replaced. When I collected the last set, they told me I'd have to pay fifty quid next time, due to the 'exorbitant' costs of electronic fobs. As a result, before going to the Satellite one evening, I'd come up with the idea of leaving my keys somewhere safe and had hidden them in a crack in a wall close to the high-rise. It seemed like the perfect solution at the time. But at 1 a.m., swaying drunkenly in front of a wall which ran the full length of the street, it dawned on me that it was a fucking stupid solution.

And if only it had been dawn. That night in the Satellite had started badly and gone downhill from there. I'd spent it in the worst of company, so that by the time I left, the darkness was upon me, as well as all around me. I was a whiskey-sodden unable-to-focus mess. To have any chance of finding my keys I'd need to eat to sober up. With this in mind, I started the forty-five-minute trek towards dopamine heaven, the nearest row of fast-food outlets. Like some mad monk climbing the Ladder of Divine Ascent, I lurched towards paradise, only to find when I made it to the row of shops, that all the shutters were down and heaven was closed for the night.

I dropped to the pavement exhausted, and must have dozed off, because the next thing I knew I woke up slumped against the shutter of the Lucky Star Chinese takeaway with a dog pissing on my leg. I kicked the dog away and it darted off into the dark, gaping maw beneath a flight of stairs. Almost immediately I was caught in the full beam of a police car. Moments later, two policemen got out and stood over me. One of them poked my shoulder with his telescopic baton, while the other started asking all the usual questions. What was my name? Where did I live? What was I doing here? What was that smell? Did I believe in God? Was I ready to go to hell? None of which I was able to answer with any clarity. One of them called me 'a waste of fucking space' and the other 'a fucking disgrace', as they picked me up and flung me into the back of their car.

The next thing I knew I was waking up again. This time, stinking of piss on top of a blue plastic mat with a thin grey blanket wrapped tightly around me like a straitjacket. From a narrow window of glass bricks high up the wall, shafts of muted sunlight cut through the dead air. I crawled across the floor on my hands and knees, pulled myself up over the stainless-steel toilet, puked, then slumped back against the wall. In the surrounding cells the other detainees were waking up, too. Someone started hammering on his door, screaming that he needed his medication. After a few minutes without response, he started flinging his body around like he was having a fit or seizure. He was going at it with such gusto you could hear his body slap and thump off the floor and walls. The prisoner in the cell next to him began pounding his door, demanding that the guy be given his medicine, so he'd *shut the fuck up*. After that, shouts began to go back and forth around the whole block. What time was it? What were yesterday's football scores? What police station was this? When someone recognised the voice of the person they'd fought with the night before, insults and death threats were reissued. People became confused about who was threatening who, and completely new fights emerged fully formed out of the air. Others started singing. It was like being in a playground with all the bampots you'd tried to avoid in school, only now they were your friends and you were all living in a big house together.

I could hear the duty officer going from cell to cell, telling everyone to calm down and offering them tea. I crawled back on to the mat and waited for him to open my little window. Instead, he opened the cell door and asked how I was feeling.

'Better,' I told him.

'Can ye remember yer name now?'

'Yes.'

'How about yer address?'

'That too.'

'Are ye sure?'

'Yeah.'

'Right. Do ye want a tea?'

'Is there any chance of a coffee?'

'Naw. There's nae chance.'

'Okay. A cup of tea then. No milk, please.'

'It comes with milk.'

'That's okay, thanks. I don't need it.'

'Naw. It's powdered tea. The milk's already in it.'

'Powdered tea?'

'Aye.'

'I didn't know there was such a thing.'

'Honest to fuck. Do you want a cup or no? Ye can have it without the water if ye want.'

'No thanks.'

'Right then, ye might as well get up.'

'Where are you taking me?'

'To get yer things.'

'Then where?'

'I don't give a monkey's where ye go.'

'I can go?'

'Aye.'

'Really?'

'Naw. We're going to frame ye for a triple murder. Aye, *really*.'

'Thanks.'

'Don't thank me. Just don't come back.'

When I returned to the wall later that morning, I still couldn't find my keys. I'd pushed them into a cavity, then scratched a mark next to the cavity with a stone. It was only in the daylight that I saw the wall was covered in scratches just like the one I'd made the evening before. People were watching me from their windows, shaking their heads and laughing, while others stopped to gawp or make hilarious comments as they walked past. To be fair, I did look ridiculous. It didn't surprise me that people were wondering what the hell I was doing. A grown man groping his way along the wall in a khaki greatcoat and brown tackety boots. I looked like some shell-shocked soldier who'd staggered up out of the trenches and was blindly trying to grope his way to safety across no-man's-land.

I'd been aware of someone standing behind me for some time, but I hadn't spoken to them or turned around to see who was there. I was focused on the cracks and crevices in the wall, on finding my keys, and wanted whoever was there to leave me alone. They still hadn't spoken either, but I could feel them staring at me, harassing me with their silence, willing me to acknowledge them.

'Are you looking for something?' they eventually asked, when they realised I had no intention of talking to them.

I turned and saw a young girl standing a few feet directly behind me, with one hand raised to shield her eyes from the sun and the other balled into a fist and dug into her hip. Petite and pretty, with an impish face and shoulder-length brown curls into which she'd stuck green plastic sunglasses shaped like stars, she looked about thirteen. Dressed in long boots and short skirt, with a hoodie beneath a long blue suede-and-fur coat she reminded me in appearance and manner of Jodie Foster's character, Iris, in *Taxi Driver*.

'Isn't everyone?' I replied.

'Too corny,' she responded, putting three fingers in her mouth and making a gagging motion.

'I've been here taking shit from people for over an hour. I've run out of original comebacks.'

'I'll tell you what daddy-o, buy me a drink and I'll help you find what you're looking for,' she winked and stepped towards me.

'Now it's my turn to throw up.'

'No, *it's still my turn*,' she said, wincing and taking a quick step back. 'What's that smell, have you pissed yourself?'

'Jesus, not this again,' I muttered.

'I'm sorry, but there's a smell.'

'I haven't pissed myself. A dog did it.'

'*A dog pissed on you?*'

'That's right.'

'Where?'

'On my leg.'

'I mean where were you when it pissed on you?'

'Outside the Lucky Star.'

'Not so lucky for you,' she smiled.

'No.'

'Why did you let it *do that?*'

'I didn't *let it*. I was sleeping.'

'Outside the Lucky Star?'

'Yes.'

'Why?'

'I couldn't find my house keys.'

'What are you doing now?'

'Looking for them.'

'Your keys?'

'Yes.'

'Here?'

'Yes.'

'In the wall?'

'*Yes.*'

'*In the wall?*' she asked again, incredulously.

'Jesus wept. Yes. That's what I said, didn't I?'

'Why?'

'Because that's where I hid them.'

'Why would you hide your keys in a wall?'

'So I wouldn't lose them.'

'Man, this is fucking awesome,' she said, and started laughing.

'Isn't it just?'

'And you don't remember where in the wall?'

'Of course I fucking don't, or I wouldn't still be standing here, would I?'

'Okay, take it easy. I'm the solution, not the problem. Buy me a drink and I guarantee I'll find them for you.'

'What?'

'Buy us a bottle of vodka and I'll find your keys.'

'Wait. First it was an unspecified drink. Now it's a bottle of vodka and it's *us*. Do you mean the informal *us* as in *you*, or *us* as in *me and you?*'

'Me and you.'

'Why would I want to do that?'

'Because I've the magic touch when it comes to finding lost things.'

'Oh really?'

'I do.'

'Are you even old enough to drink?'

'Fuck's sake, *yeah*.'

'How old *are* you?'

'I was eighteen last week.'

'What?'

'I swear, I was. *I just look young.*'

'*That is young.*'

'No it's not.'

'Okay, fine. Knock yourself out,' I told her, gesturing at the wall.

'Any clues?'

'I scratched where they are with a stone.'

'Are you shitting me?'

'I shit you not.'

'Fuck me, what a total idiot,' she said, and started laughing all over again.

After she'd managed to compose herself, she stood looking at the wall for a minute, then walked along the length of it a couple of times, before stepping back. Seconds later she strolled right up and lifted my keys from a large crack at the intersection of four stones.

'How did you do that?' I asked her, genuinely surprised.

'I looked for the light.'

'The light?'

'Yeah, the light. The sparkle. The twinkle.'

'But the sun's shining from behind the wall.'

'That's where the magic comes in,' she said, holding up a little compact mirror that she put back in her shoulder bag. 'Now you owe *us* a bottle of vodka.'

We walked down to the corner shop and she waited outside while I went in for the booze. Up ahead of me in the queue, I saw Flamenco, the American I'd been buying drinks for a couple of weeks before. Dressed in an old tracksuit and holding a *Daily Record* in one hand, and a loaf of Mothers Pride in the other, he seemed to have settled seamlessly into life in Glasgow. When it was his turn to pay and he spoke to the shop assistant in a broad Glaswegian accent, it was clear he'd got the voice down to a T, too. Then I realised I'd seen Flamenco several times before. I recalled one particular occasion when he'd been thrown out of the Brazen Head for dealing drugs. He wasn't thrown out on account of the dealing. He was knocked around a bit, then thrown out, because he was trying to pass off baking powder or some other shit as coke.

Flamenco was a petty criminal, a third-rate con artist whose real name was Larry something or other. For the briefest moment I considered following him to demand he pay me back the money I'd spent buying him drinks all night, then, just as quickly, I abandoned the idea. Most of us who frequented the Satellite were pretending to be someone we weren't. Either because we'd genuinely forgotten who we were, or because we didn't have the courage to face who we were. To enable us to maintain our charade, we drank. And when we weren't drinking, we were figuring out ways to get drink.

I was no different from Flamenco, or Larry, or whoever he was. We moved around the Satellite in our shabby clothes and bewildered heads, like extras auditioning for a TV show that no one would ever make. Limited by our perspective it was easy to forget, as we worked through our scenes, how ruinous were all the lies we told to each other to sustain the illusion. Convincing ourselves that what we didn't remember didn't matter, we drank to excess and blurred in and out of each other's lives like reflections in carnival mirrors. We considered our oblivion a blessing and a wonder. A gift to be cherished, rather than a reason to repent. Within the walls of the Satellite, we felt exalted, liberated from the consequences of everyday life. But if we'd zoomed out and up — as in an aerial shot in a movie — seen our world through God's eye, witnessed the true cartography of our lives, would we have smiled in wonder at the ragged map spread out below us, or recoiled in terror at the labyrinthine prison we'd carved out of our brief time on earth?

'Do you have somewhere we can go to drink that?' the girl asked when I walked out, holding a bottle of Glen's Vodka.

'Now that you found my keys — yeah, up there,' I said, indicating the high-rise towering above the landscape a few streets away.

We walked back to the high-rise and I swiped my retrieved fob across the sensor and pushed in through the heavy security door.

'The lift isn't working. We'll need to take the stairs,' I told her as we stood in the foyer.

'*Are you kidding me?* What floor do you live on?'

'The fourteenth.'

'No way. I'll never make it up there.'

'You don't like walking?'

'Not uphill and carrying someone else,' she said, patting her stomach.

'You're pregnant?'

'Yeah. Only two months. But I get out of breath easily.'

I was about to ask if the vodka wasn't a bad idea, under the circumstances.

But she registered the look on my face and answered before I'd posed the question.

'I'm not going to say it's none of your business, that'd be stupid. I'm here with you and you bought the vodka. But I want a drink. Okay? Unless you have a problem with that?'

I didn't know her, she'd only just turned eighteen and was pregnant, and I was about to share a bottle of vodka with her. I had all sorts of problems with that. But it was also clear she already had more than enough to deal with that afternoon. I could've turned my back on her, told her to leave, but what good would that have done? I didn't know where or what she'd come from, and I had no idea where she might end up instead. Besides, if I'm honest, I didn't want to be alone and was equally worried about where I might end up.

'I won't lie either. As you say, that'd be stupid. I do have a problem with it. But I don't have a problem with you. If you want a drink, we can have a drink.'

'I want a drink.'

'Okay. Most of the flats are empty, the building's been condemned. That's why the lifts don't work. We could try a flat on a lower floor if you want to.'

'How would we get in?'

'Some of them have been broken into.'

'Okay. Let's try one of those.'

We stopped at a flat on the fourth floor and I found a couple of teacups in the cupboard beneath the kitchen sink and there was a double mattress on the floor in the living room to sit on. The window had been smashed in with a brick and there was glass everywhere. I had to lift the mattress onto its side and bounce it up and down and kick it a few times to get as much of the glass off as possible. I opened the vodka and filled both cups, and the girl pulled off her jacket and then her hoodie to use as a cushion. Before she'd put her jacket back on, I saw she had bruises around her neck and lines of scars running like burnt sleepers on a railway track up each forearm.

'Do you ever wonder what you're doing?' she asked when she saw me look.

'Sometimes. Mostly I try not to. You know, it complicates things,' I smiled.

'I do. I'm always wondering what I'm doing. The problem is, I always seem to wonder too late. I cut myself every time I do something I regret, to remind me not to do it again.'

'How's that working for you?'

'About as well as your idea with the keys.'

'The pregnancy?'

'Bingo. That's this cut right here,' she said, pointing to a scar that was scabbed and yellowed around the edges, 'the one that's infected.'

'Shouldn't you get that seen to?'

'Probably,' she said, and tipped a little vodka from her cup over the scab.

'What about the bruises? If you don't mind me asking?'

'The father.'

'Are you still together?'

'He thinks we are. Funnily enough, I didn't think I'd make a mistake with him and have anything to regret.'

'What happened?'

'I had too much to drink.'

'I've been there before. What about today?'

'What about it?'

'Getting drunk with a stranger in a derelict flat — are you going to regret this?'

'Are you going to fuck me?'

'Would you let me?'

'Maybe. *If you had a bath.*'

'And then cut yourself again?'

'Who said I'd regret it?'

'Trust me, I don't want to fuck you.'

'I do trust you, otherwise I wouldn't be here.'

'Why are you here?'

'The same reason you are.'

'Which is?'

'I'm lost.'

'You think I'm lost?'

'I know you're lost.'

'And how do you know that?'

'I told you, I've a gift for finding lost things.'

'Yeah, so you did.'

'You know,' she said, drinking down the vodka and holding her cup out for a refill, 'this is the first drink I've had.'

'*Ever?*'

'Very funny, of course not.'

'Since you found out you were pregnant?'

'Yeah.'

She lifted the teacup to her mouth and, as it touched her lips, the room flooded with so much light that for a moment I wouldn't have been surprised if we'd floated up into the air and drifted clean out the window.

'Holy fuck,' she gasped, looking around the room, wide-eyed. Before she had the chance to say anything else, a flurry of snow ghosted in through the window from the clear blue sky and swept upwards into the room and fell all around us, as if it were materialising from the ceiling. Then, as effortlessly as it had appeared, it disappeared without a trace.

'Did it just snow in here?' she asked in disbelief.

'Eh, yeah. I think it did,' I answered, equally astonished.

She put down her cup, then crossed to the window and looked out. 'I knew this would be a special day,' she said, over her shoulder.

'Did you?'

'Yeah.'

'Who for?'

Still looking out the window, she paused for a second.

'For both of us,' she answered.

'Special how?'

She turned and faced me. 'For me, it's the day I go free.'

'And for me?'

'It's the day you help me go free.'

Certain moments can be so filled with light and love — not selfish love, not love for another person or for oneself, but a universal love — that they can lift you clean out of whatever shit you happen to be in and deliver you straight into the arms of mercy. This was one of those moments. A moment I'd never forget. That would overwhelm me whenever I thought of it. That would resonate forever. That would endure, because part of me would live on in that moment, and part of that moment would live on in me, forever.

'You look tired,' she said.

'I am.'

'Lie beside me.'

'What?'

'Lie beside me. Just to rest.'

'God knows, I could do with a rest.'

'Lie down next to me,' she smiled. And I did. I lay beside her and I fell asleep and dreamt about the year I left home.

I'd been leaving home in roundabout ways since I was twelve years old. Alcohol became my primary escape route quite early on, but it wasn't the only one, and not the first. The first time I escaped I didn't even realise I was escaping. I ran along the hallway in our house straight into a vast green plain chased down by a band of sword wielding Vikings on horseback. I can still see them now, hear their cries, see the steam from their horses' nostrils turn to vapour as they galloped after me. I was around ten years old when I first experienced these full-blown hallucinations. Within a year, during which I saw a psychiatrist once a week, all my visions had been talked and reasoned out of me. Funny thing was, when I was having them I'd wanted them to stop, and when they'd stopped, I wanted them back. In *my* need and *their* absence, I developed a fascination, bordering on obsession, with the unexplained and supernatural. It started innocently enough. I read books like *The Unexplained* and *Arthur C. Clarke's Mysterious World*. A few years later I happened to pick up a copy of W.B. Yeats' *A Vison* in a charity shop and the next thing I knew I was in the local library looking for Helena Blavatsky. At fourteen I was taking the train from my hometown through to a bookshop in Glasgow to order Aleister Crowley's *The Book of the Law*, and Francis Barrett's *The Magus*, from a bookshop. I read anything of that nature I could get hold of. I say I read it, I didn't so much read it, I swam in it. Drowned in it. I mean, I didn't really understand it. I didn't need to. I only wanted to become lost in it. Which I duly was. Lost, but not lost enough. I tried all sorts of shit back then, including chewing a gram of magic mushrooms then covering my body in hot wax, convinced I was about to have a wild afternoon with a succubus. That was a painful experience, but not in a good way, *and not a succubus in sight*. At sixteen, having yet to be abducted by aliens, failing to induce spontaneous human combustion, or managing to talk to the dead, or conjure a single spirit, I became desperate. I watched *The Medusa Touch* on TV one night, then spent a month trying to derail passenger trains and pull airliners from the sky with the palms of my hands and power of my mind. Unable to escape, I'd opted for destruction instead. Everyone's destruction. I was not a well child. I was afflicted — by life, *my life*. But nothing was having the desired effect. Then I got into Carlos Castaneda and that shit really messed me up and proved to be just the ticket I was looking for.

The prevalence of secret communications between absolutely everything began to make life gloriously unbearable, and when a blue tit perched on a fence post signalled to me one morning that it was time to abandon everything I knew, to go and find my true self, I booked a seat on a train to France. Abandonment was easy — the problem was finding myself. I wasn't convinced I had a true self to find.

I looked for it in various places. From the countryside around Carcassonne to Chartres Cathedral. I sat in the Chagall Biblical Message in Nice staring at the stained-glass windows for a week — ah, all that blue light — but found nothing. *I even tried Lourdes*. And on, from the night streets of Berlin to Amsterdam. From the ports of Marseille and Algeciras, to the Hill of Crosses in Lithuania, and places in between. Some mornings I'd wash the pollen from my sleeves with the dew. Other mornings, the blood and semen with cold tap water in a public toilet. But I never did find myself. Finally, I pitched up in Rome, and after three weeks of stealing food and begging every backpacker I saw, I scraped together enough money to buy a train ticket back to London.

Before that, an old Spaniard had offered me food and lodging if I let him hold me at night. The food was two stale baguettes and a sweaty array of putrid cheeses that he kept in his home, a foul double-sleeping bag on the ground outside the Stazione Termini. Sleeping rough in Rome was dangerous at the time, I'd already been attacked once, so for my own safety I accepted his offer. For several nights I shared his sleeping bag and food, and let him hold me. I bid him *arrivederci* the day before I was due to leave and found a way into the fenced-off grounds of a church that was being renovated and decided to sleep in there on a stone bench on my last night. I'd blagged a blanket from a hostel, which I wrapped around myself, before falling asleep beneath the stars. I thought I was safe there, on holy ground in the heart of Rome. But in the middle of the night two guys rolled me off the bench, beat the shit out of me, and stole my jacket *and the blanket*. I'd hidden my ticket and passport down inside my pants and still had those, but I was in such a state when I made it to the station the following day that at first the conductor refused to let me board the train. When he finally reneged, I could hardly get myself up the steps, and when I made it to my couchette and sat down, I was in so much pain and despair I wanted to die right there and then. I didn't feel sorry for myself. I just wanted to give up. I'd gone away a mess and was on my way back even more of a mess. I didn't see the point in taking things any further.

Back then on old Italian trains you could still open the doors while they were moving. I'd decided that at some point I'd do exactly that — and jump while the train was at full tilt. Without doubt or drama, I would have done so, if something remarkable hadn't happened.

I'd fallen asleep an hour after leaving Rome and didn't wake up until the middle of the night when I looked out the window at a vision I will never forget. The train was swinging its way round the edge of a great lake, on the other side of which was a snow-capped mountain range lifted straight out of the mind of God. Behind the mountains a pitch-black sky, untainted by light pollution and teeming with stars, curved up around the earth. They cascaded in thick, flowing mists, formed clusters, and spilled, shimmering down across the arch of the world in a dazzling waterfall of light. The lake beneath them was calm and still as glass, and each star burned just as brightly there as it did in the sky above. The entire landscape was filled with light, and as we passed through it, I was washed clean. Lustrated in an orchestra of stars and momentarily reborn, I felt something remarkable inside me that I'd forgotten was there — my beating heart.

I'd spent months appropriating the remnants of other people's lives to disguise the inadequacy of my own. I knew I'd need something close to a miracle if I had any hope of ever knowing the truth about myself. That it might happen was a long shot, but then I was nothing if not a disciple of the long shot. And as far as I'm concerned, that's what I experienced that afternoon when the room filled with ice crystals. Honestly I'd never wish our lives on anyone, but if we hadn't been living the lives we lived — lives that most would be ashamed of, with both of us helpless, but desperate to help each other — then I wouldn't have experienced such a glorious moment, or found the sleep and the dream I'd been longing for.

When I woke up, it was late in the afternoon and I was alone on the mattress. I never knew where you came from and didn't know where you went. But whoever you were and wherever you are, I'll never forget you. I pray you wake each morning to see your child's beautiful face, and that you smile the sweetest joy every time they say your blessed name.

16

How can I best describe how I felt around this time? Like I'd fallen asleep at a party and woke to discover it was over, and I was the only one still there. Not just any party, but a party in an abattoir. And now I was wandering through the carnage, being jostled by the carcasses hanging from the ceiling while I stooped to pick leftover drinks off the floor. *Minesweeping* — which was appropriate, as I'd been minesweeping my whole goddamn life and inadvertently blowing shit up for years. The sensible thing would have been to get out of there and to try to make my way back to civilisation. But civilisation wasn't back there. Civilisation wasn't anywhere.

One afternoon, while I was standing in line waiting to pay at the checkout in a supermarket, the elderly lady standing next to me asked me if I was okay. I tried to respond, but I was unable to. I just stood there, staring at her. I couldn't get myself to utter a single word in response, turning what had been a simple enquiry into a momentous occurrence. I watched her study my face, the scar on my forehead, the lines around my eyes. Then, with her right hand, she gently brushed the sleeve of my jacket with her fingers.

'Son, you look terribly sad,' she said, and the world rushed away from me.

My whole body began to tremble like I was experiencing some sort of seizure, and I stepped out of the queue and headed for the doors. As soon as I was outside,

I ran down a nearby alley and started drinking from one of the bottles of wine I'd taken without paying for. I'd made no attempt to hide them as I walked past the security guard on my way out, but he didn't question me or come after me.

Half a bottle gone and once again the drink had me believing there was a way out of the mess I was in. That I could cross back over, reborn and absolved, into the place I'd once been. Back before the days of leaning blottoed against lamp posts in the afternoon sunshine, before speaking in tongues to the rain. But alcohol produces a terrible duality in a man who is over the edge, whereby one mouthful convinces him he's about to discover the way out, and the next convinces him there is no way out. Anyway, who was I trying to fool? *I had nowhere to cross back to.* I didn't need to find a way back, I needed to find a way forward. And the only way to transform the inertia of despair into hope, to transform death into life, was to keep going. It's not true that the best way out is always through, but there are occasions when it's the only way.

Sometimes, without realising, you find yourself in an unknown country. It's like trespassing, and all manner of things can pave your way there. Alcohol, pharmaceuticals, insanity, religion, mathematics, art, but what finally pushes you over the line is most often some simple, common, interaction. The faintest human touch is all it takes, an everyday communion, like an elderly lady brushing your sleeve with her fingers. I'd crossed over into a place where I couldn't be followed. To a place where no one wanted to follow me. Such places do exist. They are everywhere, these hallowed pockets of existence. Parallel kingdoms populated by lost men and women you will never see. Except perhaps out of the corner of your eye, or if one day you yourself become lost.

December approached in omens and sigils inscribed on white bones, thin and delicate as insect wings, that drifted across my field of vision. Once again I began seeing portents everywhere. Walking through the streets I saw all manner of ghosts, or at least what I thought were ghosts. Some days I was so confused I had trouble telling who was dead or alive. Then again I often wondered if the living and the dead knew themselves on which side they belonged. I entered what is best described as a haze, from which I drifted in and out of, without agency for two weeks. I remember there was a beautiful woman who turned out to be a man in the process of transitioning. I met her in a bar where they still scattered sawdust on the floor. I had no idea what she was doing in a place like that, and I told her so. She said she'd been through so much she wanted to die, and since they killed people like her in places like this, she'd thought she'd give it a try. I thought we could save one another, and I painted her a picture of our future together with words and symbols on a beer mat. We went back to hers and danced to Donna Summer. Then she gave me head on her unmade bed while, at her insistence, we listened to Leonard Cohen sing 'Chelsea Hotel'. In the morning we went for coffee, then into town for drinks in the afternoon. Later, I lost her in a crowded bar. I didn't try to find her, and I don't think she tried to find me. For those brief hours, we'd wrested beauty from a burning star, and learned to love our love, for who we were.

In a club I ended up in one night, I met a young guy from Rotherham who was convinced I would let him fuck me. I told him there was no way that was going to happen. But he insisted — he was aggressive. I came out of the haze for a few hours and found him in my flat, sitting next to me on the settee in my living room staring at me.

'Where's the fucking bed in this place?' he asked.

'In the bedroom,' I told him.

He said he'd get it ready for us. Seconds later, I heard him yell in disgust. The sheets were bloodied. When he asked who's blood it was, I told him the truth. It was the blood of a woman I'd met on a train I'd got on somewhere, going to nowhere. She'd come back, we'd fucked, she was menstruating. Surprisingly disconsolate at hearing this, as if I'd cheated on him and broken his heart, he started crying. His anger gave way to shame. He explained how he'd been sexually abused, and that because of the resulting dishonour brought upon his family, his parents had forced him to move to Glasgow. Here the abuse had continued from day one with the full knowledge of the elders of his community. I tried to talk to him, but I entered the haze again and when I came back out he was gone. I might never have remembered he was there at all if he hadn't left a note, thanking me for listening to him.

There were numerous afternoons when I found myself in make up departments again. In Fraser's, John Lewis, Boots, or Superdrug, thickly applying rouge, lipstick, mascara, eyeshadow, and eyeliner to my face. Or on my knees, begging a terrified beautician to remake me. One afternoon, I found myself seated at the world-famous pipe organ in the Kelvingrove Art Gallery and Museum. A sizeable audience I'd drawn through melodramatic solicitations had gathered down below in the main atrium, awaiting my recital. I had no idea how to play the thing, or how I'd got up where I was. How hard can it be, though? I asked myself. When I started pulling out all the stops and banging on the keys, a wild composition of intuitive genius emanated from the great machine. At least that's what I heard. The crowd below heard something else entirely. An appalling act of blasphemy. An unholy fucking noise. There was booing. Name-calling. Hollering for blood. A guy in a suit came at me from one side, and another in a uniform from the other. I didn't know whether to run or to hide, so I ran towards the guy in the suit, and ducked under his flailing arms and kept running. Somehow I managed to get out of there without being caught. I bolted through the doors into the day and re-entered the haze. But I couldn't trust the haze, or myself while I was in it, so I took to my flat and didn't go back out. If the phone rang, I'd ignore it. If the doorbell rang, I'd ignore it. Or, too fucked to respond, I'd sit a room away, gazing helplessly in its direction through the walls. Sometimes it would ring, but it wouldn't register in my mind straight away. I would *hear* it, but what it signified — that there was someone at the door — wouldn't sink in till hours later. At which point I'd open the door and there'd be no one there.

A doctor would probably have said I was depressed, psychotic, suffering some sort of break down. A less considered view might have been that I was barking, bonkers, not the full fucking shilling. I wouldn't be so clinical, nor so droll. My way of living may not have been normal, nor my experiences run-of-the-mill. But then what is normal? Turn on your television, consider what you're doing, what you're seeing. Sit with your dinner on your lap watching bombs fall on people in a city somewhere, then switch channels and watch a couple buy a house in Cambridge. I know I'm not saying anything new here. There are countless, equally prosaic examples we could all give. Which is the point. Normal is what we're conditioned to accept, and we accept it so readily. But there's nothing normal about any of it. As for the visions, I'd seen far rougher beasts when I was a child. Bodachs, apparitions, ghosts — whatever you want to call them. Full-blown hallucinations as alive as you or me. These current manifestations weren't nearly as intense. And whatever demons I was being pursued by — and God knows there were many — I now realised that during all those lost days and nights, I hadn't been trying to hide from them. I'd been trying to find them. I wanted passage back to that land, back to myself. Preferably without winding up in prison, a psychiatric ward, or turning up dead in a car somewhere. A reckoning was at hand. I could feel it in my mad bones.

By mid-December, an Arctic front was moving in over the country, heralding the onset of the coldest winter since Met Office records began. Death was everywhere. It always is, of course, but that December the news was filled with it in a queer way. Sensational tales of weather-related executions, notable either for their heart-breaking banality, their brutality, or sheer absurdity.

There was the couple in their late seventies found, near the beginning of the month, sitting on the bench in their front garden, frozen to death. Their bodies wrapped around each other, conjoined like two figures in an unfinished marble statue. The thirty-five-year-old woman and her seven-year-old son who were returning from a shopping trip when their car spun across a stretch of black ice and hit a tree. The mother's neck snapped, and the boy and everything else went through the windscreen, decorating a four-hundred-year-old oak with tinsel and baubles intended for a different tree, and bloodied gifts unwrapped before their time. The man and his dog who fell through the ice on a lake that had frozen over. The dog escaped, but the man could be seen pounding the underside of the ice with the palms of his hands, pleading to be released, before slowly sinking down into the darkness. The six-year-old girl who died in a seemingly innocent sledging accident as she whizzed, laughing, towards her father. The man found slumped over the bonnet of his car, holding an ice scraper. His heart kaput, the engine of his car still ticking over. The petrified woman sitting bolt upright at the bus shelter across the road from her house. The children who discovered her while on their way to school, said at first they thought she was daydreaming — then they saw that her mouth was frozen in a contorted grimace, like something had scared her to death. The man found in his bathrobe sitting on the toilet in the shower block of a caravan park — a towel in one hand, an adult magazine in the other. *Man Dies A Happy Camper*, *The Sun* headlined the story. The last recorded fatality that December was a forty-eight-year-old man who died from hypothermia after apparently falling asleep in the graveyard of St Anne's Church in Limehouse, while setting up his telescope. His wife said he'd gone out to choose a spot to view the rare astronomical event of a triple conjunction.

These were only some of the weather-related fatalities mentioned in the newspapers — there were others, of course. All of them people who awoke in the morning with no idea that in a few hours or less they'd freeze to death, or break their neck, that they'd drown, or crash, or have a heart attack, or whatever.

The strange thing was, it wasn't their deaths that I found particularly notable. It was the manner of their deaths. There was something slightly theatrical about them, almost as if they'd been stage-managed, which I started to believe they might have been. That God was making macabre Christmas presents out of people's lives to pay debts due to the Devil.

At least their deaths were deemed notable, their souls coveted. Unlike those who went to sleep each night, expecting to die, and who, in a grim twist of fate, awoke each morning astonished they were still alive. I'm talking about the scores of homeless people who perished in doorways and beneath bridges. Whose corpses often weren't found until months later, rotting in abandoned buildings, or in sagging tents in woods somewhere. If they were ever found and identified at all. People whose names were never spoken, mentioned, or thought of again, except when they were entered as ciphers into obscure computer databases. If those worth a mention in the news were the big notes God used to pay Satan his dues, then the homeless were the loose change he scattered for Satan's minions.

Wrestling my own demons and making a half-hearted attempt not to add to the statistics, I'd been hiding in bed for days trying to stay warm, while slowly working my way through an early Christmas gift. A box of cheap cherry brandy with photocopied foreign labels on the bottles I'd bought for myself.

Outside, the temperature continued to plummet, bringing down trees and powerlines and causing untold transport chaos across the land and in the skies. I lay watching complex ice crystals spread across my bedroom window in beautiful, fern-like dendrites, that obscured my view of the world. After a time, I began to question if the world beyond existed at all. When I did catch a glimpse of it — if I got up to go to the toilet or to drink a cup of water or eat a peanut butter sandwich — it seemed like a mirage or somewhere I'd once seen during an acid trip, or in the memory of a dream. On my way back to bed I'd usually scrape an opening in the ice on the window, before slipping beneath the dead weight of all the blankets, coats, curtains, and other garments I'd taken from the voids and piled on top of myself. Arranging and rearranging them to get the right balance across my body for optimum warmth, only my head would be sticking out of the heavy cloth carapace that had formed across my bed. I'd look out at the sky through the opening I'd made until I fell asleep, and when I woke up the window would have iced over again. I spent days like this, drinking and drifting in and out of sleep. Glimpsing the world and then losing it, over and over, in dreams and frozen visions.

One night there was a shift in the acoustics of the world. Shop and car alarms sounded muffled and faraway. The hum of traffic from the surrounding streets quietened. The ever-present drone of speeding cars across the nearby flyover dissolved into its own darkness. Jetliners were hushed in the sky. Voices vanished. I didn't have a clock that ticked, but I'm sure if I had, it would have stopped.

I stood up and rubbed a porthole onto the frosted window and saw it advance like a great tsunami from miles off. Suddenly the horizon disappeared. Then the skyline. Then the entire city, and with it each smudge and blot of colour. In every direction the landscape drew nearer and nearer, as one by one the street lights leading to the base of the high-rise were erased like candles pinched by invisible fingers. Then distance vanished altogether, and in one great heaving sigh the entire building was engulfed. And then an impenetrable silence and I found myself face to face with nothingness and uncompassed.

A snowstorm rolled in from the west that night like a vast wall of white noise hushed by all the angels in heaven. It filled the sky and snowed all through the night and all through the next day and didn't stop until 3 a.m. the following morning. By the time it did, just under fifteen inches of snow had fallen, and Glasgow had been brought to a complete standstill.

From my bedroom window I had a panoramic view of the city and its environs, and when I looked out it was clear there was no one out there and nothing moving anywhere. The surface of the earth glowed supernaturally beneath an electric magenta sky and the air was filled with incantations. The land looked stilled and at peace. As if the last snowflake had created a perfectly weighted balance in the world the moment it landed. And in the wake of that perfect moment, all our scars had been healed and our borders buried.

Steeped in booze and desperate to piss, I made my way to the toilet. The bathroom was only twenty feet or so from my bedroom door, yet getting there was a goddamn odyssey in and of itself. Not wanting to switch the light on for fear of upsetting the night, in the gloom the numerous piles of clothes resembled the bodies of people who'd collapsed or were sleeping, and I kept stumbling over them and apologising as I crashed against the walls. Then there were the pieces of furniture, electrical appliances, toys, and bric-a-brac that I kept banging into and stepping on. I'd taken so many belongings from the voids throughout the high-rise, my flat had come to resemble the storerooms of a charity shop run by a madman. Surrounded by the wreckage of abandoned lives, I sat in the gloom of my bathroom besieged by shadows and ghosts. The bathtub was filled with liquor bottles and unopened mail, and I leaned over and picked out a bottle of White Horse. I tilted it to my lips, but it was empty. I tried a few more. Not a drop to be had. Not even a whiff of it. The horses had well and truly bolted.

I opened several of the numerous envelopes that had URGENT stamped on them in red ink, but my vision was too blurred and it was too dark to be able to make out what was written on the letters inside. I pulled on a thin cable running into the bath and the house phone came crashing out from beneath the bottles. I held the receiver to my ear with on hand and kept clicking the switch hook with the other, but the line was dead.

When I'd finished, I tried to flush, but the handle flapped uselessly through the air. I'd only just washed my hands when the water began to splutter from the taps. A few seconds later the pipes gave out a bony death rattle and the water stopped flowing altogether. I decided to switch a light on, to try and see what the problem was, but the bulb didn't burn. I thought it must have blown and tried the light in the hall, but that didn't work either. I tried a few more, flicking them back and forth, but all the lights were out. When I opened the fridge door and stared into the cold, stinking darkness of the abyss, the penny finally dropped — the utilities had been disconnected.

Realising I was probably the only person left in the building, the illusions that had sustained me until then started to give and crack, and a terrifying loneliness began seeping through the resulting fissures. A minute later the entire edifice began to crumble and loneliness flooded into the high-rise like water pouring in through a series of breaches in the hull of a huge ship. I was overwhelmed by it, drowning in it, and for the first time since the residents began leaving, I was utterly terrified of it, and desperate to get out.

Rummaging through piles of clothes in the pixelated darkness, I managed to pick out a pair of trousers, a shirt, two jumpers, and a pair of gloves and socks. After pulling it all on, I wedged myself into my greatcoat, then stuck a bottle of cherry brandy in each pocket and made my way down the fourteen flights of stairs like a man being pursued by rumours of his own death. On several floors ice had formed thick, curtained folds like sculpted marble, down the sides of the casements and across the glass on the windows in the stairwell. It ballooned in great spherical pearls over ledges, and crept along the walls and down the stairs, forming little valleys on each step. There is a light that glows from within ice that forms in abandoned buildings. Its lure increases in relation to the darkness around it. It shines from another place. It's a call and a yearning. I saw it and felt it, and I knew it would have been the easiest thing in the world to remain in that magnificent, enchanted interior, and never leave it. I had to be careful not to slip, and to remind myself to keep moving and not stop altogether.

The snow had drifted high up the front of the building and an eerie yellow glow from the sodium-vapour street lights fuzzed through the strip of wired glass set in the main door in the foyer. Pushing hard against it and creating just enough of a gap to squeeze through, I stumbled into a silence that was vast and complete, like the weight of a large, smooth stone in the palm of your hand. Everything had stopped. The entire city had inhaled a collective breath, not only of air, but of time, and holding it in its lungs, was listening to the miracle of it.

I'd fallen to my knees after stumbling out into the snow, and when I looked up I saw several angels ranged along the wall bordering the roof of the high-rise. Their shapes and features were recognisable, distinct, fully formed — and yet formless. They had their wings spread wide and were gazing down at me. Such terror and beauty, and such light. The closest to it I'd ever seen was in newsreel footage of exploding atom-bombs. Then they were swooping towards me and their voices were multitudes and their hearts devastation. I could hear them singing, *The Nine Choirs of Angels*. In unison they sang, 'We have come to abandon you …' and I turned away in terror, and when I turned back, they were gone. I knew I had to get up off my knees. That I had to keep going. I saw all this and heard it and knew what I had to do and didn't doubt or question any of it.

I walked around the city, stopping at spots where the immense stillness of the night seemed particularly concentrated and the silence poured in from the sky as thick as oil. On a street corner, in the empty car park beneath the Finnieston Crane, in the middle of a red blaes football pitch, at the flagpole in Ruchill Park, a median strip on the deserted M8, at the elevated tip of an unfinished bridge thirty feet above an area of wasteland in Tradeston.

Sinking the cherry brandy in long draughts, I was trying to dissolve the chaos inside me. Walking further and further into the white landscape, becoming increasingly disorientated the further I went. The deep snow made all the objects beneath it appear both larger and far lighter than they really were. As if everything were made of polystyrene and you could just pick it up and throw it away. I tried leaning into a lamp post, convinced I could push it over, but it didn't budge. Next I attempted to lift a car by its bumper and ended up face down in the snow. Nothing was as it seemed. I rolled onto my back and lay there for a while staring at the sky, then rolled back over onto my knees and managed to get to my feet. I'd already fallen several times and lay, staring up at that strange, hypnotic sky. On each occasion I felt like I was floating and could no longer feel the cold. I felt warm inside and would have happily remained where I'd fallen, partially submerged in the snow with the night slipping into my heart. But each time I fell, something would haul me up again. The thought that the world wasn't at peace and calmed at all, but spellbound and bewitched. That come daybreak when the dawn began to inch its way across the landscape and everyone thawed, limp and flaccid, back into the lives they'd dreamt they'd left behind, I'd be found lying dead from hypothermia in the middle of the pavement with a pile of dog shit for a pillow. Some part of me knew it was all an illusion — a beautiful one, but an illusion all the same. That nothing would ever be healed, that all our borders remained, no matter how deeply they were buried.

Determined to confront the coming day the only way I knew how, by drinking my way through the night, I reached for the necks of the brandy bottles sticking out of my coat pockets and grabbed fistfuls of air. They should have been there — that they weren't was unacceptable. Desperate to locate them, I thrust my hands into the deep pockets of that greatcoat, searching along the hems and in the corners, hoping I'd simply misplaced them down among the dust and lint, but they were gone. Unwilling to believe I'd finished the brandy, that there was no more booze, I told myself I must have lost the bottles in the snow, and pushed on, convincing myself that somehow I'd find them. I walked for miles, lovesick for all the bottles I'd lost, feeling my soul disintegrate with every step I took.

Having lit out for a destination, real or imagined, somewhere in the back of my mind, I was conscious of it drifting away from me like a wound whose pain was diminishing and I was desperate to feel again. I needed booze to find the pulse of it. To locate the hurt. Without it I was sleepwalking into a world that had been turned off, unable to learn by going where I had to go.

'*We have come to abandon you. We have come to abandon you,*' the angels sang.

When I woke up I was lying in bed in a large, high-ceilinged room that looked like it had been furnished with a jumble of furniture bought from a Salvation Army shop. It had the feel of a bedsit, one that hadn't been cleaned for some time. I figured it was probably quite early in the day, maybe late morning, but the thick brown curtains were drawn and in the sepia-toned light I couldn't be sure.

This time of year, with the winter sun so low in the sky and the landscape dusted with a russet light, the hours always felt old and far away. It was easy to confuse the morning with the evening, especially when you were drunk, and I was drunk most of the time. I'd become accustomed to losing track of the hours, of living a life where confusion was a forgone conclusion. Of going to bed early in the morning, thinking it was night, then walking out into the evening thinking it was dawn. I'd been so long in that lost place that time and order had been shot to pieces. Waking up in a strange room with no idea where I was or how I'd got there was just another example of a day that made perfect sense in a life that increasingly made no sense at all.

I got out of bed, then walked to the window and parted the curtains and looked down from the second floor of a tenement building. The flats on this side of the street were bathed in a muted, golden light, while the opposite side of the road — where there was an old, Victorian administrative building of some sort — was in complete shadow. The sky was raw and blustery and on windowsills and ledges the deep snow had begun to sag heavily, as if the city was hunching its shoulders against the cold and the wet. Unlike before, when the snow had a transformative effect on the landscape, it now lay across rooftops and around buildings like a burden.

My clothes had been washed and folded over the back of a chair, and I slipped off the bathrobe I was wearing and started to dress myself. I heard the floor creak just outside the bedroom door, then someone asked, 'Are you awake in there?'

'Yeah,' I replied to a voice I didn't recognise.

'Good. Come into the lounge when you're ready. It's the room at the end of the hall.'

I finished dressing, then walked along a dimly lit hallway past half a dozen fire doors painted with white emulsion, then entered a spacious lounge on the left. Sitting at a dining table in the curve of a bay window was a man in his late forties dressed in black jogging bottoms, a grey T-shirt, a nylon blue warehouse coat, black-leather Hush Puppies, and a brown Jack Daniels-branded baseball cap.

'I've made coffee,' he said, and invited me to take a seat, 'but there's tea if you want?'

'Coffee's great. Thanks.'

There was something in his dishevelled and thrown-together appearance that made me think this was someone who spent a lot of time on their own. He looked like a caretaker who was unsure of what he was supposed to be taking care of.

'I'm sorry,' I said, looking around the room, 'but I've no idea where I am.'

'You're in a flat just off Great Western Road, the city end. I'm Lester.' He smiled and reached across the table.

We shook hands and I introduced myself.

'Thanks for washing my clothes,' was all I could think to say.

The truth is, I wasn't entirely sure what else to be thankful for. I remembered being in a hot bath, drinking sweet tea, then falling sleep, but not much else.

'I had to wash your clothes. You threw up all over yourself.'

'Oh. Shit. Sorry about that.'

'It's all right, don't worry about it.'

'Did you wash me?'

'I helped you wash yourself.'

'Right. To be honest, I don't remember much. I remember drinking a lot of sweet tea. Thanks for that.'

'You're welcome. Do you remember lying down in a snowdrift?'

'No.'

'You lay down in a snowdrift in the doorway of the building across the street. You were freezing. You needed heat.'

'How long have I been here?'

'This is your third day. You've slept most of it.'

'How did I get here?'

'I was sitting at the window and saw you coming down the street. When you lay down in the snow and didn't get back up I went over to check on you. I would've called someone for you, but you don't have a mobile or ID.'

'And you just took me in?'

'Yes.'

'You weren't worried?'

'Not particularly,' he said in a manner that said not at all.

'Maybe I'm the one who should be worried?' I said, half-jokingly.

'Your boots and coat are by the front door — it's not locked. You're free to leave whenever you want.'

'Thanks,' I smiled, feeling ungrateful. 'Do you live here on your own?'

'At the moment. It's a friend's place. He rents the rooms out to students. I look after the place for him and he lets me stay for free. They've all gone home for the Christmas holidays. How are you feeling?'

'I've felt better.'

'I'm not surprised. You were in a bit of state. You were crying when I helped you across the road.'

'Really?'

'Uncontrollably.'

'No wonder you weren't afraid. Still, I'm surprised you didn't just call the police.'

'I thought about it. Any other time I probably would've. But you were so pissed you'd have wound up in the nick. I don't know you, obviously, but I didn't think you deserved that. Not on Christmas Day.'

'*Christmas Day?*'

'You sound surprised.'

'I am.'

'You didn't know?'

'I didn't.'

'How could you not know? Where have you been?'

'Away.'

'Away where? It's Christmas day everywhere you go this time of year.'

'I'm not sure. Out of this world.'

'And now you're back.'

'It would seem so.'

'The man who fell to earth,' he grinned.

'More like crashed.'

'Do want to call someone?'

'No, thank you.'

'You're sure?'

'I'm sure. And thanks for helping me out.'

'It's all right. I'd nothing else to do, it's not like I don't have the room. So, what's the story?'

'My story?'

'Yeah.'

'I don't really have one.'

'Everyone has a story.'

'I'm still working on it.'

'Where were you walking to?'

'I don't know.'

'Is there anything you do know?'

'I'm beginning to wonder that myself.'

'You mentioned your parents a few times.'

'What did I say?'

'You asked where they were.'

'I asked *you* where they were?'

'Well, not exactly, you just sort of put it out there.'

'Right.'

'You do know where your parents are, *don't you*?'

'I know where my father is. Inasmuch as any of us know where someone goes when they die. My mother, I don't. I've no idea. She disappeared years ago.'

'I'm sorry to hear that, about the pair of them.'

'No need. What about you, if you don't mind me asking? What's your story?'

'You mean what's a guy doing here on his own at Christmas?'

'Not at all. Glass houses and all that.'

'It's okay. I'm a gambler.'

'What sort of gambler?'

'The sort whose mother and father disown him, and wife and children don't ever want to see him again.'

'Serious then?'

'Nothing was out of bounds. Everything had a price, and the price didn't matter, not if it meant I could keep gambling. I lost everything and everyone.'

'I'm sorry to hear that. And about all of those you've lost, too.'

'Well, you don't need to be sorry, either.'

'What does that feel like, losing everything?'

'It sounds like you already know.'

'It's different. I never really had much to lose in the first place.'

'It's like walking around with a big fucking hole inside you. You must have an idea what that feels like?'

'That, I do.'

'Only your hole still has hope.'

'It does?'

'Of course. If you didn't have much in there in the first place, then at least there's still a chance you can fill it with something, hopefully something good. The hole inside me is different.'

'In what way?'

'When you lose everything that was dear to you — tear it out of your life with your own hands — the place you took it from gets messed up. It can't hold things the same ever again. You can make all the changes you want to your life on the outside, but you can't undo what you've done inside. It's a hole without hope. A big, hopeless, fucking hole.'

'People start again.'

'Yeah, people start again. But people who've done what I've done — they're never the *same* again. It's the violence of it. The things I did. It's never the same after the violence.'

'A lot of regrets?'

'Oh yeah. Big fucking regrets that I'll have to live with for the rest of my life.'

'I know a bit about regrets.'

'I'm sure you do. But you're younger, you can learn from them.'

'Yeah?'

'*Of course.*'

'You picked me up out of a snowdrift, do I look like I'm learning from them?'

'True. Sorry. I need a drink. I take it you want one. What will you have? Beer, whisky, vodka? There's lots of wine the students left.'

The last thing I wanted was a drink. To start drinking now with Lester would have been to reach the end of the road before I had reached the end of the road.

'It's good of you to offer, but I should probably get going.'

'Don't be daft. You can stay here a few more nights, can't you? The first student isn't back till after New Year.'

'Thanks, but …'

'After looking out for you like that — a few drinks, is it too much to ask?' Lester snapped.

It wasn't too much to ask, and yet it was. I hadn't asked Lester to drag me up to his flat, and though I was grateful, I was beginning to think he had his own reasons for doing so. Reasons that weren't entirely altruistic. Clearly, he was damaged and lonely. He would have recognised those same characteristics in me the minute he saw me staggering along the road on Christmas morning. Both of us alone together in this flat with an endless supply of booze would have been fatal. I wondered if he'd known that, had banked on such an outcome from the start.

'I could do with the company,' he said, softening his tone.

'Sure, okay, then. Just one or two, though,' I said.

'That's more like it, for fuck's sake,' he beamed.

Maybe Lester *was* the end of the road. Perhaps I should have stayed and drunk with him until it was all over. But I didn't. When Lester went to the kitchen to get a bottle of vodka, I stood up and walked quietly back down the hallway towards the front door. Hoping it really was unlocked, I picked up my shoes and coat, then tried the door. It opened and I stepped out onto the landing and pulled on my boots, then my coat. I did feel bad walking out on him, but there was so much bad shit around both of us, I honestly think if I hadn't, one of us would have wound up dead.

Once I was down on the street, I looked up towards Lester's flat. He was standing at the window watching me. When I raised my hand and waved, he didn't acknowledge me. He just turned and moved out of sight. I turned then too, then started walking home. Out on Great Western Road the thaw was in full flow and the heavy traffic was throwing grey sludge up onto pavements, where people slogged and skidded through mounds of slush and ice. An inky rag of long black cloud stretched across the horizon, while the pale disc of the winter sun — now barely visible behind the washed-out sky — looked set to give up on the day. In the thin, wintry light, the streets were raw and unforgiving. The city that only a few evenings before had been reimagined by the whiteout looked even bleaker than it had before. As if the snow had leached any remaining colour from it. Lonely wisps of steam drifted from rooftops where the angels had stood, and water trickled down every surface and dripped from every ledge, like the tears of a city forced to wake up before it was ready to let go of its dreams.

As I approached the high-rise I sensed that something was wrong. Even from several streets away it was clear that something had changed. It looked utterly desolate. Untenanted, not for weeks or months, but decades. If Glasgow high-rises, with drying sheets whipping the air on clothes lines strung across balconies, had once been envisioned as ships in full sail on washing day, then this vision had been well and truly scuppered. Before me was a ghost ship, a phantom preternaturally drifting in and out of view through the freezing winter mists shrouding its upper floors.

Walking up the driveway, I saw a portacabin, and parked next to it a lorry loaded with metal fencing panels. When I swiped my fob across the electronic sensor nothing happened. I tried again, pushing against the heavy metal door with my shoulder this time, but it remained locked. A laminated sheet of A4, attached with a cable tie to the metal grill covering the door, flipped and turned in the icy breeze. I took hold of it and read the notice. It was a note of condemnation, stating that the building was considered unsafe and unfit for human habitation and no longer occupied. I stepped back and looked up at its vast, sweeping façade. Normally, I would feel its brooding presence, but it gave off nothing now. The living had left some time ago and now it seemed even the dead had departed, and neither the living nor the dead were ever coming back. This brutal, concrete edifice, that had once sheltered so many lives from the sky, and later all those impenetrable voids, had given everything up to the air and was now a void itself. Stunned force. Failed dream. It would be torn down. Erased. Yet its destruction would endure like an open wound. An invisible tear that would scar the emotional and spiritual fabric of the city forever.

When I think of regret, I see everything going backwards. Life being rewound like a movie. Not just my own life, everyone's life. The great tide of life in reverse. It's not in slow motion, but it stops so often it appears that it is. It pauses each time someone returns to the moment when they made the choice that irrevocably changed the direction their life would take. The moment they were filled to the brim with regret and didn't even realise. When they reach that point they're all alone and can't move, and there's absolutely nothing they can do about it. Theirs is the loneliness of an empty church. Of a sheet of newspaper twisting in the wind on a street corner. Of Sunday morning sunshine on the side of a building. They can't move from that place, because they can't let that moment go. All they can do is watch as all around them life winds back up and starts moving again, while they're left in that place forever, a tsunami of regret crashing in their heart.

17

All those letters in the bathtub with *URGENT* stamped on the front had been notices of one kind or another. That the water supply was going to be turned off. The electricity disconnected. That I was going to be evicted and had to vacate the flat. That legal proceedings would commence if I didn't respond. That legal proceedings *had* commenced. When my eviction notice expired and the housing association still hadn't been able to get hold of me, they turned out the lights and called time on the high-rise the day after Boxing Day. I'd worn out all the couches I could sleep on, as well as most of the friendships I could rely on, when I'd been made homeless the first time. With the high-rise in darkness, and my options limited to none whatsoever, I had no choice but to make my way to the Windsor Hotel. A couple of days later, I made an appointment to see my housing officer.

'Hello, I'm Sheena.' The woman sitting across the desk from me in the small interview room started as soon as I closed the door behind me. 'I've looked at your case and frankly I'm not sure what you think we can do for you.'

Sheena looked to be in her mid-sixties and must have been close to retirement. She certainly seemed ready for it, the way she eyed me with the weary resignation of someone who'd dealt with so many deadbeats over the years that she automatically regarded everyone who walked through the door with another hard-luck story as a waste of time.

'You have to do something. I'm homeless,' I responded, as I sat down.

'Again,' she said, looking up from the folder she had open in front of her on the table.

'I'm even more homeless now.'

'I'm not sure that's possible.'

'It's possible, *honestly*.'

'Getting back to your point, we don't have to do anything.'

'Surely you'll help me out?'

'In what way?'

'What about my disturbance payment?'

'What about it?'

'I'm due a disturbance payment.'

'Were due.'

'What's changed?'

'We had to force the lock to gain entry to your flat. The state of the place was appalling. You're lucky we're not charging you a disturbance payment.'

'It wasn't that bad.'

'Yes, *it was*. In over forty years as a housing officer I've never seen anything quite like it. There was so much *stuff*. Your flat was uninhabitable.'

'The entire building was uninhabitable. You're demolishing it.'

'That's not the point. There are procedures to follow. Why did you hoard all that junk anyway?'

I wanted to tell her the truth. That it wasn't junk. That I'd kept it because it talked to me. That each item had its own story. That they'd whisper secrets to me from the lives of those who owned them, and that I planned to use all those found secrets to build a new life of my own. But I didn't tell her the truth. I told her I'd no idea why I kept it all. That it was a dumb thing to do.

'Anyway,' she went on, 'you were offered a settlement at the start of the process. You didn't accept it.'

'Was I?'

'Yes.'

'I was in a bad place back then.'

'You're not in a great place now.'

'I didn't want to leave. Now I do.'

'*Now you want to leave?*'

'Yes.'

'You can't leave somewhere you've already left.'

'I know. I've come to terms with the situation.'

'We're a bit past the coming to terms phase, don't you think?'

'Are we?'

'We gave you every opportunity to sort this out. Wrote you countless letters, emailed, texted, phoned, visited. You didn't respond. Never answered the door.'

'Okay, fair enough. You're right,' I said, changing tack. 'I'm sorry. I should have got in touch. I didn't mean to leave it as long as this, but I was at my father's bedside for weeks.'

'His bedside?'

'Yes,' I said, lowering my gaze as if his ghost had just entered the room.

'What's wrong with your father?' she asked with a sigh.

'He's dead.'

'Okay. I had no idea. There's no mention of this in your notes.'

'There wouldn't be. I've been away for a while. I only got back after Christmas. This is the first time I've spoken to anyone about it.'

'You couldn't have phoned?' she asked.

Something about the way she made her case — with statements that seemed conclusive yet were left open — gave the impression that despite her hard-bitten manner there was still a little charity in Sheena's heart that she longed to dispense. That she wanted to be proved wrong. I was sure she'd once cared for those who lived in the high-rises. Back in the Seventies, perhaps, when the tower blocks still had an air of aspiration and community spirit. Before the heroin dealers moved in, making a killing out of misery, and addicts and thieves out of teenagers who'd grown up high and were determined to remain so any way they could. Before weed farms and pill labs were set up. Before they became no-go areas. I'd just have to work a little harder to remind her she cared.

'I know, I should have called. But I had to manage his care in the months before he died, then I had to arrange his funeral. I was overwhelmed. Afterwards, I could hardly tie my laces for grief, let alone deal with anything else.'

'There was no one to help you with any of that?'

'No one.'

'No other family members?'

'No.'

'Were you close to him?'

'Inseparable. I was by his side right to the end.'

'And now you don't have anyone you can stay with?'

'No.'

'How about savings? Do you have any savings?'

'I did, but my father died penniless. I spent everything I had on his funeral.'

'So, you've no money and nowhere to go?'

'Can I be honest with you, Sheena?'

'I'd like that.'

'I've totally messed up.'

'I know you have.'

'It's my own fault.'

'Yes it is.'

'What else could I do though? He was dying. I had to take care of him.'

'I understand that.'

'You do?'

'Of course I do. We're not here to make people's lives more difficult than they already are.'

'I know you're not.'

'Do you?'

'Absolutely.'

'We get all sorts in here, claiming all sorts of things. You can't imagine.'

'I can imagine.'

'The lies — not to mention the verbal abuse.'

'Awful.'

'We try to help, but some people seem determined to mess their lives up.'

'My mum used to say to me, *Son, there's nothing rarer than a person who can be trusted never to throw away their happiness.*'

'Is your mum dead, too?'

'I don't know.'

'You don't know?'

'No idea.'

'Why not?'

'She disappeared.'

'Disappeared?'

'Yeah. When I was a teenager.'

'Right.'

'I suppose she didn't think she had any happiness to throw away.'

'It's not been easy?'

'It's not.'

'I can see that.'

'I know you can.'

'Yes. Yes.'

'You'll help then?' I asked, a little too eagerly.

'Did I say that?'

'No. But …'

'But what?'

'Well …'

'Honestly, I must be going soft in my old age.'

'You're not old.'

'Tell my knees that.'

'I swear, I'll sort myself out.'

'I really shouldn't do this.'

'Everyone deserves a second chance.'

'Believe me, they don't.'

'Three strikes and I'm out?'

'All right, given the circumstances, yes, I suppose I could help. But you have to stay in touch from now on. And keep your appointments, okay?'

'Definitely. Yes. Of course. Thank you. I swear on my father's grave,' I gushed, the tears swelling in my eyes.

'Okay, okay. I'll process your home loss and disturbance payment and put you forward for a new flat.'

You might be wondering if I was uncomfortable building such a mawkish fiction around my father's death and attributing things to my mother that she never said. No, I wasn't. Given the circumstances I found myself in, I thought it was reasonable. Neither of them had been there for me in life, I figured the least they could do now was be there for me in death. Besides, we compromise the truth and rewrite the past in the direction of necessity every day. If we didn't, most of us probably wouldn't make it past midnight. And, gradually, as well as somewhat unexpectedly, it was becoming clearer to me that I did want to make it past midnight after all. That I was still curious about what lay ahead. What I did feel terrible about was lying to Sheena. But on this I convinced myself that if I managed to put even a little hope back in her heart, to sit alongside the charity she wished to dispense, then surely it was worth it for both of us.

I was grateful for the money, but I never did move into the flat I was offered. I took one look at the new development and decided it wasn't for me. I wasn't entirely sure who it was for. It was billed as being state of the art, the first in a flagship housing project the Scottish government hoped would revolutionise affordable housing across the country. Each flat had biometric, fingerprint door locks. Smart lighting that was voice activated, and underfloor heating that could be controlled via an app on your phone. To turn the taps on and off, you swiped your hand across an electronic sensor. Even the internal walls were movable, so that you could change the layout of the apartment to suit your familial needs. And all of it was wired to the internet, so that everything in it and everyone that used it could be constantly monitored. The idea was that by making your life easier to live, you'd have more time to live it. This might work for those who could afford to imagine they had something to live for other than the daily struggle to exist. But the people I'd lived alongside in the high-rise would have been undone by such vacant confidence tricks. In fact, that struggle was all they had. Their daily routines, no matter how mundane or arduous, were heroic, and gave them a handle on their existence and kept them going in the world. Moving them into automated homes would only diminish their reasons for living. Having swapped the malaise and concrete of the high-rise, where at least they could see what they were fighting against, for the cardboard-cut-out deception of some mediocre, fascist architect, and the blurred ennui of technology, it would only be a matter of time before they ran amok and began tearing their fake homes apart. I decided instead to stay where I was at the Windsor.

18

The Windsor was nothing at all like its name might suggest. It wasn't even a hotel. It was a privately run hostel for the homeless and couldn't have been more removed from its aristocratic namesake. A grim place with its own brutal system that it was easy to get sucked into, then spat back out of, damaged beyond repair for the rest of your life. Most people couldn't handle living there for more than a few weeks and would wind up back on the streets. Others, who didn't want to go back to the streets, would commit jailable offences and make sure they got caught in order to escape its remorseless grip. At least in prison you ate three times a day and there were guards and some sense of order, even to the violence. Whereas in the hostel and on the streets the violence was casual and indiscriminate. Others left in their dreams or nightmares, overdosing their way out. Some by mistake, some intentionally. Home to countless human car crashes, the Windsor was a scrapyard for individuals who'd wrecked their lives.

In the time I was there, there were three fatalities. One guy overdosed. One fell out of a fourth-floor window after drinking himself senseless. Another had a heart attack after a booze-and-spice binge. He sat on the floor in the hallway from Saturday evening until Sunday afternoon, hunched over like a sack of rotting onions, his trousers soaked in piss, and no one noticed he'd died. Or they had noticed and didn't care. I'd seen him myself on the way back from the showers on Sunday morning and had assumed he'd passed out or was sleeping. It wasn't until one of the residents walked into the TV room and announced — during an episode of *Songs of Praise* — that there was a dead guy lying in the hallway that anyone took any notice.

'Ah didnae dae anything, honestly. Ah just knocked his shoulder on the way past and he keeled ower,' he said, worriedly. His booze-soaked head jerking nervously from side to side like a needle on a seismograph.

When we trooped out to have a look, he was lying there like a mannequin that had been knocked over onto its back. Rigor mortis had set in, and his legs and arms were sticking up in the air like a dog that wanted its belly rubbed.

'Poor bastard,' somebody said.

'Fucking lucky bastard,' someone countered.

'Some cunt should stuff the cunt and mount him outside as a warning tae other cunts tae stay away,' someone else joked.

An old guy, who till this point had remained slumped against the wall, holding a bottle of wine that spilled onto the floor each time he nodded off, stood upright and yelled, 'Buy him flowers! For fuck's sake, *buy him flowers!*' before folding back against the wall, sobbing to himself. Silenced by this sudden outburst, we stood there trying to avoid looking at the dead guy and each other.

'There's no gonnae be any flowers for him,' someone eventually muttered.

At which point someone started singing 'The Lord's My Shepherd' and the rest of us hummed along.

Nothing inside the Windsor worked properly and I don't think the place had ever been cleaned. There was always litter and spillages of some sort on the floors throughout the building. Lager cans, broken bottles, cigarette butts, vomit, piss, blood, even shit and syringes. Water trickled out of the taps and showers — if it came out at all. The toilets didn't flush properly, and the seats and cisterns were covered in fag and roach burns. Even the room numbers were fucked-up.

A few years before I stayed at the Windsor, there had been a guest who didn't like the room he'd been given. He claimed it was giving him nightmares, cursing him, stopping him from moving on with his life. He'd asked to change room, but there were no other rooms available and no one would swap with him. Instead, the guy got a screwdriver and switched his room number with one he preferred. Same room, different number. It didn't help him, though. In fact, switching those first two numbers must have only made matters worse, because he kept looking and continued switching numbers until he'd changed them all. There were four floors and eight rooms on each floor. He must've been up all night, wandering around with his screwdriver, trying to work out the maths so he could turn off the light in his head and get some sleep. He never did work out the numbers. Confronted by the night manager, he stuck the screwdriver in the guy's neck. The manager died at the scene, and he received a life sentence for murder. Now he sleeps in a room behind a metal door with no number at all. While at the Windsor, the room numbers remain as confused as the dreams of those who sleep in them.

Every Thursday afternoon there were counselling services available. An outside agency would come in and talk to the residents about overcoming whatever had precipitated their fall from grace. Addiction, sexual abuse, chronic illness, bereavement, etc. Take-up wasn't great at the Windsor though, where the notion of falling from grace was met with either derision or outright bafflement. Many of the residents were of a younger, irredeemable breed. They weren't interested in being in anyone's *good grace*. Had never whispered to themselves, *there but for the grace of God go I*. As far as they were concerned, *divine grace* came — if it came at all — in liquids, powders, pills, or from turning tricks for a tenner. They weren't looking for it, because they didn't know it existed. They'd never experienced it. Chaos was woven into their DNA, just as it was woven into the fabric of the Windsor. Chaos was normality. These people needed wholesale relocations, completely new identities. Witness-protection schemes to shield them from their mothers and fathers, from their own lives.

———

All over the world there were people staying in places just like the Windsor. Men and women walking around with pockets full of emptiness. And no matter how deeply they dug their hands in to take hold of it, they came up with nothing. Trying to fill their pockets didn't work either. But that didn't stop them trying. And the more they tried, the emptier they felt. In this respect, I was fortunate. I'd been wandering away from life for some time now. Had crossed a line into the world of the missing. But I was sure there were ways back. That there were ways out of death in life, other than death itself.

Towards the end of January, I agreed to a certain amount of medical intervention and attended a few AA meetings. The AA didn't work for me. In part, I couldn't get past the quasi-religious orientation of the Twelve Steps, but mostly I didn't have the required animosity towards my addiction. These were good people trying to go clean against all the odds, and sitting amid the sincerity of these men and women, I couldn't help but feel the deep shame of the traitor. I did stick with the medication, I also signed up for some additional counselling sessions in which I fared better. Besides acknowledging whatever's killing you, counselling aims to enable you to make your own choices, to reach your own decisions and act on them. The first choice I was told to make — and act on — was to find a job. There was obviously no way back to *The Examiner*, so I found a job as a cleaner in an office building. I didn't mind the work — in fact, I enjoyed it. I found the vacuuming particularly therapeutic, and I loved the smell of Pledge in an empty office in the morning. It smelled like — harmony. The hours suited me too. I worked Monday to Friday from 4 a.m. to 6 a.m., finishing my shift and leaving before any of the employees had started arriving. In theory, I was back in the land of the living. However, with the combined side effects of the Naltrexone I'd been prescribed — principally insomnia, wild dreams (when I did sleep), and feeling mildly high — and rising for work during the witching hour, I felt like I still had one foot in the land of the dead. Which suited me fine. I felt far more comfortable in their company, and it made the transition back to some sort of normality easier as I moved through the initial stages of recovery. The job also meant I didn't have to dip into my disturbance payment. Even though by this time I'd moved from the Windsor to a bedsit, my lodgings were so basic and cheap, most weeks I even managed to put a little extra in the bank.

It was near the end of February and the weather in Glasgow could change dramatically over the course of the day. In half an hour you could see hail and high winds, followed by sunshine that made the city glisten clean as early blossoms in April and feel as warm as May. Street corners were meteorological vortexes that would spin you in and out of time and seasons, as if entropy and memory were entwined.

Most days after work I'd wander around until the pubs opened. I'd usually sit outside the pub beneath the Kelvin Bridge drinking a beer and watching the river flow, wondering about the world and my tiny insignificant place in it. Unlike some medication, Naltrexone isn't designed to prevent you from drinking altogether. Its objective isn't out and out abstinence. It blocks the opioid receptors in the body and reduces the effects of alcohol. Basically, it aims to limit the amount you consume by taking away the pleasure and pain derived from drinking, limiting the chances of an all-the-way-down-to-the-bottom-of-the-bottle relapse. That was my take on it, anyway. You could drink your way through its effect and back to oblivion if you chose to. It wasn't a cure. There are no cures. You had to meet it halfway, which I was happy to do. I wasn't looking to be healed, only for a little rest on the road to wherever I was going.

On the walk back to my room, I'd pass a hospital. Quite often I'd go inside and sit and drink coffee in one of its cafés and think about my father. I'd try to imagine what it must have felt like for him in the hospice. Alone, amid such clinical surroundings. The lack of agency. Knowing he would die soon and not knowing anyone around him. Entrusting his death to strangers. I'd wonder if he thought about his own mother and father, if he remembered them at all. If he remembered his own childhood at all. If he could still picture himself as a young man, a boy, a toddler. If he'd felt any comfort in his final months. Any peace. I hoped he had. I'd watch the patients, doctors, and visitors come and go and occasionally I'd get up and follow one of them along a corridor or into the lift or wherever. I'd stand off to the side or further behind, watching them benevolently like a guardian angel, trying to transmit strength and comfort to the weary and distressed. It was remarkable how easily I moved around the hospital without being stopped or asked what I was doing. In fact, I soon realised by the manner in which people smiled and greeted me, that many of them assumed I was a doctor or medical professional of some sort. After a week of familiarising myself with the layout, instead of just observing people from afar, I'd stop every so often to talk to patients — who were wandering along the corridors or standing outside, gripping their moveable IV-stands and smoking cigarettes — to ask how they were doing and offer succour. I'd clasp their hands in mine and look directly into their eyes until the space between us seemed to vibrate, as if charged with electricity. Often there'd be a confused look in their eyes, a combination of suspicion and supplication, as they tried to figure out who the hell I was and what I was doing. But, providing I held on, it would always give way to an overwhelming sense of peace, an understanding that couldn't be explained, only experienced.

If you only look for death, all you'll see is death. But if you look for life, though at first it may seem harder to find, if you keep trying, you start to notice it's everywhere. Even at the Windsor, for all its squalor and degradation, I witnessed moments of incredible humanity. Men who had nothing, sharing their tobacco and putting their arms around men who had even less than nothing. Trembling alcoholics, clutching their bottle like it was the most precious possession they owned, would recognise that desperate look — the deep, physical and emotional need for a drink — in a stranger's eyes, and pass their bottle to them without saying a word. I saw a junkie share the last of his heroin with another junkie once. Too fucked to stand, they were both on all fours, cutting it up on the floor in a back corridor. One man's arms were covered in scabs and he was having trouble finding a vein to insert the needle. The longer he took, the more his hands shook. The blood was trickling down his arms from several spots where he'd tried to insert the syringe, and he was crying with pain and frustration and looked ready to stab the syringe into his heart. I watched as his companion, who'd just managed to shoot up, took off one of his shoes, then a sock, which he wrapped around the other man's arm like a tourniquet. When the man's veins were pumped enough, he found a spot for the needle and slipped it in for him. Most people would consider such offerings as dismal and degrading. I saw the bloodied, beating heart of humanity. Considering where these men were in their lives and the hold addiction had on them, to me their acts were all the more remarkable and counted among the most humane things I'd ever seen anyone do.

Kindness and tenderness would come from the most unexpected quarters. There was an old man who couldn't walk after an attack of gout that went untreated during a prolonged spell of sleeping in the park. All day he'd talk about the lost angel he used to visit in some graveyard every afternoon, about how she'd smile at him and look out for him. Then one afternoon he'd been too drunk to make it to see her, and while begging for booze money later that same day, several school kids had beaten him up, resulting in several days spent in the park and the gout. If only he could see his angel again, then everything would be okay, he'd say to anyone who'd listen. Most of the residents ignored him. Others like me offered their sympathies, but never considered how they could help him. One afternoon, two young guys in their late teens said they'd had enough of his fucking whining, and declared they were either going to stab the old bastard or go and get his fucking angel, so he'd stop fucking moaning about it. If I'd had to place a bet — and such bets were placed at the Windsor — considering what these guys were known to have done to others, it would have been on the old man being stabbed. I don't think anyone could quite believe their eyes — least of all the old man, who started crying — when they carted in his lost angel later that night on a wheelchair they'd stolen. It turned out they'd got him to draw directions to where it was in the Necropolis in the East End. His angel was a solid-stone, three-foot-tall statue that stood on its own near a tree, partially hidden by a bush. Presumably, it had been removed from its original spot at some point in the past and never returned, and now it was on the move again. Within a week of being reunited with it, the old man was up on his feet walking around. When I left the Windsor, his angel had assumed pride of place on a shelf in the large alcove in the TV room, where it smiled down on all the residents — home at last.

19

It was around this time I had the dream where I met Mia again. I was in a pub on Sauchiehall Street, when I overheard the barman tell a regular about a young woman who'd died in the back lane. A heroin addict, found slumped against one of the bottle bins.

'Poor lassie. I knew her. Well, kind of,' the barman said.

'How did you *kind of* know her?' the guy standing at the bar asked.

'She'd come in at opening time and have a drink and we'd talk.'

'What was her name?'

'I don't know.'

'You never asked her?'

'No. She'd have a drink, we'd talk. Then she'd go and shoot up in the toilets. It never seemed right to ask her name.'

'*What the fuck?*'

'*I know.*'

'How accommodating of you.'

'I said, *I know*. With anyone else I'd never have allowed it.'

'Really? Why not? It's only heroin.'

'No way. Not a chance.'

'I'm being sarcastic.'

'This lassie was different.'

'Different how?'

'Well, she was beautiful.'

'You had a thing for a junkie.'

'It wasn't like that.'

'What *was* it like then?'

'She was smart.'

'Aye, *dead* smart.'

'You could talk to her.'

'Not so much chat now.'

'You can be a right bastard.'

'And you can be a right idiot.'

'Honestly. It broke my heart, the look on her face when she'd come out the toilet. She just looked lost.'

'No wonder she looked lost — she'd just shot up. She probably hadn't a clue where she was.'

'I wasn't even working — the last morning she came in.'

'Shame.'

'I wish I had been.'

'Why?'

'Just to be there.'

'Fuck off and pour me another pint, for fuck's sake.'

The barman didn't say anything else about her. He poured the guy another pint and then they started talking about something else and that was the end of it.

I had no way of knowing if it was Mia who'd been found in the alley, and the truth is, I wasn't sure I wanted to know. Yet I found myself in one of those inexplicable moments when you have no choice but to see something through, regardless of how senseless the endeavour may seem. I had to go looking for Mia, and not only her, but for the others I'd known too. Suddenly every one of them was a touchstone — suddenly their damnation was my damnation, their longing my longing, their salvation my salvation. And so I set about drinking my way through the Naltrexone and went looking for them in some of the places I'd passed through, in memories that lingered like dreams. Determined to accomplish what I'd set out to do, this time I was going all the way, until there was no way back.

I hadn't returned to the George Hotel since the morning I'd left. I'd passed it a couple of times, but I'd never gone in. When I arrived, the rays of the sun were angling off the ridge of its roof like light through a prism. Shielding my eyes, I stepped quickly towards the entrance and pushed against the revolving door, but it didn't budge. I tried again, and when it still didn't budge I looked down and saw it was held fast by large metal brackets bolted into the ground. The sun dipped behind the skyline, and I stepped back and looked up at the front of the hotel again. Grey netting covered the alcoves, as well as large stretches of cornicing along the edge of the roof where the masonry was crumbling and falling away. Some of the windows had been boarded up and torn curtains fluttered like tattered flags from others that were smashed. The siege was over. The George Hotel had surrendered and closed for good.

After the George, I went looking for Mia in some of the places where she used to deal drugs. I wound up at the Kingdom Bar in the Saltmarket, yet another area where the wrecking ball was waiting in the wings. One side of the street dripped with late evening sunshine and looked like an Edward Hopper painting that had been dumped in a skip. The other side — where the Kingdom was built in beneath a railway bridge — was in shadow and looked like a scene Goya might have painted if he'd lived in Glasgow. Three old men who resembled characters that could have staggered out of one of his *Los caprichos*, were huddled close together next to the doorway. Sharing a bottle, a smoke, and a rotisserie chicken, which they picked and tore at with their fingers, I watched them as I approached with a mixture of disgust and awe. As I went to enter, I thought one of them spoke to me and I stopped.

'Is he going in?' he asked, then bit the last of the meat off a bone that he put into his coat pocket after inspecting it.

'It's not if he's going in, it's if he's coming out,' one of his mates said, taking a long drink from their bottle.

'Out, in, he can dae the fucking Hokey-Cokey, it disnae matter. It's where he ends up that counts,' the third one said, then sent the dead butt of the cigarette arcing towards the middle of the road with a decisive flick.

I waited to see if they were going to address me personally, but they went back to their bottle, then turned their backs on me. Just as I was going in through the door, I could have sworn I heard the one with the broken teeth say, 'Son, this isnae a dream anymair — it's the real thing,' but when I turned, they still had their backs to me and were silent.

The last time I was in the Kingdom I'd stood next to a guy at the bar who kept pissing himself. He just stood there, drinking and pissing his trousers, and no one said a thing to him. It was that sort of place. Not necessarily where people were given to pissing themselves, or to wantonly pissing on the floor, but where they looked after their own. That night it had been made clear that if I protested in any way there would be consequences. Because the drink was so cheap, every hour in the Kingdom was happy hour or unhappy hour, depending on your situation. And at the end of your night, the staff were as likely to call you an ambulance as a taxi. I walked to the bar and stood looking around. Mia wasn't there, and neither was the guy who'd pissed himself. There was only one other customer. I asked the barman for a double whisky and a beer, then drank them both down. I wanted oblivion. I wanted the lights to go out. The Kingdom was exactly the kind of place I wanted to be.

I ordered the same again, then sat down near the other customer at a small round table covered with hammered brass. The guy's face was pockmarked like the table, and he had a scar etched all the way from under his left earlobe to the corner of his mouth. He could have been anywhere between forty and sixty-five years old. Heroin had sucked his soul from his body and lodged itself in his marrow, and without his soul it was impossible to determine his age. He was there and yet not there, hovering and vibrating in the air, like a sepia-toned, antique image of himself that could disappear at any moment.

'The last time I was here there was a guy who kept pissing himself,' I said to him, without considering what I was doing.

'And?' he asked, nonchalantly, without turning to face me.

'He pissed on my shoe.'

'So what?'

'I'm looking for him.'

'Why, do ye want him tae piss on yer other shoe?'

'I want him to apologise.'

I didn't know what I was saying. It felt like I was watching a scene from a movie I was in and screaming at myself to stop.

'Why did ye no ask him tae apologise at the time?'

'I felt sorry for him.'

'And ye dinnae now?'

'No.'

'Was he wearing gloves?'

'Yeah, fingerless gloves.'

'And a long black raincoat?'

'Yeah, that's him. *That's the guy*.'

'Well, ye should feel sorry for him. That's Lee. He's always pissing himself. Can't help it. Injury he sustained during the first Gulf War. He's a bona fide veteran.'

'Maybe he is a veteran, but it still doesn't give him the right to piss on my shoe.'

'And maybe ye should get a grip, ye daft bastard. Who the fuck do ye think ye are, coming in here with this shite? There's nae "maybe" about it. He's an authentic veteran of the wars. Show some fucking respect. Anyway, did he actually piss on yer shoe? Did he stand over it and urinate on it?'

'Not exactly. He was pissing next to me.'

'Didnae think so. Lee wouldnae dae that. Ye should have moved.'

'Yeah, I suppose I should've. Still.'

'Still *what*?'

'Just, *still*.'

'Fuck's sake, you're a right messed-up cunt, aren't ye? Walking in here with a fucking death wish, but without the balls or any idea how to make yer wish come true. Am ah correct?'

'More or less.'

'Well, at least you've come tae the right place.'

'Have I?'

'Aye. And am the man tae give ye what ye want.'

'Okay, good,' I said.

'Oh, *really?* It might not be that fucking good for ye. What ah give ye depends on the mood am in. See this, this is ma good side,' he said, running his finger along the scar that curved from his ear to the corner of his mouth like a maniac's smile. 'This side will show ye the way tae heaven.' He turned the other way now. 'But this side,' he said, pointing to the opposite side of his face, which, apart from looking like it could have belonged to someone born a century ago, was flawless, 'this is the bad side. This side, ye should fear. This cunt will deliver ye straight tae hell.'

'And how would they do that?' I asked.

He held out his right hand and opened it to reveal two identical white pills. 'To hell, ah give ye this,' he said pointing to one of them. 'To heaven, ah give ye this,' he said pointing to the other.

'They look the same. How do you know which is which?'

'Ah don't need tae know. This is *my* fucking kingdom. In this place I am God and the Devil. I *decide* which is which.'

'How much are they?'

'Twenty quid a pop.'

'I'll take either — I don't care which.'

'Where are ye from?' he asked.

'Not around here.'

'Ah know that much. Am sure ah know ye though.'

'I don't think so.'

'Did ye ever stay at the George?'

'Yeah. For a few weeks.'

'Mia, *right?*'

'With Mia, yeah.'

'Ah knew ahd seen ye before,' he said, and grinned across all of his face. 'Mia used tae work for me. Wasn't she always holding yer hand? Keeping ye safe. And now here ye are, all fucked up and no one tae look after ye,' he laughed.

'Do you know where she is?'

'No one knows where she is. She disnae know where she is,' he laughed.

'You haven't heard anything?'

'Naw. My advice. Go home.'

'It's too late for that now.'

'Ah suppose it is,' he grinned.

'How much for both pills?' I asked.

'Since it's for yerself, thirty.'

'I'll take them.'

'Aye, yer on yer own now, kiddo,' he said, and handed me the pills.

'I know I am,' I said, swallowing them both and disconnecting the wires, so that nothing made sense anymore.

The next thing I knew I was being carried out of an Optimo Espacio gig at the Barrowland Ballroom on a stretcher, while a rendition of 'Clair de lune', sounding like it was being performed on a theremin by a madman, echoed out into the night. The air was filled with floating amber atoms, and the ballroom spun around me like a grand carousel, as I was borne through the crowd towards the main doors. They might not bury the dead at night in Coatbridge, but they were clearly happy enough for them to rise from their graves whenever they felt like it. When they carried me down the stairs and put me in the waiting ambulance, Johnny was sitting at the foot of the stretcher smiling down at me, with music pouring from his mouth.

The paramedics were asking if I knew what I'd taken.

'God's essence,' I told them.

They rolled their eyes at my reply and their eyes kept rolling in their heads.

'Who gave you this essence?' one of them asked.

'He did,' I smiled, looking at Johnny.

Johnny took my hands in his, and holding them to his cold chest, whispered, 'What falls away is always and is near. I wake to sleep and take my waking slow. I learn by going where I have to go.'

When we reached the hospital and they lifted me out the ambulance, Hands was there, waiting for me. His beatific mug floating directly above mine, his unattached appendages gripping the trolley and wheeling it along the hospital corridors, as we speed-bombed beneath the fluorescent strip lights zipping by overhead like white lines on a highway.

'Fucking looking good, bro. Looking good. Hang in there now. You've almost found yer style,' he grinned and winked.

He was still there when they wheeled me into a room an A&E room, but as they hooked me up to the electronic monitoring equipment and attached an IV drip to my forearm, he atomised into a fog of tiny stars, then disappeared.

A female nurse appeared in his place on one wide side of the gurney, which was placed in the centre of the room, and then a second nurse appeared on the other, their faces leaning in close to mine as they talked. Even though they were right beside me, I couldn't make out their faces or hear what they were saying. I was lying in a garden, listening to voices through a cloud.

'How do you feel?' I finally heard one of them ask. It sounded as if she was talking with a mouthful of cotton wool.

'Like I've been through all this before,' I replied.

'Feelings of déjà vu?' the other nurse asked.

'All over again,' I smiled up at them.

'Do you know where you are?' a doctor who had appeared enquired.

'I've no idea anymore,' I said.

The three of them walked to a corner of the room and began conferring with one and other. When they turned around to look at me, I saw the doctor was the Afghan, and the nurses were Loretta and Lynn.

'Philosophical detachment?' I heard Loretta ask the Afghan.

'Definitely,' he agreed.

'Readjustment?' Lynn asked.

'Certainly,' the Afghan concurred.

'What do we need?'

'We need that IV filled with Buckfast. Gallons of the stuff. And drugs. Load it with drugs. And a priest. No, a witch doctor. And a song. We need a farewell song. We need him gone from this world for good this time. Agreed?'

'Agreed,' Loretta and Lynn responded in unison.

'Fine, let's get to it, then,' the Afghan affirmed, then they all left the room as Harry Nilsson singing 'Everybody's Talkin'' played through the tannoy.

As soon as they'd gone, I sat up and unhooked myself from the machine, then walked out of the hospital and into a black cab that was parked outside. When I closed the door and looked in the driver's mirror, I saw Irene's painted face smiling back at me.

'Where to honey? Down to the Anchor?' she asked.

'No. Home,' I said. 'I want to go home.'

I heard the crack of a whip and the cab lurched forward and I was thrown back into the seat. When I sat up, Linda was sitting beside me and we were speeding our way through the streets. Our pupils were black lenses in wide-open eyes that saw the city in one prolonged exposure. Coloured lights traced the sky like flak in a firefight, while every few minutes the deep orange glow of flares lit up the night. It felt like we were passing through a war zone. A covert war sponsored by those who wanted to hypnotise humanity and murder what remained unknown in our dreams, using bullets dipped in psychosis and gift wrapped in neon. Through a litany of hands touching, kisses that dissolved and lingered, it was understood there would be no words, in case they heard us, reprogrammed the volatile message of the drugs, and infected us with some form of post-club St Vitus's dance.

As we approached the high-rise, I could feel it loom towards us long before I could see it. A dark, brooding monolith towering above the landscape like an enormous, inverted fossil. Not one that stretched below the surface of the earth, mapping in fossilised layer after layer, the stories of the dead. But one that reached up into the sky, mapping in floor after floor, and layer after layer of torn linoleum and wallpaper, the stories of the dispossessed.

We got out of the taxi and stood looking up at the infinite sweep of the building's façade, scanning each unlit window as if we were looking for something we'd lost. I looked towards the roof of the high-rise and saw Pete and Martha standing on the ledge. Holding hands, they leapt off the building and flew up among the stars, where they blinked out and disappeared into the mystic.

When I lowered my head and looked round, I was standing inside the high-rise and Mia was by my side. We put our arms around each other, then we were climbing the stairs, kissing and tearing at each other's clothes. Time kept stopping, as if it had been frozen, then abruptly moving on and speeding up, as if fast-forwarded. It seemed to take forever and yet only a moment for us to make it to the tenth floor, where I'd set up a fractured bedroom scene, beside a wall of frosted glass in the corner of the landing. The furniture was scattered, disarranged. It looked like a section of a bombed-out building lifted from *The End of the Affair*. Desperate to reach the only stable point in the room, we dropped to the floor and crawled all the way to the single bed. Sick with a deep chemical fear that was pouring into whatever sanity I had left, I hesitated. I knew if I hesitated too long in this moment I would wake up and never find my way back there. I put my arms around Mia and pulled her close. She moved over the top of me and held herself there, full of violence and mercy. Her body glittered from scattered particles of light drifting up from the surrounding streets and refracted by the frosted glass. Pause. Rewind. Forward. Memory-flickers. A glitch in the machine. Men dream oblivion, even in love. Dear God, I wanted love though. Her face, her parted lips, and in the half-light her eyes sparkling everything. I turned her over and kissed every inch of her. Each blemish and freckle a brilliant star in a chaotic universe. Every spontaneous act of love, no matter how destructive, is an attempted jailbreak. At least that's what I told myself.

Mia asked me to put my hands around her neck.

'Harder,' she insisted, 'clutch me harder.'

'I can't,' I whispered.

'You can. Strangle me. Please strangle me.'

'I don't want to.'

'Yes, you do. *You do*. Strangle me — *you have to*.'

I was strangling her, and she was coming and so was I, and for a moment Time put its arms around us and held us there, away from the world. Heretic hearts. Men dream destruction, because something has made them afraid of love.

The next day, after waking in my room and standing in front of a mirror, touching the bruises on my skin and pulling ECG electrodes off my chest and stomach, I was reminded of something I once heard about memories, I think it was in a movie. *That nothing separates memories from ordinary moments. It's only afterwards they become memories, due to the scars they leave.* Even now I'm not sure if that night was all just a dream, or a dream of something that really happened.

Le Corbusier wrote: *On our side, from top to bottom, we have a perpetual tear. We are but half and only feed life halfway. Then the second half comes to us and binds itself to us. And good and evil comes to all those who encounter each other.*

20

I was standing in the hallway in my father's flat, a ground floor maisonette situated on the far edge of town. The first block to go up in a planned housing estate, it was also the last. The remainder of the build had been rescheduled, for an as yet unspecified date, after government austerity cuts hit the local council's budget and the private housing company involved went bust. The taxi driver had refused to drive me in to the estate due to the ice and condition of the roads, and I'd had to walk the last half-mile from the single carriageway.

The only access was along a makeshift road on which the earthworks had been completed and the surface laid, but never rolled. It ran about twenty yards past the lone block of flats, where it stopped and heaved up into a huge mound of abandoned macadam. A dead-end of unlaid road that contained as much pathos and mystery as any highway photographed by Robert Frank. The pavement running parallel to the road had been kerbed, but not slabbed or surfaced, and was little more than a gravel path. I walked along it and stood in front of my father's block. Even the lone street light outside the building was defective. The plastic lamp-covering swung open like a broken jaw, and there were wires hanging out where the light should have been. Everything here was unfinished, ragged, frayed, incomplete. A godforsaken place of loose ends that would probably never be tied up, and all the more beautiful for it.

I walked into the kitchen and looked around. It was austere and clean and tidy, apart from a lone mug on the worktop in which mould had cultivated, then dried out. I picked up the mug and blew into it and a cloud of bluish dust powdered my face like I'd inadvertently performed an occult ritual. Through a gap, where the net curtain on the window above the sink had caught on the rusted cutlery drainer, I looked out onto a borderless swathe of marram grass that had grown to waist height. You would never have known there was a yard if it wasn't for the four clothes poles staking out an obscured square of garden. The poles were strung with lines of rope that were sagging in the middle. Hanging in the centre of one was an empty bird-feeder, while on the others there were rows of old wooden dolly pegs that looked like little pagan effigies. Everything was covered in a heavy white frost and the big interlocking crystals of the hoar made the entire landscape look ossified. It was the time of the day in January when it feels like it has only just brightened and it's already growing dark again. That raw blue hour full of foreboding and thoughts that drift towards the sorrows. Beyond the garden there was nothing but miles of fields — land the farmers had abandoned long ago — then marshes, then the estuary. The estuary was the problem. The land here was waterlogged. You could grow in it, but nothing endured. The crops never made it to maturity. Before too long everything went under.

The heating hadn't been on in the flat for months, and the walls were withdrawing all the warmth from my body, so that I felt colder inside than I had outside. Watching my breath unfurl and expire in the failing light, I got the feeling my father wasn't the first man death had caught up with here, and that he wouldn't be the last. This was a place for those who were beyond praying or being prayed for.

A couple of weeks before he died, my father had managed to ask my aunt Mags if he could record some thoughts for me on a cassette tape. There wasn't long until the council reclaimed the flat, and I'd told her I'd pick the tape up there, as I wanted to see where he'd been living. She'd given me a key to the back door and said that she'd left the tape along with the machine he'd used on the dining table in the living room. I had no idea what his home would look like. I hardly knew him — had nothing on which to build a picture — and hoped to glean something about who he was from what he'd left behind. But the there wasn't much to see. After a brief look around, what struck me most was the contrast in how we'd both been living. Whereas I had accumulated and arranged as many objects as I could around myself in an attempt to build some sort of fictive existence, my father seemed deep into the process of dismantling his life. Renouncing everything he possessed in order to let go of his existence. The flat had been leased to him uncarpeted and unfurnished, and apart from a few white goods and essential pieces of furniture, that's how it remained.

Alive at the same time — not so far from one another, geographically — yet poles apart. Initially, I felt a final defeat in the contrast, a small desolation of the heart. And then I wondered if we were so far apart, or if we were both looking for the same thing. I'd been trying to find it by accumulating things and climbing, while he'd been trying to find it by discarding things and digging.

I walked through to the living room and sat down on the only chair at the dining table in front of the window. The tape machine — an old portable desktop cassette recorder — was in the middle of the table with the tape in it. There was no power lead, but there were batteries in the machine, and when I pressed down on the play button the tape began to turn. I paused the tape and gazed out of the window into the distance towards the estuary. The sky was a vast canvas that had been scratched and scored with a blunt grey pencil. A blustery riot, beneath which the horizon looked feeble and far away. Judging by the lack of curtains or blinds in the windows of the flat above, no one lived there either. Liberated by the barren solitude of this very last meeting place, I felt as if we'd finally made it to the end of the road, together.

He'd begun to slip into dementia in his final weeks, but even at that late stage, I'd read that periods of lucidity were not unknown, and that a complex constellation of factors unmapped by science can bring the sufferer back to the world. However, they've often travelled so far that when they do come back, they don't know where they are and speak in tongues. Like terrified supplicants, desperate to be understood and to understand what the hell happened to them to take them out of the life they once led. I didn't know why he'd left me the recording, and with the above testimonies in mind, had no idea what to expect. I took a deep breath, exhaled, then pressed down firmly on the button and the tape started turning. For a few seconds there was a noise like gas hissing through a pipe, then there was a slight crackling, and then I heard my father's voice.

'Testing … one … two … one … two … test … Oh I don't … I don't …' There was a heavy sigh, and then, 'Hello … this is your father speaking … If you're listening … then … I'm already, I'm already … I'm ready … I'm dead … ' He said with a hollow laugh, like someone who's forgotten the punchline of the joke they're telling, or have realised in the telling that it's not at all funny.

'The old grey gone … doesn't matter anyway … not now … Though something I wanted … A quote I wanted to … The boy … I remember … A boy has … has … has … fuck fuck fuck… *fuck it to God* … has never … never … never … *A boy has never wept nor dashed a thousand kim …*'

He spoke the last sentence breathlessly, as if in hurry to get it out before he forgot it.

'That's it … *that* … *is* … *it* … could just leave it there … but …'

On the tape, his voice sounded nothing like it had when I'd gone to see him. Though faltering and hesitant, it had something of the quality I remembered hearing as a boy. A strong, sing-song lilt — part Fife from birth, part Cork from blood — that swung his words through the air like the hand of a drunk conducting the ballad in his head. I'd forgotten how much emotional resonance it had once held for me, and hearing it again for the first time in over twenty years, my heart heaved and crashed like the waves of the North Sea out beyond the estuary.

'But there are other things ... I can't remember most ... but of course there are ... most I don't want to though ... not on account of ... anyway ... no shame in anything ... but shame ... Some words though ... yes ... some words ... for my ... my my my ...'

He started humming a tune here.

'No ... not bloody Delilah ... bloody Tom ... Jones ... *shit shit shit* ... couldn't bloody stand him ... Did know a Delilah though ... No ... A Delia ... *A fucking Delia* ... Now she's gone too ... Oh Christ ... songs ... So many fucking songs ... Sean South ... Wichita Lineman ... Ring of Fire ... Johnny Cash ... *He knew* ... brilliant ... What were those words though? ... Words for ... my ... my ... my son ... Some words ... for you ... my son ...'

The words came out and up, hovering then freeing themselves from his body like the gulls I could see catching the wind above the estuary.

'I was wayward ... Your mother was wayward ... We lost our way ... but there was no darkness in it ... not at first ... We loved each other so much ... and no darkness ... Not in the love ... but then in the waywardness ... Yes ... Then more wayward and more dark ... more dark in the love ... in the lovemaking ... Yes ... but never in the actual loving ... and never in our love for you ... Not in the actual love ... at least not for you ... Never darkness in our love for you ... Never dark in there ... but then in our love for each other a darkening ... yes ... and in the waywardness and the sex ... And then it was all wayward and all dark ... Part of your mother was always away ... It was just how she was ... Never here ever ... and then she went and I knew she'd never come back ... Not this time ... Not really ... That night ... we both went away ... that Christmas Eve ... Said goodbye to love ...

'Oh why-to-fucking-Christ him though? ... Why did it have to be him? ... It was him I saw that night ... *My brother* ... It was my brother ... He was the Devil ... Of all the people why did she have to choose my brother? ... And you the only light and all alone in the dark ... Oh fuck ... The words ... the words ... the fucking words ... *Where are they?* ... We couldn't ... We just ... just couldn't ... not for ourselves ... Never after that ... Nothing after that ...

But always you … When we travelled back from England together … I wanted to stay … I did … but the thought of seeing him again … I had to leave … I had to …'

There was a short pause.

'Christ … Where are the fucking words going? … The words … When you … It was pride and fear … Pride and fear that won over love … Oh fuck … Oh fuck to Christ though … Please forgive me … As God is my witness … I always loved you … always … always … I loved you … Son … *my son* …'

There was fumbling, then another heavy sigh, then the sound of my father lying back in bed. The recording didn't end, but there were no more words, only the sound of his laboured breathing. I sat for a minute looking out across the estuary, then I noticed a white envelope on the table behind the tape machine. I picked it up and opened it. Inside there was a photograph, on the back of which Mags had written a brief note.

I promised your father I'd never discuss his brother with you. It's the one thing I was able to keep my mouth shut about. But I think you should know now. Your dad had a brother. That's him in the photograph.

I turned the photograph over. It was the same image that had fallen out of my copy of *Duino Elegies* the night before I'd gone to the Afghan's, only this wasn't a photocopy. This was the original or a print of the original. Where there was an opaque strip on my copy, on this one there was a man. A man whose face I didn't recognise. Not at first. And then I felt him. Felt him before I recognised him. His lips millimetres above mine. The disorganised static of his face in the darkness. Its visual burn, branded on my soul.

I let the photograph fall from my hand to the floor and stood up. The tape was still turning and I could hear my father breathing as I walked along the hallway into the bathroom and stood staring at the person reflected in the mirror above the sink. Hung on the wall next to the mirror was a piece of religious memorabilia I'd noticed earlier but not looked at properly. A small wooden plaque engraved with a quote from the Gospel of Thomas. *If you bring forth what is within you, what you bring forth will save you. If you do not bring forth what is within you, what you do not bring forth will destroy you.*

I continued to stare at myself, and after a minute or so, was astonished to recognise myself. I tried to say my name, but couldn't. It sat in my mouth like a terrible lie I'd been told. I realised I had no idea who I was — that I'd spent most of my life hiding from myself. Spent it creating a version of myself that bore no resemblance to the person looking back at me now. Or pretending to be someone else altogether, a priest, a doctor, a writer. The ham acting and layers of cosmetics. So many personas that I couldn't remember half of them. The terrible deceits and denials of identity. I'd demanded honesty from the world — yet had rarely been honest with myself. I'd changed details here, conveniently forgot something there, recounted my life and lied to myself. I'd looked hard at everything and everyone, but refused to look at myself. I'd hidden from the truth and filled my life with illusions until I could no longer see anything but illusion.

Clenching my right hand into a fist, I punched the mirror and smashed it into dozens of shards and slivers. When I looked down into the sink, I saw a pile of mouths, noses, ears, cheekbones, and eyes staring up at me. Disconnected. Fractured. Impossible to put back together again — ever.

Pete was right. Sometimes you wake up out of a dream you didn't want to leave and the life in front of you is emptiness, and everything you ever loved is back in that dream, and it hurts so much because you know you can never go back there. I'd woken up out of such a dream — only what hurt, what made it unbearable, wasn't leaving the dream, or being unable to return to it — it was realising that I didn't have a dream to go back to.

21

I left Glasgow in early May on the afternoon the high-rise was demolished. At around six that morning I walked through the Botanic Gardens — the same place where I'd scattered the pages of my novel. The world was green again, and those discarded pages seemed written a lifetime ago. In their place, clouds of cherry blossom drifted across the paths and lawns like confetti, while swallows slalomed through the air and wood pigeons cooed softly to one another in the trees, their mellifluous purling unravelling my knotted heart. A lone cuckoo issued its melancholy call for the spirits of the dead to return to their loved ones — and dawn broke in earnest through the scattering clouds, flooding the park with a light that illuminated the landscape right down to the tiniest detail. Suddenly everything was visible. I felt like a diseased tree that had been cut back. Raw and sensitive like an open wound, I could feel the spring sing and vibrate all around me as if I were in a vast cathedral. Life hurt in a way that made me glad to be alive again — and ashamed to have wished so much of it away.

The week before, I'd booked a flight to Istanbul. The destination wasn't important. It just happened to be the flight with a departure time closest to the time the high-rise was scheduled for demolition. I'd arrived at the airport early, checked in my bag, and had been one of the first to walk through to the departure lounge. I could see the Airbus on the apron outside the terminal with its jet bridges attached, and all the ground-handling equipment and vehicles busying around the aircraft, readying it for take-off. But even once they'd made the call to say the gate was open, and I'd lined up to board clutching my passport, I still wasn't convinced I'd make it out.

Haunted by some of the choices I'd made, by things I'd done and said, or that I'd failed to do and say, I couldn't quite shake off the past. I felt like I was being followed and kept looking around, expecting retribution to show up in the form of some vengeful equaliser. There were so many people I'd met and forgotten or didn't even remember meeting. That I'd wronged or who felt they'd been wronged by me. The Devil himself perhaps, intent on collecting the debt he felt he'd always been due. I saw them all trailing behind me in a long procession. Real. Imagined. Invented. A parade. I wondered when it would end. All the people who come and go from your life, but never leave. It never ends. A cortège. I saw memories shot from the sky like defenceless birds. It ends when it ends.

Even once I'd taken my seat and the plane had taxied onto the runway, I still wasn't convinced I'd make it out. There was that hesitant moment, when the plane seems to pull back and brace itself, before roaring forward to take-off. Then the heart in the mouth, when its wheels clear the tarmac and you question the entire physics of manned flight, and in that questioning, worry you'll unravel the secret of its deception and herald catastrophe. On each occasion, I was sure some force was determined to keep me tied to the past, to drag me back down to earth.

And then there was that feeling of complete unfettered elation and freedom when you feel as light as the air around you and sense the weight of all that land falling away beneath your feet. And then you know — *you know* — as you climb out of your old life, that you've made it up into the sky.

—

I'd booked a window seat, and throughout our ascent — like a sniper fixing a bead on a target — I'd fixed my gaze on the high-rise with a mixture of excitement and dread. I could see it down to our right and was aiming to watch it fall, when suddenly we banked hard to the left and Glasgow was upended like a ship pitching into the sea and the high-rise angled out of view. It looked like everything was about to start sliding across the surface of the earth and I closed my eyes and imagined the city's buildings and its inhabitants toppling and falling through space. I don't think I believed this would actually happen, and yet when I opened them again and looked down, I was genuinely relieved to find that the world had been righted and everything was just as it had been a minute before. Everything, besides the high-rise.

A tall plume of dust dispersed into the sky where it had once stood, and before I could see what remained we entered a bank of cloud. Inside the plane, the drone of the engines fell away. It was so quiet in there, so peaceful. All I could hear was the beat of my heart. One beat, then another and another and another, and then we broke through the roof of the clouds and all the light in the sky flooded into the cabin. A light so intense and complete — like the glare after the detonation of an atom bomb — that for a moment everything disappeared.

Later that morning, after walking through the Botanic Gardens, I'd stopped in at the Satellite for one last drink. The Satellite had saloon-style swing doors, and as I walked towards it, I saw they were jammed open. When I entered, I saw the fire-exit doors were also open. I'd never seen the fire-exit doors opened before. Until then I'd never even noticed there was a fire exit. But now, like some revealed alignment, an elongated path of light stretched from one doorway to the other, out into the disused car park at the rear of the building.

All the tables and chairs had been removed, as had the jukebox and most of the pictures that hung on the walls. The interior still smelled of cold earth and spilled beer, though now it was mixed with the dry dust of the warm morning and the scent of buttercups and freshly cut grass. Dandelion florets parachuted through shafts of sunlight, and dust sparkled in the air, before settling on the few lonely bottles still standing on the gantry behind the bar. There was a feeling of weightlessness inside the place, as if the Satellite really were spinning through space now. Abandoned and crewless, but for its solitary barman. It felt like the end of something and the beginning of something. That I'd wandered into a memory just before it disappeared. I stood at the bar, the only and perhaps final customer to be served at the Satellite

'Is the place closing?' I asked the barman.

'Yeah. Today is the last day. No point staying open now the high-rises are coming down. It was dying a death anyway.'

'It's funny, I used to think I might die in here.' I'd imagine that I'd stop breathing and no one would notice. That I'd go out in a corner or face down on a table and not come back, and everyone would think I was asleep and keep drinking and the Satellite would keep turning.

'You used to drink in here?'

'Yeah, a lot.'

'You were in here a lot drinking, or you drank a lot when you were in here?' he joked.

'*Both*.'

'I've only been here a few weeks — the brewery brought me in to wind the place down — but from what I've heard, your chances of dying in here were pretty high.'

'It was always a possibility. But then there was always the chance of resurrection too.'

And there was. Especially when we entered the golden hour and forgot about all the years we'd thrown away, and how few summers we had left. The golden hour had nothing to do with happy hour. Any hour could turn out to be the golden hour. You never knew when it might be, but if you hung around long enough one would eventually come along, and during those hours we would live again. Great plans and projects would be thought up and agreed with total strangers. Everything seemed possible, and in the darkrooms of our souls, where we'd thrown all our discarded dreams, we'd bring them back to life, helping one another develop them on our paper hearts. Often there'd be tears of revelation as the images of those old negatives emerged. Grown men and women weeping like exiles allowed to return home. Joyous, after finding their way back to themselves, having come so far and lost so much.

'Not such a terrible place then?' he smiled in response.

'Not such a terrible place at all. Well, not all the time,' I countered.

For of course, the possibility of death was also always present. Three or four drinks later, when the booze started to burn the wrong way and the light in the bar or your eyes started to fail, it would turn sinister. You'd look at the man or woman sitting next to you, the same person who only a moment before you were falling in love with or loved like a brother or sister, and you'd no longer recognise them. Now you'd see the darkness in their face and realise they were just as capable of murdering or raping you as helping you carry your dreams out of the Satellite and back into the world. Yes, during those golden hours, time played terrible and magnificent tricks on us.

'It's a shame they took the jukebox, I would have liked one last song,' I said to the barman.

'What would it have been?' he asked.

'My last song?'

'Yeah'

'"The Impossible Dream", Elvis.'

'And your last drink?'

'One of those,' I answered, indicating an almost empty bottle on a shelf behind the bar.

'On the house,' he said after taking down the bottle and pouring me the last of the White Horse.

I thanked him and took a seat in one of the booths facing the fire exit. Clutching the glass with both hands, I looked down into the purling folds of amber swimming in that strongest of drinks. All the weather of the human heart was contained in that one glass. A fit haunt for saints and sinners, and all the runners-up in the world too. Toxic and intoxicating, breathing in those unholy fumes, I felt the hurt and the shame and the glory of it all — and for the first time in my life, it was no longer lost on me.

Looking out through the exit doors, I could see across the deserted car park and beyond to a broad parched lawn that dipped before sloping up and off past the side of a high-rise towards rows of brown, pebbledash houses. I knew the sad song of this landscape. The lament of forgotten housing estates everywhere. With their uniform rooftops, vandalised play-parks, graffitied bus shelters, and burnt-out litter bins. Quiet afternoons, spooked by phantom ice cream vans and the ghosts of kids with toy guns. Evenings, haunted by the melancholy glow from buses drifting through their streets, as empty and mournful as the one church. The only bar permanently closed and half the stores in the one row of shops boarded up. The locals living shrunken lives beneath a shrunken sky. Burdened by a sun that reminds them of the places they'll never make it to, and a moon only good for howling at.

I knew this landscape and understood I'd given something of myself away with every measure of it I'd drunk. Not just this landscape, but the one just like it that I'd grown up in, and I knew I had to leave and never return.

The late morning sun filled the fire exit with a blinding light. Just beyond it, I heard empty cans and bottles being blown across the car park. The souvenirs of broken dreams. A noise like wind chimes in a gentle breeze. The sound of promised heatwaves, of temporary reprieves, of lives lived beneath distant stars. And then from somewhere far away, the liquid peal of church bells and the plaintive chant of bagpipe music, sweet in its unending mercy, drifted across the land. I knew this music too. And knowing there is always as much lost as gained in everything we do, I drank down the last of the White Horse and stood up, a living revenant, and walked towards the light.

'Mate, *you're going the wrong way*,' the barman shouted after me.

'No, I'm not,' I called back over my shoulder and kept walking.

As my eyes adjusted to the light in the cabin I looked out through the porthole and experienced a trick of the mind. I was on board the plane, flying parallel to the brilliant fusion of orange and yellow light stretched and scattered across the rim of the horizon, and at the same time, lying on the roof of the high-rise, looking up towards the undercarriage of the plane just as the high-rise was demolished. Between the horizon and the rooftop, the explosion and the sky, I couldn't tell whether I was falling or flying. In the end, as in the beginning, I felt both at once — and I was filled with wonder.